ANITBEET PRODUCTIONS PRESENTS

Love's *Deadly* Masquerade

A Novel by *Yani*

Vanessa is a beautiful, young woman with a bright, and promising future. She's never known love until she meets Eric, who sweeps her off of her feet. But is he the man of her dreams, or the monster of her nightmares? In the blink of an eye, Vanessa finds herself the victim of Eric's brutal assaults physically, mentally and sexually. With the help of strangers, she makes an escape. Soon after, she learns that her fairytale introduction to Eric was a disguise for something much darker and sinister. Reality sets in that once you deal with Eric, the only out is a deadly one. No one is safe once they've made contact with Vanessa and Eric won't stop until the blood trail ends with hers. "Love's Deadly Masquerade" shines a light on domestic violence fueled by possessiveness and past demons. It's a story that every woman needs to read.

Yani

Love's Deadly Masquerade

By Yani

Published by Anitbeet Productions

ISBN **978-0-9969666-3-4**

Printed in the U.S.A

www.theauthoryani.com
www.anitbeetproductions.net

Yani

Yani

Dedication

This book is dedicated to my three children Destiny, Demetrius and Dallas. Without you, there would be no me. You three inspire me and motivate me to keep going no matter how tough things get. I love you all more than words could ever say. This one is for "us".

Yani

"Is it true that when kicked down, a kind word or gentle smile can help you stand again? Friends become strangers while strangers become friends. Love turning into hate and vice versa in the end…"

1

The ceiling fan oscillated from high above, blowing a cool breeze meekly about. While the room's temperature should have felt like a cool, autumn's day, to Vanessa it felt hot as hell, like the middle of summer.

"Bitch, you must have lost your fucking mind having a man in my house while I'm not here." Eric barked from the bathroom as he ran the sink water. "I swear, you never learn. You'd think by now you'd be tired of me going upside your muthafucking head. But you must like it. Yeah, I think you like this shit." He soaked Vanessa's wash cloth in the cool water before partially wringing it out. He then checked his appearance in the bathroom mirror before heading back to their bedroom.

The mere sight of him caused Vanessa to back pedal on the floor towards the corner, positive he was coming to deliver more blows that still had her feeling dizzy. Her ribs ached as well as her back from the rapid kidney punches he gave to her after she tried, to no avail, guarding herself against his assault. She was afraid to look up at him, afraid to speak and even more-so, afraid to breathe, worried that he may have fractured her ribs. It wouldn't have been the first time.

"Why was that nigga in my house, V-Dot? Huh?" Eric asked as he walked over to her slowly.

Vanessa shook her head getting ready to make her plea for him to spare her anymore punches. "Please Eric, I swear. He was just an insurance salesman doing door to door sales," she whimpered in a hoarse voice.

"So the fuck what!" Eric bellowed. "You should've left that nigga outside. But you brought him in my house!"

"It was raining out, I was just…" Vanessa was cut off by Eric's strong hand going around her neck.

"I don't give a fuck if the Bloods and the Crypts were having an all-out gun battle out this muthafucka. You think I worked my ass off all these years to get everything I have just for you to bring some bum-ass nigga in here to take my shit?" Eric spoke through clenched teeth while getting all the way in Vanessa's face.

"Please…" Vanessa managed to squeal, feeling a bit of darkness begin to take over. *Oh my God, this is it. He's really going to kill me this time.*" Vanessa thought to herself. She didn't bother fighting him back, knowing that would only make things ten times worse. Eric stared at her a moment longer before shoving her into the wall and standing up. Vanessa let out a dry, ragged cough, trying desperately to get in air to breathe. She wanted to scream, but she knew better with that as well. There was no screaming in *his* house. No way would she ever raise her voice louder than his.

Eric picked up her dampened wash cloth and threw it at her, hitting her in the face with it. "Clean yourself up and clean up this damn room," he said calmly before casually walking out of their bedroom as though nothing happened.

Vanessa placed the cold rag on her face and began to sob. For the life of her, she couldn't understand what she had done in her life that was so horrible that karma was dishing out this kind of wrath on her. At twenty-two years old, she had suffered and endured more than most women who were twice her age.

"*Why me?*" she asked herself before coughing again. She spat in the wash cloth and wasn't surprised when she saw the red spots of blood.

Yani

Vanessa thought back to when she first met Eric two years before while she was in her junior year of college. She was with her best friend Arianna shopping in the King of Prussia Mall when they crossed paths with him inside of Saks Fifth Avenue. Though Vanessa was immediately attracted to him, she was sure that he was going to go for Arianna instead.

Eric appeared alluring to Vanessa, standing over six feet tall and having a medium, muscular build. He had a honey brown complexion almost looking as though the sun has placed golden, glowing kisses on his skin. His deep, chocolate brown eyes almost took her breath away when they initially made eye contact, and the dimples in his smile nearly made her melt inside.

She noticed that he was coming over to her and Arianna and she pretended to be smitten by a faded pair of 7 for all Mankind jeans.

"How are you ladies doing?" Eric asked in a deep, friendly voice filled with sex appeal.

Arianna hadn't noticed him until he came over to them and gave him the once over before smiling. "We're good. How are you?" she asked with a seductive grin, ready to shift into a flirtatious mode.

"I'm good also," Eric replied. He mostly ignored Arianna as he stared intently at Vanessa. "What's your name, sweetheart?"

"Vanessa," she said with a blush as she looked away from him.

Eric studied her as he made small conversation with her, immediately seeing that she was younger than him and quite shy. He watched her as she tentatively picked up different pairs of jeans, checked the price and then placed them back on the rack. He could tell she wanted to shop, but her pockets were holding her back.

"You should get those jeans. Not too many ladies have the right look to pull those off, but I think they would be perfect on you."

"You think so?" Arianna replied with a slight grin as she looked at her friend, not at all pleased that Eric seemed more interested in Vanessa than in her. "She needs to put some meat on her bones with her little boney ass," she chuckled at her one woman comedy show. Vanessa shook her head and rolled her eyes, slightly blowing off Arianna's comment as she prepared to put the jeans back on the rack.

Yani

"Not at all," Eric replied. "Petite, slender women make the best models and I can definitely see you ripping the run-way in a pair of these."

Vanessa blushed. "I wasn't going to get them anyway. I was just checking them out real quick."

Eric picked the jeans up that she had just placed back on the rack and looked at the size. "How about I get them for you?" he offered with a charming smile.

Arianna's eyes bulged knowing that the jeans her best friend was just looking at had to be over $200. Envy boiled inside of her but she clenched her teeth to hold back on another snide remark, not wanting to appear jealous of the offer. Instead she told herself the guy was just bullshitting, expecting Vanessa to turn him down so he could put them back without embarrassing himself.

"Oh no, you don't have to do that," Vanessa said quickly.

"Oh, I know I don't *have* to. But I want to. How about this?" Eric said quickly. "You letting me take you out to dinner can be your way of saying thank you for buying these jeans for you."

Arianna was now standing behind Eric and looked at Vanessa wide eyed. She quietly stomped her feet and mouthed dramatically, "Bitch, you better say yes! I swear to God, if you say no, I'ma punch you in the throat. Tell the man yes!"

Vanessa peered at Arianna and then smiled nervously at Eric unsure of what she should say. Eric sensed Arianna's influence behind him and turned to her. She quickly rubbed her hand across her neck as though she was doing and saying nothing and gave him a friendly smile. When he turned his attention back to Vanessa, Arianna gave her an evil eye and mouthed again, "You better take them damn jeans!"

"You're really serious?" Vanessa looked at him suspiciously.

"I'm really serious. I want to get to know you better and though this is one of my favorite stores, this isn't exactly my idea of a first date, you know what I mean?"

Vanessa took a deep breath and thought to herself, *"Screw it, how often will something like this happen to me?"* "Okay…" she replied hesitantly. She retrieved the jeans from the rack and was about to place them over her arm when Eric stopped her.

"I'll carry those for you," he said with another charismatic smile that almost made her heart stop.

"Thank you," Vanessa said shyly as she smiled as well.

"You're going to need a shirt to go with that as well as a pair of shoes…"

Before Vanessa knew it, Eric was paying for her a Dolce & Gabbana blouse along with a Chanel hand bag and a pair of Chanel low heel stilettos. Vanessa thought she was in a dream by the way he helped her try the shoe on and didn't seem the least bit impatient as she made up her mind about what she wanted. Arianna tagged along enviously feeling like the third wheel, not understanding for the life of her what Eric saw in Vanessa that he did not see in her.

Though they were best friends, Arianna always felt a need to compete with Vanessa. They were equally beautiful young ladies who had both grown up in the "Brickyard" section of Germantown. "Cradle to the Grave" is how they always said they would be, meeting when they were in the second grade. They were enemies at first, getting into a small fist fight in the school yard of Kelly's elementary school over a double-dutch game. They would later become the best of friends after Arianna saw a few girls from Morton Homes trying to jump Vanessa one day and she jumped a fence to intervene. Ever since then, they were thick as thieves and inseparable.

Arianna was a "red-boned" female mixed with Italian and Black. Her great-grandfather was a full blooded Italian who shunned his daughter when she got pregnant by a "Black Mooly". Practically her entire family disowned her in her Chicago home-town. When she was asked for her hand in marriage, Inga quickly accepted and moved with Barry to Philadelphia. Tragically during the race riots near Girard College in the late 1960's Barry was killed while Inga was pregnant with Arianna's mother, Josephine. "Josie" wasn't exactly mother material. She was more attracted to running the streets and bar hopping than raising Arianna, so Inga took care of her and raised her as though she were her own. And while Arianna was indeed intelligent, she used her strikingly beautiful appearance to get most of what she wanted in life. She stood at 5'8 and had a soft, creamy complexion like a cup of coffee that had been heavily diluted with milk. Her hair was naturally thick and curly, but she kept it bone straight and wore it just past her shoulder blades. She was curvy and slightly bow-legged with dimples and dark seductive eyes. In her mind, any man who was not attracted to her was either dumb as hell, or gay.

Vanessa on the other hand, was shorter than Arianna and petite. She was barely 5'6 but had an athletic body from playing sports all through grade school and even in college. She played badminton, volley ball and ran track. She was the color of a coconut shell with smooth skin and dark shoulder length hair. And though she was twenty years old, Arianna often joked that if she were to put on a school uniform and pull her hair back into a pony-tail, she could pass for a high-school freshman.

Arianna sat on a bench and began playing with her cell phone while pretending not to be jealous of the mini shopping spree Vanessa was getting from Eric. *"I hope his card declines,"* she thought to herself as an evil grin crept across her face. But when Vanessa and Eric were walking over to her carrying shopping bags while grinning and giggling like the pair had been dating for months, she knew that wasn't the case.

"So what time can I pick you up tonight?" Eric asked Vanessa as they slowly walked through King of Prussia.

"I guess 8 o' clock sounds good."

"Alright, I'll make dinner reservations for us and I'll see you at 8pm." They exchanged phone numbers and then Vanessa texted him her address. "Would you ladies like a ride home?"

"No thanks," Arianna said quickly. "We have some other stops to make, right Vanna?"

Vanessa cut her eyes at her best friend. She hated when Arianna called her that and Arianna knew it. "Yes, we have a few more stops to make. Call me later when you are on your way."

Eric smiled and gave her a warm embrace. Vanessa thought she was going to melt when she smelled his Izzy Miyake cologne. Arianna rolled her eyes again and looked at her non-existent watch on her wrist to drive the point home that she had run out of patience.

Eric parted ways with Vanessa and she walked away with Arianna with a bit of a bounce in her step.

"You are such a cocky bitch," Arianna said with a smirk.

"And you are a hater," Vanessa smiled.

"I can't believe he bought all that for you and didn't know you from Adam. You better watch it, that fucking credit card is probably stolen," Arianna said.

Yani

"Ugh, you are such a hater, shut up!"

"You think I'm joking. What man does that? Just walks up to a strange girl that he doesn't know shit about and spends over a stack on her in Saks? This ain't Pretty Woman and you are not Julia Roberts."

"Hay-ter," Vanessa said again in a sing song manner.

"Yeah, whatever. Watch he tries to fuck you in the ass tonight," Arianna said before laughing loudly.

Vanessa burst out laughing with her. "You are a horrible, HORRIBLE person, girl. Just horrible! You wouldn't be saying that if he had bought this stuff for you."

"Nah, but you probably would."

"No I wouldn't because unlike you, I'm not a hater," Vanessa replied as she continued to smile.

"Yeah well, you better take your mace with you because ol' boy definitely finna steal your virginity tonight." The two of them laughed together as they took the escalator down to the food court. "You're laughing like I'm joking. But you gon' learn tonight. You gon' learn about that long dick," Arianna mimicked Kevin Hart.

"Alright, alright, alriiiiight!" They both said at the same time before leaning into each other and laughing.

They went over to Chick-Fil-A to grab something to eat before heading home.

Later on that night, Vanessa nervously got dressed for her first date with Eric. She obsessed over how she should wear her hair, her accessories; hoop earrings or diamond studs, lip-gloss or lip-stick. Arianna sighed and shook her head before propping herself up on her pillows.

"You need to get a damn grip girl, shit. It's not that deep!"

"It is that deep. I'm not like you, going out on dates with different guys every other day," Vanessa replied as she checked herself out in the mirror.

"Well maybe if you did, you wouldn't be tripping."

Vanessa turned around. "How do I look?"

Arianna looked her over. "Your outfit is cute but honestly, you look like a kid playing dress up in her big sister's cool wardrobe. Take that pony-tail out of your hair and put some make-up on."

"I don't like make-up," Vanessa frowned.

"Well, you're going to like it tonight. You're rocking a Chanel bag and Chanel shoes. Bitch, if you don't at least put some eye-liner on and some mascara and make your lips look kissable," Arianna suggested as she pushed her friend down in the chair.

"He liked me without make-up, though!" Vanessa whined.

"Vanna baby, I love you to death. But trust me when I tell you, he may have been attracted to you in Saks today, but he also dropped over a stack on one outfit to take you out. He wants to show off his lady not his little sister. Now hold still so I don't poke you in the eye with this pencil." They both giggled before Arianna started fixing Vanessa's face. She quickly undid her ponytail and ran her fingers through hair before parting it on the side and re-styling it.

"Hot-damn, girl! Eric is gonna be on that ass tonight!" Arianna grinned as she admired her handy work.

Vanessa smiled as she looked at herself in the mirror. She hadn't been done up like this since her senior prom.

They heard a knock at the door and Vanessa jumped up. "Oh my God, that's him. I'm nervous."

"Girl, have a seat in here while I get the door. You want to wow him when you make your grand entrance," Arianna said before leaving the room so she could answer their door. The two of them shared an apartment in a duplex near La Salle University where they went to school.

It was their way of being adults and not having to stay in their parents' homes while completing their education. It was more of a benefit for Arianna than Vanessa since it kept her from having to deal with the unbearably strict rules her grandmother set for her in hopes that it would keep her from traveling down the same path as her mother, Josie.

"Hey Eric!" Arianna said with a smile after opening the door for him. She gave him the once over just as she had done at Saks Fifth Avenue earlier and thought to herself that he looked good enough to eat. He was wearing a pair of faded blue jeans with a pair of Prada sneakers, a white Polo shirt and a blazer. He even smelled better than he did earlier.

"How are you…?" he winced not remembering her name.

"Arianna…" she replied with a frown. "I'ma let you slide on that one, home-boy. Just don't let it happen again," she joked in a flirty manner. She called for Vanessa to come out of the room for her date.

Eric smiled at her but turned his attention to Vanessa. His smile widened as he gave her the once over. "You look beautiful."

"Thank you," Vanessa blushed. He took her by the hand tenderly and kissed her on the cheek making her blush some more.

"What time should I expect you?" Arianna asked.

Vanessa looked at Eric and then looked at Arianna. "Um, I don't know. Are we just doing dinner tonight?" she asked Eric.

"Whatever you want to do afterwards is fine with me as long as I get to spend as much time with you as the night allows me to."

Vanessa blushed again. "You don't have to wait up, I'm a big girl," she said to Arianna.

"Yeah, uh huh. Okay," Arianna replied as she walked them to the door. She watched from the window and her mouth damn near hit the floor when she saw Eric open the car door to what she estimated to be a 2012 Infiniti. Vanessa sat inside and he closed her door before jogging around to the other side and getting in. Arianna watched the car until it disappeared down the street.

"He's probably a drug dealer. Yup, that nigga's a trap king," she smirked before closing the blinds and going to pop some popcorn for her mini marathon of *Law & Order SVU*.

Though Vanessa was nervous, she hit it off very well with Eric during their drive to Chima's Brazilian Steakhouse for their dinner date. Eric made her feel at ease as they both talked of their child-hoods. While he didn't look it, Eric was 25 years old and worked as a partner with one of the top Financial Brokerage Firms in the Tri-State area. He had no children, had never been married and for the last five years, he had been more focused on establishing a career and a good life than starting a family and settling down. He told Vanessa that he dated off and on but hadn't met a young lady he could see himself with for a long time.

Vanessa thought that he was too good to be true. Most of the guys that she knew who were his age had done at least one bid in jail, were barely making above minimum wage at a mediocre job with hardly any aspirations for anything better than the next get rich quick scheme; a party promotor or an "up & coming" rap star from Philly with a mix-tape always coming soon but never arriving. And then there were the DJ's hustling at hole in the wall bars and clubs or alley-way block parties, guys with multiple children by multiple women who still lived at home with their mothers; back bedroom or basement dwellers who only left home when their chick of the moment let them stay with them. Because of the same scenarios she constantly ran into, she gave up on dating and focused more on school, hoping to enroll into law school after she graduated with her bachelor's degree in criminology.

Eric was impressed with her aspirations as well as they sat in Chima's talking some more while waiting for their dinner. At first, Vanessa was afraid to order after she had seen the prices. Not wanting to over step her boundaries, she asked him to recommend a dish stating that she had never been to the restaurant before. Eric ordered the Picanha-top sirloin for Vanessa and a salmon steak for himself with a bottle of Chateau Montelena Estate Cabernet Sauvignon- 2010 wine and two salads.

"I'm only twenty," Vanessa whispered to him after the waiter poured both of them a glass and walked away.

"It's okay, I won't tell if you won't tell," Eric smiled. "You've never had wine before?"

"I've never drank, smoked, nothing," Vanessa said bashfully.

"Well, first things first: sip, don't gulp. But when you sip it, don't swallow it right away. Close your eyes and let the flavor dance around your mouth for a moment. Let it play a sweet melody on your tongue almost as though it's singing to your taste buds," Eric said softly. He watched her intently. "Now swallow it."

Vanessa did as he said and then slowly opened her eyes. Looking into his eyes, she felt hot, and aroused. She felt his seduction wash over her body and felt as though she was getting to know him intimately without having him touch her physically.

"Was it good?" he asked her in the same soft voice, snapping her out of her trance.

"Yes," she replied trying hard not to bite down on her lip and trying even harder not to stare at his.

Eric sat back and smiled as though he read her thoughts and could sense what she was feeling. He took a sip from his glass and then swirled it slightly before sitting it down and looking back at her. "When do you turn 21?" he asked.

"In June. My friends want to throw me a big party, but nah. I'm just not into that."

"Well, how about I take you to one of my favorite vineyards and we can go wine tasting together. You'll love it. That's normally around the time that I grab a few bottles for the winter and the fall anyway, so if things work out for us, we can make it a date."

Vanessa smiled. She was liking Eric more and more even though she had just met him. "Maybe we can."

They ate their dinner and desert continuing their conversation, sharing stories, laughing, and enjoying each other's company as they got to know one another. After Eric paid the bill, he drove them over to Warm Daddy's where they listened to the live band and had a few more drinks. Eric then noticed that it was almost 1am and decided to bring the evening to a close.

He pulled up in front of her residence and got out of the car so he could open her door. He walked her to the front door and she turned to face him.

"I had a wonderful time tonight. I honestly can't think of any other time I went out on a date and had this much fun with a guy who genuinely seemed interested in me and was such a gentleman. Thank you," Vanessa said with a smile.

"You don't have to thank me, Vanessa. That's what a man is supposed to do, and if a man isn't doing those things for you, he isn't a man."

Vanessa blushed and looked away from him for a moment. Before she realized it, Eric leaned in and kissed her softly. She hesitated momentarily, but then kissed him back. He pulled away before giving her another peck on the lips and then brushed her hair behind her ear.

"I'll call you when I get in, okay."

Vanessa nodded unable to speak, feeling like her breath had been taken away.

Eric waited for her to go inside before getting into his car and driving away.

Vanessa floated to the bedroom that she and Arianna shared and plopped down on her bed grinning from ear to ear. She replayed the night over in her head mainly focusing on their kiss as she continued to smile. She was snapped out of her daydream by Arianna's groggy voice.

"GTD or naw?" Arianna asked in a husky voice.

"GTD?" Vanessa asked confused.

Arianna clicked the lamp on by her dresser. "Got the drawls, dawg!" She burst out laughing, imitating Tommy from the T.V show *"Martin"* and Vanessa laughed with her.

"You're so goofy! No he didn't get the drawls, girl shut up!" Vanessa went into the bathroom and changed into her night clothes before crawling into bed and dishing the details of her date with Eric.

That night, Vanessa was positive she had found the man she was looking for; charismatic, smart, funny, and ambitious, good looking, kind and gentle. She was positive Eric was the man of her dreams. Little did she know he would turn out to be nothing more than a hellish nightmare from which she could not escape…

2

Eric had gone out for the night like he normally does after him and Vanessa gets into a physical altercation. Once before, Vanessa had tried to leave him and because of that, he put locks on the door that could only be unlocked from the inside as well as the outside with a key. And of course, he was the only one who had the key. So Vanessa literally was a prisoner in her own home. As punishment once, Eric locked her in the house with only one bottle of water and a half of a can of plain Pringles. He also took her cell phone so she couldn't call anyone and disconnected the internet so she couldn't get on any of her social media pages, send emails or anything. For two days she practically starved as she tried to ration out the chips, choosing to sleep off the hunger so she didn't suffer too much.

On the eve of the second day, Eric came home as though nothing had happened, with her favorite Beef with Garlic Sauce Chinese food, a shrimp roll and a mango

Nantucket. He purposely opened the food to let the aroma fill the air, teasing her senses and awakening her hunger even more. But before he allowed her to eat, he demanded she performed oral sex on him.

Eric forced his throbbing member in and out of her mouth with such vigor, becoming more and more aggressive each time she gagged and sounded as though she would vomit on him. Seeing her eyes getting teary and hearing the gagging noises she made turned him on even more. Without warning, he ejaculated in her mouth and on her face. He then laid her on her back and pushed her knees to her chest before entering her hard and deeply. She clawed the sheets, grimacing against his strong thrusts knowing better than to scratch his back because that would result in a hard slap to the face or him possibly choking her as he fucked her harder and deeper. He seemed to enjoy seeing her face covered in his cum and that made him pound her even harder. Not being able to take the look on his face any longer, she closed her eyes trying hard to separate herself from that experience.

After he ejaculated the second time, Eric flung her legs off of him as though she was just a whore whom he had picked up off the street, and walked out of the room not saying a word. Vanessa never felt so degraded and humiliated. It wasn't until almost two hours later that the sexual escapade came to an end. But by then, her food was already cold. Vanessa had lost her appetite and just wanted to take a shower.

Vanessa laid in the bed as that memory danced around in her head. Her constant thoughts and questions of "why" were endless and always resulted in no answers. She stopped believing she was a good person and began to tell herself this is what she deserved. The best way she knew to comfort herself was to tell herself that it could always be worst. She could be dead. *"But is death really worse than what's happening now?"* a voice said inside of her head. She ignored it and rolled over in the bed before closing her eyes and thinking back to when times were happier between her and Eric…

They had been dating for six months and Vanessa couldn't be happier. And though she had spent nights at his place, they still had not had sex. Eric was well aware that she was a virgin and did not pressure her into being with him intimately. Sometimes Vanessa thought that he was tempting her with the coconut oil body massages he would give to her, the way he would walk around his house with no shirt on looking as though he had just stepped out of a Melanin Adonis God Catalogue. But at night when they would go to bed, he would only wrap his arms around her and sleep. While Vanessa had never experienced sex, she was indeed feeling sexually frustrated.

"Why don't you just tell him you want to fuck for goodness sakes?! Sheesh!" Arianna asked one day when they were in their apartment.

"Oh my God, Ari! Do you have to put it that way?" Vanessa shook her head as she folded her clothes.

"I'm just saying! This man got you all horny and shit, damn near leaving a trail of pussy juice behind you as you move about, complaining about the lack of dick action you're getting. Say something! Shit, closed mouths don't get fed, and closed legs don't get fucked."

Vanessa shook her head at her friend. "You're a whole mess."

"Yeah well, at least my coochie ain't dying from dick deprivation," they both laughed at her comment. "Aw shit, what if he has a little dick and he's scared you might laugh at him." Arianna roared with laughter. "I bet that's it! He's a little midget, limp-dick, leprechaun mofo!"

"Nah, that's not it. I felt it up against me when we were sleep and it definitely wasn't little," Vanessa replied with a mischievous grin.

"Oooh, girl! How big was it, could you tell? Was it on some Idris Elba shit from the movie *"Takers"* when he got out the bed and you could see that big Black Mandingo Warrior dick behind his drawls! That print was like POW!"

"God help this girl," Vanessa chuckled. "I'm not telling you! All I'ma say is he definitely ain't small."

"Then he's probably a two pump chump… shit, you better hope his ass ain't gay."

"Here you go! He's definitely not gay."

"Shit, you don't know. Niggas hide that shit too well these days. And it don't even be the obvious fagalicious fairies you gotta worry about. Those the ones who are cool with me because they accept their gayness, they ain't trying to hide it. It be those fine niggas with the deep-ass Barry White voices, talking about just cause they let a bitch eat they ass or stick a finger up they ass, that don't mean they're gay, knowing muthafucking well they're a jail sentence away from getting butt-fucked like Bubba's bitch. You better watch that nigga," Arianna warned.

Yani

"If you don't shut up, Arianna I swear on my life, I'ma punch you in the throat. Eric is not gay." Vanessa rolled her eyes starting to become annoyed.

"Alright, if you say so. But if his dick ain't little and he's not a two-pump chump or gay, you got another problem."

"And what's that, Ms. Know-It-All?" Vanessa retorted.

"He might be fucking somebody else. And this ain't me on some hating shit either, Vanna. I'm dead up. When a nigga ain't worried about getting pussy from the chick he's with, it's because he's getting pussy from somewhere else. Don't believe me if you want to. All jokes aside, that's some real shit. Any nigga on the street will tell you that. All that I'll wait for you shit, it's no rush, or whenever you're ready, is a bunch of bullshit. One thing a nigga not gonna go without is some pussy. He might go without food, a haircut, hell a nigga will even go without washing his fucking drawls. But he for damn sure ain't gonna go without getting any pussy from somewhere. So remember this, if I ain't teach you nothing, I taught you this; what you won't do, there's twenty thousand bitches lined up waiting to do that and more. Eric is young, fine as hell, has his own place, his own car, don't have a bunch of ratchet kids by a bunch of different ratchet-ass baby-moms running around. He has good credit, never been to jail and got money. What bitch wouldn't be throwing the pussy his way?" Arianna looked at Vanessa with the screw face as though she should know better.

"Does that include you?" Vanessa asked her best friend seriously.

Arianna stared at Vanessa for a moment before smiling. "I'll tell it to you like this, if you wasn't my home-girl and I didn't love you like a sister, I would have fucked that nigga months ago and had a toothbrush, a drawer and closet space in his house. I'd have the keys to his car, know when he gets paid and what percentage is going to be mine." And with those words, Arianna went into the kitchen to get her a bowl of ice-cream.

Vanessa thought on Arianna's words. She began to wonder if what she said was true. What if Eric wasn't worried about having sex with her because he was getting taken care of by someone else? What if holding onto her virginity left her inexperienced and unable to satisfy her man, which would ultimately cause him to look for sexual satisfaction from another woman. She was falling in love with Eric and didn't want to lose him over sex. She sat down on the bed and began to devise a plan to seduce him for her 21st birthday that was coming up in a week.

The night of her birthday, she pretended she had a serious craving for some cookie dough ice-cream and begged Eric to get her a half-gallon from the market. While he was gone, she quickly showered again and put on the sexy lingerie that she purchased from Victoria's Secret earlier that day. It was a black, lacey bodysuit that accentuated her cleavage and was see-through in the midsection as well as in the crotch area. She made sure the day before she got herself a Brazilian bikini wax and waxed her legs as well. She was just placing the bow on her tummy when she heard Eric's car pull up in the drive-way. She hurried to put the six inch heels on and ran into the kitchen almost stumbling and falling twice. She posted up on the kitchen counter in a sexy pose and waited for Eric to come into the kitchen. Vanessa could hear that he was talking on the phone and began to get nervous as he got closer to the kitchen. When Eric saw her, he stopped in mid-sentence.

"Yo, I'm going to have to call you back…" he said as he peered at Vanessa. He disconnected the call and sat the phone and the bag on the kitchen table before looking Vanessa over, immediately becoming erect as he gazed at her body.

"Damn baby, is it my birthday or yours?" he asked as he walked over to her.

Vanessa giggled nervously. "Mine," she replied as Eric kissed her neck. "But I don't mind sharing." They kissed each other but Eric pulled away from her.

"Are you sure about this? I don't want to rush you into anything."

Vanessa nodded. "I'm sure."

Eric kissed her again before picking her up and carrying her to his bedroom. Vanessa thought she would be terrified but she felt completely safe with him at that moment and wanted to be with him intimately more than anything in the world. She watched Eric as he undressed like a wide-eyed toddler seeing an amusement park for the first time. The only thing she could think of was how absolutely amazing his body was. She marveled over every inch of him feeling like she would lose her breath. She wanted to take in every second, every minute; memorize every detail, scent and taste so she could play it again and again in her mind and never forget.

Eric was gentle and passionate with her so much so that Vanessa thought she would cry. She had never felt such ecstasy before in her life. When it was over, she clung to him shaking as they looked at each other. If she had not been sure before that night, she was absolutely positive at that moment that she was in love with him and there was no doubting it.

Eric kissed her again as he looked in her eyes. "I love you, V-Dot." He laid next to her, pulling her close as he wrapped his arms around her.

"I love you, too," Vanessa replied as she snuggled close to him before falling asleep.

3

Vanessa wiped her eyes as she reminisced on the night her and Eric first made love. And as usual, she couldn't help but to wonder how someone who had been so tender, loving and kind to her, could turn into such a monster. She slowly got up and winced before grabbing her side. She took a slow, deep breath, praying that her ribs weren't fractured again. The excuses of falling down the steps were getting tired and she had already used that excuse twice at Einstein Hospital, Chestnut Hill Hospital, Abington Memorial Hospital and Temple University. They were eventually going to either figure she was very clumsy or was lying her ass off.

After a moment or so, Vanessa slowly made her way downstairs to the kitchen and put the tea kettle on the stove to make herself some chamomile tea. She sat down at the counter and laid her head down, closing her eyes. She felt weak physically and mentally, though she was positive that was not always the case with her. Vanessa could recall conversations that she had in her high-school classes with other students about domestic violence and the stand that she took on it. She believed a woman who stayed with a man who beat her was dumb as hell and no amount of fear in this world would cause her to stay in a situation that was harmful to her. And now look at the irony. She couldn't help but wonder if God was punishing her or making her see first-hand that her viewpoint on domestic violence was incorrect. Fear can be overpowering, and sometimes no amount of strength can get a woman to see the light when she is in this kind of trouble. It's easy to say what you'll do in a situation when you're not actually in that situation. And now Vanessa found herself in this situation and didn't know what to do to get herself out of it.

That passing thought made her reflect on the day that Eric hit her for the first time.

The brokerage firm that he worked for was having a Black Tie party and Eric wanted to take her with him so she could meet some of his partners and friends. He convinced her to wear a black Diane Von Furstenburg dress that was form fitting and low-cut in the back. The dress was long with a slight flare at the bottom. She wore a pair of open toe, strappy four inch heels, and carried a clutch handbag. Eric walked into the gala like a proud man with his beautiful woman on his arm. But they hardly spent any of the evening together. Eric was mostly with his partners talking business and left Vanessa alone for primarily the entire night. After feeling stupid while standing in a corner watching everyone mingle, and losing sight of which way Eric went, she went over to the bar and ordered herself a glass of champagne. She was sipping it and casually bopping her head to an old P. Diddy song playing when a gentleman sat down next to her and ordered himself a drink as well. Vanessa vaguely paid him any mind as she wished Eric would come back from wherever he was so they could either dance together or go home.

"How are you doing?" the man asked her in a friendly voice.

"Oh, hello," Vanessa smiled. "I'm doing pretty good tonight, and yourself?"

"I'm well, thank you. Nice party. Could have done better with the DJ, though," the friendly man chuckled.

Vanessa swallowed her drink back almost choking on it as she tried to suppress her giggle.

Yani

"I'm Antoine, by the way," the friendly man said as he extended his hand to shake hers.

"Vanessa," she replied with a smile and shaking his hand.

"So Vanessa, are you with one of the firms here?"

"Oh, no. I'm just a guest. I'm here with my boyfriend, but he seems to have disappeared on me. I guess he's drumming up some more business so I'm not too upset."

"Ahh… the beautiful ones are always taken. What a shame," Antoine said before drinking from his wine glass. "Well, shame on him for leaving a pretty lady alone in a room where the wolves could descend at any moment."

Vanessa chuckled. "I'm a big girl, I can take care of myself."

Antoine smiled. "I don't doubt that for one second." He finished his drink and extended his hand to be shaken again. When Vanessa went to shake it, he brought it up to his lips and kissed it briefly. "It was a pleasure meeting you Ms. Vanessa. Enjoy the rest of the party."

"The pleasure's all mine," Vanessa smiled. She was still smiling as Antoine walked away. She checked him out a little longer before turning back to the bar to finish her drink. She never saw Eric approaching from the direction Antoine was headed in.

"See something you liked?" Eric asked from behind her.

Vanessa turned towards him and smiled. "Hey, babe." She stood up to kiss him on the cheek but the look in his eyes made her feel as though something was wrong. "Did everything go okay with your co-workers?"

"Everything was fine. Are you ready to go?" Eric asked flatly.

"Yes, sure if you're ready, I'm ready." Vanessa stood up and Eric sat a twenty on the bar for the bartender. He instructed him to keep the change and he and Vanessa waited for the valet to bring his car around.

The silence felt awkward to Vanessa so she cleared her throat. "Is everything okay?" she asked.

"I don't know, you tell me," Eric replied as he looked at her.

"What's do you mean?"

"Who was the dude at the bar?"

"Oh, Antoine? He was just a guy that was buying a drink and he asked if I was enjoying the party. I told him I was here with my boyfriend and was having a pretty good time. He cracked a joke about how they could have hired a better DJ and when he finished his drink, he told me to enjoy the party and left," Vanessa explained wondering why Eric would let that bother him.

Eric laughed sarcastically as the valet handed him the keys to his Infiniti. "Antoine. You on a first name basis with these niggas now?"

"Eric, why are you getting bent out of shape over a friendly guy who was buying a drink near me and was just being cordial."

"I ain't bent out of shape over no nigga being cordial. That nigga wasn't being cordial. He kissing your hand and you smiling at him, checking the nigga out while he's damn near across the fucking room. I'm not bent out of shape, try fucking annoyed," Eric snapped.

"First off, you need to stop cursing at me, Eric. I'm not talking to you like that so don't talk to me like that," Vanessa replied becoming upset.

"What? I'll talk to you any fucking way I want. Fuck wrong with you."

"Whatever, Eric. I don't know what your problem is tonight but like I said, don't talk to me like that. Getting mad over a guy kissing my hand is so petty. It's not even that deep."

"I'm petty? I'm being petty, now? You're calling me petty? I leave you alone for five minutes and you in the party acting like a hoe."

"Acting like a what?!" Vanessa repeated looking at Eric as though he had lost his mind. When Eric stopped at a light, she opened the car door to get out. Eric snatched her by her arm and pulled her back to her seat. "Get off of me!" Vanessa yelled at him as she yanked away.

"Close the damn door, where the hell do you think you're going and I'm talking to you? Close the fucking door, NOW!"

The look on Eric's face slightly frightened Vanessa. The light turned from red to green and the cars behind them began to honk. Vanessa slammed the car door shut and folded her arms across her chest.

"I know you better not slam my fucking door again," Eric practically growled. He continued to snap at her about Antoine from the party for the duration of the ride home. When he parked in the driveway, Vanessa got out of the car and slammed the door again. She marched over to the front door and used her key to unlock it. No sooner than she made it to the living room, Eric snatched her by her arm and spun her around before slapping her in her face. Vanessa cried out and stumbled back in her heels almost falling. She put a hand to her face feeling the sting from his slap and looked at him with tears in her eyes. When she got over the shock of him slapping her, she cocked her fist back and swung back at him but Eric blocked it.

"Bitch!" Eric barked. He punched Vanessa in her face, knocking her to the floor. Before Vanessa had a chance to brace herself, he was on top of her. "Bitch, I will break your fucking neck in here, swinging on me like you're tough!" Vanessa struggled to fight back, screaming for him to get off of her, but that only infuriated him some more. He put his hand around her throat and squeezed. Her legs kicked beneath him trying desperately to kick him in the groin.

"Oh bitch, I see you have to learn the hard-way," Eric said as he snatched Vanessa by her hair and dragged her from the living room to the stairs. Her arms and legs flared as she screamed and begged for him to stop, but her cries fell on deaf ears. As Eric tried to drag her up the stairs, she clung to the banister. He used his fist to beat on her knuckles to make her let go. He then yanked her away, and dragged her up the stairs. He stopped momentarily between steps to slap her in the face again. When they got to the bedroom, Vanessa tried to scramble to her feet but Eric punched her in her back and in her ribs, knocking the wind out of her. He then grabbed her by the neck again, lifting her in the air and throwing her to the floor.

"You better not ever fucking disrespect me like that again! Ever! You hear me!" he yelled before kicking her like a dog.

Vanessa curled up in a ball with her arms covering her head and her face to protect herself from any other punches or slaps he may have delivered. She cried and sobbed as she peeked from behind her arms to see where he was.

"Shut the fuck up," Eric said calmly before walking out of the room. Vanessa listened for his footsteps and heard him when he walked down to the kitchen. She laid on the floor a little longer, struggling to catch her breath while wondering what the hell had just happened. Who was the monster impersonating the man she slept with almost every night and had loved more than anything in the world? When she felt like she could move, she sat up slowly and placed her hands to her head as she felt dizzy and nauseous. She crawled hurriedly to the bathroom and lift the toilet seat up, vomiting everything she ate and drank that evening. She rest her head against the cold porcelain bowl and began to sob. Vanessa stopped when she thought she heard Eric coming back upstairs. She quickly shut the bathroom door and locked it.

"V-dot, open the door," Eric said as he twisted the door knob. His voice sounded much calmer than it did five minutes before.

"No!" Vanessa said back as she choked on her sobs.

"Vanessa, please. Let me in. I just want to talk, babe."

"Talk? With what, your fists? I think you've said enough."

Eric placed his hand on the door and leaned on it. "I'm sorry, babe. I don't know what came over me. Just please, let me in so I can make sure you're okay. Let me make this right, please. I never meant to hurt you, I swear. I'll never put my hands on you again, I promise. Please, open the door so we can fix this. Please, Vanessa. I love you."

Vanessa closed her eyes and listened to him. Though she loved him, she was terrified of him at that moment.

She began to think that maybe she did gawk at Antoine as he walked away a little longer than she should have. She knew she wouldn't have appreciated it if she caught Eric kissing another woman's hand and then gazing at her body as she walked away. *"But he still shouldn't have hit me,"* she thought to herself. She then thought that maybe she should hear him out. *"If you listen to the bullshit he's about to spew when you open that door, you are a fool. Once a beater, always a beater! Trust me."* a little voice said in her head. She silenced it as she slowly unlocked the door and opened it. She was shocked to see Eric with tears cascading down his face.

He looked at her and winced. "Aw damn baby… I…" he shook his head unable to find the words. "I can't believe I did this to you. I swear, I've never done anything like this before. I swear, I've never, ever hit a woman before. My mother raised me better than this. I have sisters and would break a muthafucka up if I ever heard they had done something like this to them." He reached his hand out to her face to wipe her tears away and Vanessa flinched and moved away from his hand.

"How could you do this to me, Eric? I didn't do anything! I thought you loved me," Vanessa cried.

"Vanessa, I do love you. I guess I was more stressed over the party tonight than anything else. Not with you or Antoine, just some things that happened with the discussion I was having with some of the guys we were trying to do business with. Some of the senior partners were spitting my ideas like they were their own and was shutting me outta things. I took it out on you. I shouldn't have done that." Eric hung his head in shame and put his hands to his face. "I fucked up, babe. I fucked up bad and if you wanna leave, I guess I don't have a choice but to respect that and let you go…"

Vanessa stared at him for a moment, her heart aching. The better part of her knew she should run and never look back. But too much of her loved him. Vanessa loved him hard. He was her first love and the only man she had ever loved or been in love with. She understood that no relationship is perfect and felt that they could get through this with a little counseling and maybe even praying together.

She reached for his hand and held onto it. Eric grabbed it and fell to his knees in front of her. He buried his face in her abdomen and cried like a baby.

"I promise we'll fix this. I love you more than anything, Vanessa. I've never loved a woman the way I love you. You mean everything to me and I swear I'll never fuck up like that again. I promise you."

Vanessa was speechless as she stroked the back of his head. She promised herself at that moment that if he was willing to work with her, she was willing to forgive him and try to fix their relationship so they could be stronger together.

"I love you too, baby. But this can't ever happen again, Eric. I mean it. If it does, I'm gone. Do you understand me?" Vanessa said sternly,

"It won't happen again. I swear. It won't." Eric stood up and kissed her gently. He then sat her down on the toilet and left the bathroom before returning with her bathrobe and a towel. He turned the tub water on and poured some melon scented bubble bath in the water, running her a hot bubble bath. He then undressed her gently and helped her step into the bathtub. He took his time washing her body, squirting the hot, bubbly water down her back and over her chest, soothing her. Afterwards, he helped her from the tub and gently dried her off before placing her robe on her and carrying her to their bedroom.

They made love that night as they did on her birthday just two months before. And he held her in his arms like he had held her the very first time and Vanessa began to relax, foolishly believing that things were going to be like they were before that dreadful evening.

4

The tea kettle began whistling and Vanessa got up from the counter. As she was fixing herself a mug of hot tea, she heard Eric pulling into the drive-way. If her ribs weren't so sore, she would have ran back upstairs and got in the bed, pretending to be asleep. Instead, she continued fixing her tea, already knowing what to expect when he came in the door: an apology, possibly some flowers and then the script would flip to how if she had not disrespected him the way that she did, things would not have taken an ugly turn. *"How long are you going to let this go on? What is it going to take? A punch that does more than leave a bruise? A kick that does more than leave your ribs sore?"* Vanessa shook her head to silence the voice inside of it just as Eric came inside.

He walked over to her quietly and kissed her on the cheek without saying anything as though nothing happened earlier. She kept her mouth closed as well not wanting to say anything that would set him off and cause him to unleash another ass whipping on her. She glanced up and noticed that there were no flowers or apologetic gifts. She stirred the honey and sugar in her mug and then blew softly on it before taking a sip.

Eric looked through some papers and then sat a stack of mail on the counter before heading over to the stairs. "Are you coming to bed?" he asked.

"As soon as I finish this tea, I'll be right up," Vanessa replied softly. And without responding, Eric went upstairs without her.

Vanessa sighed and sipped her tea. She wished she had someone she could call and talk to. Because she was an only child, she had no sisters she could cry to and no brothers to protect her. And with the connections that Eric had within the police department and in other places, calling the cops was out of the question. The only person she had in her corner since she was a little girl was Arianna and they barely talked to each other because Eric kept her on such a tight leash. He claimed Arianna ran the streets too much and was an educated hoe. But Vanessa knew what the problem really was. Arianna wasn't afraid of Eric and made a damn good point to let him know if she said the word, she'd blow his fucking head off and not think twice about it. She had tried to get Vanessa to leave Eric and did not hold her tongue when it came to speaking on her disdain for him.

Vanessa sipped from her mug once more as she thought back on the big blow up between her, Eric and Arianna. It was after the first time he beat her…

Vanessa had spent so much time at Eric's house that it was almost as though she didn't have a place with Arianna anymore. She still paid her half of the rent, not wanting to leave Arianna hanging, but it had gone from her living at the apartment and spending the night at Eric's, to her living at Eric's and spending the night at the apartment.

The fall semester wasn't going to be starting for a couple of more weeks so she wasn't sure if Arianna was home or if she had company, so she text her phone: *"hey chica, you busy?"* Moments later, her phone was ringing.

"Ting-a-ling-a-ling, school bell ring, LSU seniors up in this thing!" Arianna sang into the phone to the tune of Shabba Ranks reggae hit *"Ting-a-ling-a-ling".* She burst into a loud laughter. "Heyyy sis!"

Vanessa smiled as she grabbed her purse and her keys. Hey, sis. What are you doing?"

Yani

"Nothing girl, just watching that episode of *Grey's Anatomy* when dude had the bomb in his chest. You gotta love Burke. He hit that floor mad quick when ol' girl snatched her hand out of that guy's chest." Arianna laughed again.

"Yeah, that was always my favorite episode, too. Hey, is it okay if I hang out over there today?" Vanessa asked.

"Oh, I guess you and Eric got tired of fucking like rabbits and now you want to adopt me," Arianna said sarcastically. "This is still your home, baby-girl. I'm not going anywhere, today. Come hang out. We can gossip about these little mid-west White girls moving into the La-Salle dorms plotting on some big black cock. You better watch your man, girl!"

Vanessa chuckled lightly. "Okay, I'm on my way." She disconnected the call and left a note for Eric letting him know where she was in case he got in before she got back. She threw her sunglasses on to hide the bruises on her face planning to stop at Rite-Aid and grab some foundation to cover up the bruise near her eye and on her cheek. She knew if Arianna saw her bruises, she would be ready to draw blood and Vanessa could not handle that drama today.

She dabbed the make-up on while sitting on the back of the bus trying to be discreet while grateful that it wasn't crowded. She didn't have a clue on how to wear make-up but tried her best to make sure the bruises were covered well.

She was shocked to see Arianna waiting in the doorway for her as she walked up the street. "Hey chica!" she said with a huge smile on her face.

Arianna looked at Vanessa crossly wondering why she would be wearing sunglasses on a cloudy day. "Hey boo, what's up with the shades?"

Vanessa touched them tentatively. "Oh, Eric bought them for me and I couldn't wait to wear them so… sun or no sun, I was wearing these bad boys today," she laughed nervously.

Arianna chuckled with her suspiciously. She knew something was up and hoped it wasn't what she thought it was. She opened her arms to hug her best friend and was more than slightly mythed when Vanessa winced and cringed after she squeezed her. Arianna backed away and looked her bestie over. "Are you okay?"

Yani

"Yeah, I'm fine. I just called myself working out with Eric yesterday at the gym and I'm feeling it today, that's all," Vanessa lied.

Arianna knew she was lying and she was now positive that there was something more going on. "Take the glasses off, Vanna."

"You know I hate when you call me that," Vanessa replied, refusing to take the glasses off.

"Never mind that shit. Take off the glasses," Arianna said more sternly. "Take them off, now."

Vanessa was moving too slow with taking the shades off so Arianna snatched them off of her face. Her mouth hung open and she gasped. "Vanna… seriously?! SERIOUSLY!"

"Ari, it's not that deep, really I'm fine," Vanessa said as she reached for her sunglasses.

"The hell you are?! What the hell kind of work-out were y'all doing yesterday? Because judging by that black eye and your sore ribs, I'm going to guess boxing and you were the punching bag! Did Eric do this to you?"

"I'm fine," Vanessa replied, avoiding the question.

"You are not *fine*!" Arianna snatched her friend by the arm and pulled her into their apartment and slammed the door behind them. "Why the fuck is he putting his hands on you? Don't he know I will put two in him with no fucking regards as to where they bury him?!"

"It was an accident, Arianna. He didn't mean it."

"Oh!" Arianna said sarcastically. "Forgive me for thinking the worst! Tell me more about how you tripped and your face hit his fist!"

"Arianna, please. I didn't come over here for this. I don't want to talk about it. We had a misunderstanding last night but we're going to work it out. Everything will be fine."

"Everything will be fine when you leave that woman beating bastard where he is and get as far away from him as possible. Tell me you didn't fall for the bullshit apology routine."

Vanessa sat down in a chair and covered her face as the tears slid out of her eyes. She was confused and an emotional wreck. She came to her best friend with the hopes that Arianna would take her mind off of what happened the night before, not to be badgered and ridiculed for something she felt as though she had no control over.

Yani

"Vanessa, you're like a sister to me. Cradle to the grave, sis. Cradle to the grave! There is no way I can sit by while you let this happen. You're better than this! You deserve better than this. And just because he has a few dollars and showers you with fancy shit and fucks like a porn star, that does not give him the right to beat on you! His wallet ain't made of gold and neither is his dick!" Arianna preached angrily.

"Will you just drop it, Arianna!? Damn, that's why I didn't want to say anything to you because you always go off on some ghetto, Shakespearean monologue, and I can't deal with that right now. So please, just drop it. I just want to hang out today like we used to, watch re-runs of *Grey's Anatomy* or *Law & Order SVU*, eat popcorn, pizza and ice-cream and gossip about the new White girls moving in on campus. Can we just do that, please?" Vanessa asked her best friend with tears in her eyes.

Arianna thought Vanessa was being stupid. But if she didn't want the stress of talking about whatever happened between her and Eric the night before, she would grant her that pass. But eventually they would talk. Arianna would see to that.

"You're terrible at putting on make-up," Arianna said flatly with a half-smile.

Vanessa smile with her. "I know…"

Arianna cleaned up Vanessa's face and gave her a heating pad to put on her side to ease the pain from the bruises on her ribs. They sat together talking and laughing as though nothing had happened. Vanessa's phone went off quite a few times with phone calls and text messages from Eric but she ignored them. Even though the night before she said she would forgive Eric and they could work on fixing whatever had been broken so their relationship could last, hearing what Arianna said brought her back to her senses. She decided that she would leave Eric. She didn't want to be one of those weak women who constantly went back to her abuser. One time was enough.

Vanessa had fallen asleep but was awakened by the sound of Arianna's very loud and angry voice.

"Hell no, you can NOT come into my damn apartment. Now you better get your ass out of here before I call the cops on you!" Vanessa heard Arianna saying. She knew that it was Eric and jumped from her bed with her heart racing. She was afraid to leave her bedroom but she didn't want the argument between Eric and Arianna to escalate nor did she want the nosey neighbors to start peeking out of their doors.

She swallowed past the knot of fear in her throat and took a deep breath before going into the living room.

"Vanessa, what happened babe? I thought you said we were going to work things out last night?" Eric asked, sounding sad and confused.

Vanessa opened her mouth to speak but didn't know what to say. She looked at Arianna, who was staring at her as if she would go upside her head if she even thought about bringing Eric into their apartment, and then she looked at Eric who looked heartbroken. He looked as though he was under a lot of stress and just needed someone in his corner to reassure him things would be okay. She was his woman and it was her job to be in his corner and have his back.

Vanessa sighed and shook her head. "It's okay, Arianna. Let him in."

"What!? Are you fucking…? SERIOUSLY!" Arianna stopped talking abruptly and laughed sarcastically before opening the door wider for Eric to come in.

Eric walked over to Vanessa and held her hands. "When I got home and you weren't there, babe I was so worried. I was scared in fact, because I thought that you changed your mind and decided to leave me after all."

Vanessa shook her head. "I thought about it and what happened last night was…" she paused as she tried to find the words to say. "I can't even find the words to describe what happened last night. But I can't do this again. I can't let what you did to me slide like it's okay because it's not."

"It's not okay, V-Dot. I understand, I fucked up last night. I messed up, but I promise you, it won't happen again."

"Oh nigga, please. You heard what she said so get your woman-beating ass the fuck up out of here before I call the cops," Arianna snapped as she snatched open the front door.

"Ari…" Vanessa started.

"Look shorty, I never had a problem with you before, but if you keep talking to me like I'm one of these nut-ass niggas on the street, you about to have a problem with me today," Eric said with base in his voice as he glare at Arianna.

Yani

"Yeah you talk real tough when you up against a female. Let's get one thing straight, I'm not fucking Vanessa. You put your fucking hands on me, nigga…"

Eric advanced towards Arianna and Vanessa tried to grab his arm to stop him as her heart raced, but he yanked away from her. Before Vanessa or Eric had a chance to react, Arianna had a knife at his throat. Vanessa screamed.

"Arianna, no!" Vanessa cried out.

"Now what, bitch. Take one more muthafucking step and I will cut a second smile across your throat, nigga. Try me!" Arianna said through clenched teeth. They stared daggers at each other for what seemed like an eternity to Vanessa.

"Arianna, please…" she begged. "He's not going to do anything."

"Oh I know damn well his punk-ass ain't going to do anything except walk out of this bitch or he'll be carried out of this bitch if he tries something," Arianna replied never taking her eyes off of Eric. She saw the way he glanced from the knife back to her eyes as though he was contemplating who was faster. An evil grin crept across her face.

"We're going to leave, Arianna. Just please put the knife down," Vanessa pleaded.

"You are not leaving with him, Vanna."

"Ari, it's okay. We're just going to go somewhere and talk. I'll be okay. He's not going to hurt me."

"He already has," Arianna grimaced. She held the knife to his neck a little longer before stepping away quickly. Eric straightened out his shirt and walked over to the front door. It was so tempting for Arianna to stab him in the back but she managed to restrain herself.

As Vanessa was about to walk past her to leave out behind Eric, Arianna stopped her. "Vanna, listen to me. If you leave with him, he's going to sweet talk you, wine and dine you, offer to give you the moon and the stars but never act on his promises. And as soon as you get comfortable, he's going to beat you again. Trust me, honey. Don't leave with him."

"We're just going to talk, Arianna. That's all."

"What is there to talk about?" Arianna asked hysterically. Vanessa huffed and folded her arms across her chest, shaking her head. Arianna threw her hands in the air out of frustration and waved her towards the door. "Fine, do what you want. But I'ma tell you something;

when he whips your ass again- and he will- don't come crying to me because I don't want to hear it. It's one thing for him to beat your ass by surprise. It's another for him to beat your ass because you went back and let him."

"Whatever," Vanessa said as she marched past Arianna. She slammed the door and left with Eric.

5

The night that Vanessa was reminiscing over, she made the second biggest mistake of her life, which was choosing a man over her best friend. The first biggest mistake was going home with Eric and allowing him to convince her to stay. Arianna's words never rang truer at that moment. He did exactly what she said he was going to do; he wined her, dined her, and gave her the world. But as soon as she got comfortable and thought their relationship was moving in the right direction, the beatings started. At first it was once every few months. Then it turned into every few weeks. Now it was routine for her to get slapped in the mouth or popped upside of her head like an insolent child being scolded by a parent. She walked around as though she was stepping on glass, knowing that the smallest misstep could grant her an ass whipping that would leave her as she was at that very moment, sore and feeling defeated.

Vanessa drank back the rest of her tea and washed the mug out, dried it and put it away. She turned out all of the lights and made her way upstairs slowly, grimacing against the pain in her back and ribs from his punches and kicks. She wished she had the courage to leave. But where would she go? He knew who all of her friends were and where all of her friends lived. And he had threatened her numerous times that if she even thought about skipping out on him, he would see to it that her body was never found. The only thing she could think to do was to try to co-exist with him as peacefully as possible to warn off anymore beatings. *"Or you could always kill his ass,"* the voice in her head said. This time the voice was so loud and clear that she stumbled as she made her way down the hall. She shook her head to clear it and made her way into the bedroom, hoping Eric was asleep.

She slipped her robe off and hung it on the back of the chair before easing into the bed with him praying that he was asleep and didn't force himself on her again. She was just getting comfortable when he punched her in her back.

"Watch your damn feet," he grumbled in a sleepy voice.

Vanessa put her hand to her mouth to muffle her cries knowing that if she disturbed his sleep anymore, he would surely beat her again. She hugged her pillow close to her face and scooted to the edge of the bed. Tears fell into her pillow and she closed her eyes praying for an escape… praying for death.

Vanessa awoke the next morning to a bed filled with rose pedals. Instead of smiling at the romantic gesture, she grimaced. Next to the bed was a breakfast tray with her favorite, strawberry topped French toast with scrambled cheese eggs and turkey bacon. Though she was hungry, she wasn't in the mood to eat. Just as she thought of dumping the food in the trash, her stomach rumbled and she felt sick, so she forced herself to eat the food.

She was about half-way through her breakfast when the nausea became stronger. It hit her like a ton of bricks. She ran to the bathroom and vomited in the toilet. She was about to get up to rinse her mouth out when the need to vomit came again. She puked until she felt empty inside, fatigue and weak. After she was able to compose herself, she ran the cold water in the sink and splashed some on her face. She then looked at herself in the mirror and it was as though her reflection spoke back to her. *Jesus, look at you. You're only 22 years old and you damn near look 40. Wouldn't it be a shame if you were carrying that bastard's child?*

Yani

Vanessa stared at herself as that last statement echoed in her head. She walked back to the room and looked at the calendar on the wall.

"My last period was…" Vanessa mumbled aloud as she tried to think back to the last time she used a tampon. She closed her eyes and then remembered it was more than two months prior when she and Eric had one of their episodes. She remembered when she went to the bathroom afterwards that she at first panicked thinking he had caused internal damage. But was relieved that it was just her menstrual. "…two months ago… that can't be…" she panicked.

She sat down on the side of the bed feeling sick. "Oh my God, no. Please God, no. I can't handle this right now. I can't," she said almost breaking down in tears.

"Can't handle what?" she heard Eric ask from the doorway.

Vanessa jumped when she heard his voice. "I… my um throat is hurting and I feel a little congested like I'm coming down with the flu or something. I'm just not in the mood to be battling anything like that right now," Vanessa lied. She then averted her eyes to the floor.

"I'm sure you'll be fine," Eric replied before kissing her on the forehead. "I have a meeting to go to. The keys are on the table for you to lock up when you go to the market. I bought some orchids from the flower shop for you to plant out front since you said you like the way they bloomed last spring. Is there anything else that you need?"

"No, I'm fine," Vanessa said softly. Eric kissed her on the head again and then left the room. When she heard the front door close, she listened for the sound of his car backing out of the driveway and peeling off down the street. She hurriedly got dressed before snatching her pocketbook from off of the hook in their walk-in closet and grabbed the keys to lock up the house. She had enough on her mind and on her plate. The last thing she needed to be worried about is whether or not she was pregnant with Eric's baby. And if she was, then what? Apart of her believed that would be the golden light for him to see to make him stop beating her. *"Or, what if he beats your ass while you're pregnant and kills the baby? Did ya think of that lil' possibility?"* the voice in her head said.

"Shut up," she said aloud, jumping at the sound of her own voice. That was the first time that she answered the voice in her head out loud. Hearing her own voice in the previously quiet bedroom left a feeling of craziness floating around.

"Great, now I'm talking to myself, answering voices in my head. I guess losing my mind is yet another thing I'll have to worry about," she grumbled as she headed downstairs to leave out of the house.

"Oh no, honey. You lost your damn mind the minute you went back to Eric after he beat your ass the first time…"

"Shut the hell…" Vanessa caught herself and shook her head as she locked the door. Before walking completely away from the house, she began searching her purse for her debit card.

"Hey Vanessa," a friendly voice spoke.

Vanessa jumped, unaware that anyone was out at this time of day.

"Oh, I'm sorry. I didn't mean to startle you," the neighbor said to her.

"It's okay. That's my fault for not paying attention to who was outside. Hi Mr. Tremaine," Vanessa spoke back nervously.

Tremaine gave her a friendly smile to calm her down. "No need to be so formal. I'm not that much older than you."

Vanessa looked at the ground and then shook her head. She knew she needed to hurry up and get to the store. The last thing she needed was for Eric to double back home because he forgot something and catch her talking to another man. Regardless if that man was the neighbor. She did not want to get another ass whipping.

"It was good seeing you again, Mr... um... Tremaine. I should go. Enjoy the rest of your day."

"You do the same," Tremaine replied. He watched Vanessa as she walked timidly and nervously down the driveway. Even if he didn't hear the commotion next door periodically, he could tell by the way she carried herself that the lovely couple wasn't so lovely. Apart of him told him to mind his business. But the better man in him wouldn't let him live it down if something serious had happened to her because he didn't intervene to help her. He jogged down the driveway to catch up to her.

"Vanessa! Wait up a second!" he called after her.

Vanessa glanced nervously over her shoulder and then stopped. "Please don't let Eric have someone out here watching me and they go back and tell him I was talking to this man. Please," she mumbled to herself.

"I wanted to ask you something. I know you're in a hurry so I won't take up too much of your time." He fell silent as he tried to find his words. Vanessa stared at him wishing he'd hurry up so she could go on about her business. Finally, Tremaine just spit it out. "My wife and I were wondering if everything was okay with you in that house."

Vanessa knew what he was talking about and fidgeted for a moment. She had hoped for a long time that the neighbors could not hear the way Eric was beating her ass in that house for the last year and a half.

"What do you mean?" she stammered.

"I don't mean to intrude, it's just my wife told me that she could hear…"

"Hear what?" Vanessa interrupted him, feeling even more embarrassed.

Tremaine sighed, "Vanessa, you can try to hide the black eyes and the bruises on your face when you leave out of the house, but Camille and I know. And we've known for quite some time now. We hear how he beats you over there and for a while…"

Vanessa began walking away. "I have to go."

Tremaine gently grabbed Vanessa's arm and reflex, along from the expectation of getting hit from all of the times that Eric grabbed her by the arm, caused her to flinch as though she was protecting herself against being struck in the face. Tremaine let her arm go feeling sorry as he saw the fear in the young woman's face and how easily her eyes became teary. He knew at that moment that Vanessa was living in constant fear.

"Vanessa…" Tremaine said softly. "My wife and I just want to help you."

"If you really want to help me, just let me go on about my business. Please. If Eric catches me out here talking to you…" she said in a whisper before trailing off.

"Maybe my wife can speak with you…" Tremaine insisted.

"I really have to go," Vanessa turned away from him and hurried down the street to head over to Shop Rite inside of the Cheltenham Mall. She picked out the items she needed to fix dinner for her and Eric that night and then went over to the aisle where she found the pregnancy tests. She grabbed two and threw them in the basket with the other items before hurrying over to a cashier.

Yani

No matter where Vanessa went, she was always nervous and afraid that she was being watched. Eric had warned her numerous times that she had better watch what she was doing when she wasn't in his presence because he always had people watching her. She looked nervously over her shoulder, hoping that there wasn't anyone watching her and saw her purchasing a pregnancy test. She didn't want anyone telling Eric before she had a chance to tell him.

Vanessa noticed a man standing by a rack filled with various magazines. She began to wonder if he was watching her for Eric. He gave her a friendly smile. She waved at him tentatively and began placing her items on the counter.

"Jeez Louise, you need to chill, honey. The man was just checking you out. You keep acting looney and folks are gonna start thinking you a little loca," the voice in her head said.

"Hush, damn it," Vanessa mumbled under her breath.

"You say something, sweetheart?" the cashier asked Vanessa as she looked at her with a raised eyebrow.

"Nothing," Vanessa mumbled. She let out a deep sigh and shook her head. *"See… told ya!"* the voice taunted.

"I didn't get much sleep last night and I'm just saying out loud what I picked up to make sure I got everything," Vanessa lied. She tried to relax a little but the idea that she was talking to herself in public was not sitting well with her.

"Oh don't worry. Chile sometimes, I'm so tired I start seeing shit. I start ducking shit that don't even be flying towards me." The two ladies laughed together as the cashier continued ringing her items up.

"Oh my, now that would be funny," Vanessa giggled. She swiped her debit card and paid for her items.

The cashier handed her a receipt. "Get some sleep, sweetheart, and enjoy the rest of your day."

"Thank you, you do the same," Vanessa replied with a genuine smile. She left the store with a bit more pep in her step and feeling upbeat.

"Is it true that when kicked down, a kind word or gentle smile can help you stand again? Friends become strangers while strangers become friends. Love turning into hate and vice versa in the end?" Vanessa mused. And this time it wasn't the *"she"* inside of her head. "I think I might write that down when I get in the house," she said aloud, not at all bothered by the sound of her voice.

Yani

Vanessa was definitely feeling better by that small, friendly exchange at the market. She walked in the house and began putting the food away when she came across the pregnancy tests. Worry and fear washed over her as she remembered her main reason for going to the store in the first place.

"Back to life… back to reality…" the voice sang in her head.

Vanessa picked the test up and looked at it, suddenly feeling the urge to use the bathroom. She decided she might as well get it over with rather than drive herself even crazier thinking about the what-ifs.

She read the instructions and followed them, waiting for what seemed like an eternity for the test results to come back and let her know what the woman within already knew.

When the five long waited minutes had finally passed by, she picked up the two tests from off of the counter, taking them both just to be sure. She looked from one test to the other, shaking her head in disbelief.

"I'm pregnant…" she mumbled. She stared at the pregnancy tests as if they would burn a hole in her retinas.

She continued to stare feeling as though eternity was right around the corner.

"What am I going to do?" she asked out loud.

"Bitch, are you stupid? Talking about 'what I'ma do?' You better fucking run! Because Eric will kill your ass if you don't…"

The voice was silenced by the doorbell ringing. Vanessa jumped, damn near letting a scream escape from her mouth. She was startled by the sound of the doorbell interrupting the silence in the house. She hurriedly grabbed all of the items from the pregnancy tests and ran down the stairs. She stuffed everything under much of the trash in the kitchen's trashcan and then took a deep breath before walking over to the front door.

"Who is it?" she asked politely.

"Hi Vanessa, it's Camille from next door…" a friendly female voice said from the other side of the door.

Vanessa hesitated, not knowing what to say. "Can I help you?" she replied through the door.

"I was hoping we could talk… maybe inside. Or you could come over to my place…" Camille said back. She looked at her husband and shrugged her shoulders. Though she wanted to help Vanessa as well, she wasn't about to make a fool out of herself talking through a door.

Yani

She was about to give up and walk away when she heard the door unlock and creak open. She turned back around and smiled at Vanessa.

"Hi Ms. Camille," Vanessa replied. There was an awkward silence as Vanessa weighed her options. Eric wasn't due home until almost 6 o'clock and it was barely noon. She didn't see the harm in letting her in the house. After all, it wasn't like the night before with the insurance sales guy.

"Yeah, Eric catch your ass in here with that damn woman and he might be on some bullshit, accusing you of having a lesbian affair and then beat your ass for that. I wouldn't put it past him," the voice in her head smirked. Vanessa took a deep breath and closed her eyes briefly to keep from speaking out loud against that voice.

"Come on in," she said to Camille, opening the door wider for her. Camille walked inside and Vanessa shut and locked the door behind her. She then led her to the kitchen. "Would you like a cup of coffee or some tea?"

"Coffee is good. Thank you, sweetie," Camille replied.

Vanessa put on a pot of coffee as an awkward silence filled the kitchen. She sat down at the counter across from

Camille with their mugs of coffee, a small bowl of sugar and a container of cream.

"So what brings you by today, Mrs. Camille?" she asked, breaking the silence.

"Oh please, call me Camille," she took a sip from her mug as she tried to choose her words carefully. "Well, to be honest with you, Vanessa, I had been wanting to come over here for quite some time, but I just wasn't sure when would be the right time and I didn't want to seem intrusive." Camille looked up from her mug at Vanessa as though she was studying her facial expression. She could tell that Vanessa was not only afraid, but nervous as well. She cleared her throat and continued. "Both Tremaine and I are worried about you, forgive my bluntness. We can hear what's going on over here, the way Eric beats you and honey, we are worried." She took a hold of Vanessa's hands to stop her from fidgeting. Vanessa bit her bottom lip to fight back the tears.

"I know it is so easy for a person on the outside to ask you why you have not left him yet. Trust me, I know. It is much easier said than done. But you are much too young, too smart and too precious to just allow a man to beat on you. God did not put you on this Earth to be that man's punching bag. You've got to get out while you can before something irreparable happens to you!" Camille told Vanessa as she squeezed her hands.

Vanessa sniffed as the tears fell. "If God didn't put me on this Earth to be a punching bag, why is He allowing this to happen to me?" she asked as her voice cracked. "Why is this happening to me? What did I do?"

"Oh Vanessa…" Camille started to say.

"No, you don't understand! Every day, I'm afraid to speak too scared that he might slap me or punch me or choke me until I pass out. You talk about God as if I don't know God. But for the last two years almost, it feels like God doesn't love me."

"He does love you, baby. Trust me, God loves you very much. This is a test sweetie, that's all. It's a test of your strength, it's a test of your will and a test of your love for Him," Camille said to Vanessa.

"Ha!" Vanessa laughed sarcastically. "Then that makes God no different than Eric. He's making me go through this abuse as a way to make me show how much I love Him. How is that any different than the reasoning behind why Eric beats me?"

Camille was silent for a moment as she thought over what Vanessa said. "I know it may seem that way. But believe me when I tell you that God gives you signs to let you know if a situation or a person is right for you and it's up to you to see those signs, understand them and then do what needs to be done to avoid harm. Yes, God will wrap you in His arms and cover you with love and protection. But you have to do what's necessary, you understand me? God puts people in your life for two reasons. Some are placed in your life as blessings, and some as lessons. But you have to be open to the lessons and the blessings and take the right things from each!

"Now I would like to think that today, He woke me up with the courage to speak His word to you, to give you the courage to stand up, Queen! Stand up, Queen! Walk out of here with your head held high, your shoulders back, your dignity and pride and strength in tack, and say I am mother of all things on this Earth and will not be disrespected or harmed by no man!

"A man is supposed to stand by your side and love and protect you and honor you. Not beat you, and leave you broken and defeated!" Camille continued to minister to Vanessa.

Yani

For the first time in a long time, Vanessa felt stronger than she had felt since before the first day Eric first put his hands on her. Everything Camille was saying to her, resonated throughout her body. She swallowed back her tears.

"Where would I go though? I don't have much money and he knows where my mother lives and knows who all of my friends are, the few that I have left since I started dealing with him. I have no brothers and sisters. I don't have anywhere to go."

"You leave that to me and Tre', honey." Camille stood up and took a business card out of her back pocket. "I want you to take this card. There is a woman named Marcella that I want you to call. You speak to her and speak to her only. And when you do, let her know Cammie and Tre' sent you to her and she'll take care of the rest."

Vanessa looked at the card for a moment without saying anything. "Now, you mean leave now?" she asked as she looked up at Camille.

"No, unfortunately, Marcella doesn't get in until after 6pm. But if you are ready to leave tonight, what time does Eric get home?"

"He gets home just after 6pm," Vanessa replied as her heart raced.

"Okay, Tremaine will knock on the door to show Eric his "man-cave" in the basement. They've talked to each other about it over the last couple of months and it's finally finished. Knowing how men are, not to mention all of the cool electronics and technology Tre' has in the basement as well as how it's set up, I'm sure we can steal him away for a good hour. And that's when you run. You run and run as fast as you can. Don't take any clothes with you, don't take any shoes or anything with you. Not even your debit card in case he tries to track you down through your purchases and ATM withdraws. Just you and the clothes on your back. No matter how hard it gets, no matter how tired you get, no matter how much the devil creeps in your mind and starts to fill it with BS lovey-dovey memories to get you to miss him and lead you back to the abuse, you keep running. You understand me?" Camille said firmly.

Vanessa nodded her head as she tucked the card in her back pocket. She then remembered the new pregnancy that she was dealing with. "I'm pregnant!" she blurted out.

Yani

Camille stared at her for a moment and then cursed under her breath. "How attached are you to this pregnancy?" she asked.

"What do you mean? Like, are you suggesting that I get an abortion?!" Vanessa asked feeling horrified.

"No, not at all. I just don't want to have Marcella put herself under fire to help you escape and then you start contemplating what kind of family you might have had and let that be something that leads you back to the abuse," Camille explained.

"Oh no, if you have a means to free me from this man, I'll take the help and never look back," Vanessa said quickly.

"Do you understand what I mean when I say run and never look back?" Camille asked Vanessa.

"Well… I think I do," she replied hesitantly. "Run and never come back to Eric."

Camille took a deep breath and placed her hands on Vanessa's shoulders, staring at her intently. "Sweetie, what I mean is, you will have to sever ties with everyone. It's the only way to ensure your safety and not compromise the network and any other battered women who have been helped with leaving their abusers. Is that something you can handle?"

Vanessa froze. *"Leave my whole life behind? My friends, my mom... Arianna... Could I really just walk away from them like that?"* Vanessa thought to herself.

"Shit, you better rethink this, Vanessa. I mean, maybe if you just tell Eric that you're pregnant, he'll come to his senses and keep his hands off of you for the sake of the baby. But leaving your family behind, shit if you thought talking to yourself was crazy... this is fucking nuts!"

Out of frustration, Vanessa let out an aggravated grunt. "Shush!" she said aloud. Camille looked at her confused. Vanessa tried to calm herself as she thought over what Camille said.

"If this isn't something you can deal with, you can always try calling the police, filing for a restraining order and go stay with friends or family until you guys go to court," Camille suggested.

Vanessa laughed, "A lot of his good buddies are cops. So that won't work," she shook her head. "No, this works. If I can get away from him and keep this baby safe in the process, I'm with it."

Yani

"Okay. So tonight I'm going to be in my garden tending to my rose bushes. When I see Tre' taking Eric down in the basement, I'll flag you to leave out of the back. You don't have to worry about contacting me to let me know you got to Marcella safely. She will contact me to let me know. But go straight to her. No pit stops, no cell phone, nothing. You understand?"

"Yes Mrs. Camille," Vanessa said as she nodded her head. Camille came around the counter and hugged Vanessa tightly.

"Everything is going to be okay, sweetie. Just trust God. Trust that he will never leave you or forsake you. He will see you through this, okay?"

Vanessa cried as she held Camille and nodded her head, too choked up to verbalize how grateful she was that Camille and Tremaine cared enough to help her get away from Eric.

Camille left and went to her house. Vanessa paced around for the rest of the afternoon, nervous as a cow in a meat factory. It seemed like time moved slower than usual and 6pm was never going to get here. She wasn't sure if she was feeling butterflies in her stomach from being so anxious to finally be escaping from Eric's abuse, or if the morning sickness was a silly name for something that doesn't just happen in the morning.

Vanessa decided that if she went about her normal routine, that would help move time along. She took out lamb chops to cook with rosemary for Eric along with string beans to make with baked potatoes in garlic and butter. Just as the food was finishing and she was pouring Eric a glass of wine, she heard him pull into the driveway. Her heart began to race in her chest and her palms started sweating. She looked at the clock as it felt like her body was going to separate into a billion pieces and fly into a gazillion different directions.

"Keep calm, Vanessa. Just act normal. Don't give off any signals," she said to herself.

When she heard his key turning the lock to the door, she put on a somber facial expression, not wanting to look too happy or excited.

"Hey babe," Eric said as he came in the house. "Smells good in here. What's for dinner?"

"Oh, just some lamb chops cooked in rosemary, string beans and white potatoes cooked in garlic and butter," Vanessa replied softly.

Yani

"Sounds good," he said before kissing her softly on the lips. "You feeling any better?" he asked.

"Huh?" Vanessa asked, forgetting that she told him she thought she might be coming down with the flu earlier.

"You said you felt like you were getting sick. Are you feeling any better?" Eric asked.

"Oh… I feel a little better. It's probably something I ate yesterday," she managed a slight smile.

"Oh okay," he replied just as his phone rang. He picked up. "Yo, Tremaine. What's up bro?" And like all of his conversations around her, he left the kitchen and went into the front room to keep Vanessa out of his business. Vanessa peeped out of the window and saw Camille come out of the house and begin to tend to her rose bush just as she said she would. Vanessa admired how happy she appeared to be. She figured it must be nice to be married to a man that not only loved and respected her, but worked with her as a unit. She saw Camille as a very beautiful woman, tall and shapely. Though she wasn't very busty, she had very wide hips with a large backside. She was as dark as a Hershey candy bar, her skin smooth and rich with melanin. She could tell by the way Tremaine hugged and kissed her whenever she saw them together, that he loved and cherished Camille very much. She craved to experience that kind of love, but knew she would never have that with Eric.

Vanessa began feeling even more nervous. Doubt started to creep in her mind as she begin to think what she was about to do was wrong, not to mention unfair to her unborn child to cut his or her father out of their life.

"Would you rather the child grows up in the home and sees you getting slapped around. Or worse, he smacks the child around?" the voice in her head asked. She didn't think that would happen… but then again, she didn't think Eric would be knocking her around like the way he was doing either.

Before she could finish thinking her next thought, she felt the sting from Eric's hand as he slapped her in her face. She cried out and stumbled into the bench, which barely caught her. She clung to the side of the counter to avoid completely falling on the floor.

"I'm talking to you and you're staring off into the heavens like some fucking retard. What the fuck is your problem?"

"I'm sorry, I didn't hear you," Vanessa cried. She lightly touched the corner of her mouth and wasn't surprised to see spots of blood on her fingers. She looked up at him with contempt.

"Oh what, you want to challenge me like you're a man now? Do I need to knock your ass back to reality?" Eric asked as he walked over to her quickly.

"No," Vanessa replied as she coward against the counter. Eric stared at her for a moment longer before sipping from his wine glass.

"Tremaine finished his basement. I'm about to go over there and check it out. I won't be gone too long. Cover my food up and go upstairs in the room until I get back," Eric replied as if he were speaking to a child instead of the woman he claimed to love.

Vanessa stood up and fixed his plate before placing it on top of the stove with a lid over it. She then quietly went over to the stairs and made her way up to their bedroom. She peeked from behind the curtains and watched Eric go down the stairs of their house. She could hear him exchanging words with Camille.

"How you doing, Camille?" Eric replied with charm as he smiled. If Camille didn't know any better, she would have assumed from the smile on his face that he was every woman's dream man.

"Oh, hi Eric! How are you this evening?" Camille spoke in return with a smile.

"I'm good. Tremaine told me he finished doing his basement. I'm about to check it out."

"Oh you're going to love it. I just finished dinner also, so feel free to fix yourself something to eat while you're in there."

"Thanks, Cam. I appreciate it." Eric walked into the house and shook Tremaine's hand before following him down into the basement. Vanessa tapped on the window and Camille looked up at her. She then watched the door for a moment to see if Eric would come right back up. When he didn't, she signaled for Vanessa to run.

Vanessa backed away from the window and ran down the stairs. She was about to go into the basement to leave out of the driveway when she stopped by Eric's plate. She lift the lid covering his food and stared down at it before making a guttural sound in her throat. She then hawk-spit in his food.

"Muthafucka!" she said venomously. That was the first time she had ever used that kind of language before and it felt good. She ran down the stairs to the basement and left out, closing and locking the door behind her. All she had was one hundred dollars cash. She haul-assed down the driveway until she got to the end and even then, she didn't stop running. It was almost as though she couldn't stop running. She felt like a runaway slave. In her mind, she kept saying again and again *"I'm free! I'm free!"*

"Not yet," the voice in her head echoed as air pumped in and out of her lungs.

"Shut up, bitch!" Vanessa said quietly. She heard a horn beep and tires screech as they strained to come to a halt.

"Stupid bitch! Pay attention to where you're running!" the driver yelled at her.

"FUCK YOU!" Vanessa shouted back, before taking off running down the driveway.

Camille was still tending to her bush in the front of her home. She was saying a little prayer that Eric stayed down in the basement for at least another half hour. That would give Vanessa a chance to get to Marcella and start her route. She began walking into the house when she heard Eric coming up the stairs.

"You hooked it up real nice down there. The surround sound with the sub woofers and the three flat screens are a perfect set up for a good fight night or super bowl. Man, you got me thinking I need to get myself my own little man-cave in the house." He and Tremaine laughed like they were old war buddies. Camille was almost in a panic when she saw Eric headed towards the front door.

"Oh wow, I wasn't expecting you to leave so soon. You're not watching the game?" Camille asked casually as she took her gardening gloves off.

"No, I'ma go kick back and relax with my lady tonight. Do the romance thing since she isn't feeling well," Eric replied.

"I completely forgot the game was coming on tonight. It's the Bulls vs the Cavs. Is Derick Rose still hurt?" Tremaine asked as he opened a beer.

"I think he did something to his elbow. I can't even keep up with all of the injuries this man done had this season," Eric replied.

"Yeah it ain't like back in the day where Iverson dislocated his shoulder and was expected to be out for the rest of the season but came back two games later. These cats ain't got that kind of heart anymore."

"How about that…" Eric replied. Before he knew it, Tremaine had him talking about sports for another twenty-five minutes. He finally looked at his watch. "Yeah, let me head on out of here. I know my food is probably cold by now. I'ma see you for that Mayweather fight in a couple of weeks."

"Oh most definitely," Tremaine replied, shaking Eric's hand as though they were good friends. Eric said good-night to them both and went back to his house.

"Babe!" Eric called out as he closed the door behind him and locked it. "She better not had fell asleep and my damn food on the stove all cold," he said. He went upstairs into the bedroom. "V-dot…" he looked around, puzzled. "Well where the hell is she?" He looked in the bathroom and then the other bedrooms, all which turned up empty. "I know this bitch ain't leave the house and not tell me where she was going," he grumbled as he made his way back down the stairs. "Vanessa!" he called down into the basement even though he knew she wasn't down there because she had a fear of basements. He remembered how she screamed and begged him to let her out of the basement when he locked her in there one time after she burned his dinner.

Eric walked past the stove when he noticed his food was uncovered. He was about to cover it up but took a double take.

"What the fuck?!" he exclaimed. "Did this bitch…?" he stood there staring at the thick wad of spit in his food feeling a fury rise within him. How disgusting did a bitch have to be to spit in a person's food? He swore when he got his hands on her, he was going to fuck her up something fierce. It then occurred to him that she left him and the spit in his food was her way of saying "fuck you" to him before leaving. He slapped the plate over in anger causing the plate to flip, fall to the floor and break while spilling its contents all over the place.

"You bitch! You fucking bitch! Where the fuck are you?!" he snapped as he stormed from the kitchen to the living room. He kicked the trash can over as he passed through, his anger causing him to miss the pregnancy tests that Vanessa put inside earlier. He left out of the house and jumped in his car figuring she hadn't gone far. He would find her and bring her back home so they could talk… so they could have a nice, long face to fist conversation.

Yani

Camille was watching from her kitchen window and saw when he left out the house to go find Vanessa.

"And there he goes…" Camille replied as she watched him back out of his drive-way. "Bet money he is going to try to see if he finds her at Broad and Olney or Cheltenham depot or something."

Tremaine slipped an apple slice in his mouth. "You know damn well he is, that controlling sonuva bitch. He's probably mad because he never saw the shit coming. Did she get to Marcella's yet?"

Just as Tremaine was asking his question, Camille's phone went off with a text message coming through. *"Package received,"* it said.

"Yup, she just got there."

"Good," Tremaine replied as he looked out the window. "Let's just hope she keeps going…"

6

Vanessa was huddled over the toilet bowl puking her guts out. The morning sickness seemed to be getting worse with no relief in sight. She had been gone from Eric for almost two months but had only made it to her second stop due to the pregnancy slowing her down. The women who were helping her were very understanding and took special care of her to avoid any stops to a hospital.

Even though she was told to sever ties from her past, she knew there was no way she could walk away from her mother without a word and not run the risk of her mother putting out a missing report on her. After losing her father tragically when she was 16, Vanessa and her mother were extremely close. After explaining that to Marcella, she was allowed to make one call.

"Mom, I just want you to know that if you don't hear from me for a while, I'm okay. I had to leave Eric, mom. You kept saying it was something about him that you didn't like and I guess mothers always knows…" Vanessa

99

trailed off for a moment and took a deep breath. "I just want you to know that I'm okay and I love you. I'll try to be in touch soon. And if Eric comes to you asking if you know where I am, please tell him you have not heard from me. Okay… I love you, mommy." Vanessa hung the phone up as the tears stung her eyes. It pained her to leave that voicemail but she figured it was better than actually talking to her mother and having to dodge or avoid questions or outright lie to her.

Vanessa managed to make it to a small suburban town just outside of Baltimore. Her first stop was in Delaware. At first, she thought she was being passed around like a cheap date until a woman explained to her that she was traveling through a modern day "underground railroad" for battered women. Each stop was secretive and the destinations were never revealed to the woman traveling through, nor was her final stop. She was provided with food, shelter, money and even clothing.

Though it was strongly forbidden, Vanessa wanted desperately to reach out to her mother again or even Arianna to let them know that she was alright. She imagined that her mother was beside herself with worry, sure that Eric went to her with some sad, sob story about how she had left him without so much as a word or explanation, faking concern and worry, pretending to give a damn about her whereabouts when really he was probably upset that she got the drop on him and he couldn't find her.

Many nights she had gotten lonely, and while she did not miss the abuse she suffered from his hand, she sometimes missed lying next to him and feeling his arms around her. She remembered what Camille said about there being times where sweet memories would creep into her mind trying to override all of the horrible memories of the abuse, and foolishly try to convince her to return home. To help her cope with those feelings of heartache and her longing to be near him, she thought of her unborn baby and let the memories of the bruised ribs, the busted lips, the black eyes and the constant fear that he had her living in, snap her back to her senses so she could keep moving through this journey that would help her start a new life.

One afternoon, while she was in a car waiting for her caretaker to pick up a few things inside of Walmart, she noticed that she left her cellphone in the car. Vanessa bit her bottom lip as she looked from the doors leading inside of the store to the cellphone, contemplating whether or not she should call her mother just so she could hear her voice and let her know she was okay. She decided against calling her mother, knowing that Eric would more than likely try to sweet talk her into giving up any information that she had. She knew it would be a cold day in hell before he went to Arianna to find out if she knew where she was. Vanessa figured Arianna could pass the word along to her mother to let her know that she was okay. She also wanted to let Arianna know she was going to be a God-mother.

Vanessa snatched the phone up and dialed Arianna's number quickly as she kept an eye on the doors to Walmart.

"Who's this?" Arianna asked in a groggy voice, not recognizing the number.

"Hey, chick! It's me! Vanessa!"

"Oh my God, girl! Where the hell are you? Your momma is two seconds away from putting out a missing person's report on you!" Arianna exclaimed as she sat up in her bed.

"I can't talk too long," Vanessa said quickly as she continued to watch the doors. "I just wanted you to know that I left Eric."

"It's about damn time!" Arianna interjected. "I kinda figured that when your mom called me saying how Eric came to her crying and shit saying that you decided to take a trip to Miami for a little while claiming you needed time and space from him. Shit, I thought he had pulled some Lacey Peterson shit. I said if I ain't hear from you in the next 48 hours, I was filing a police report."

"Shhh girl! I just said I can't talk long! I can't tell you where I am. There are some people who are helping me get away from Eric. I wasn't even supposed to call you, but I couldn't just leave things the way that they were. I just want you to know that I'm okay. I'm on like an underground railroad for battered women…" Arianna burst out laughing. Vanessa giggled with her. "I'm serious, chica. Don't tell my mom too much. Just tell her I love her, I'm okay and I will do my best to get in touch with her. And tell her she's going to be a grandmother. And you're going to be a Godmother."

Arianna gasped. "Girrrrl! And your mom told me she dreamt of fish, looking at me all suspicious and shit. Awwww girl, I'm so happy for you even though you're carrying the spawn of the devil. Is that what made you leave?" she asked.

Yani

Vanessa saw her caretaker coming out of Walmart. "I've gotta go! Don't call this number back for any reason. I mean it Arianna. I love you, girl. But before I go, I want to say I'm sorry I didn't listen to you that day you pulled that knife on Eric. I was wrong and I never should have put a man over you. I'll never let that happen again. I love you, sis."

Arianna became teary eyed. "I love you too, sis. Cradle to the grave, boo. Cradle to the grave."

Vanessa kissed in her ear and hung up. She quickly deleted the number from the call log and put the phone back as though nothing happened. Then she closed her eyes and pretended to be asleep. She heard the car door open and shifted in her chair.

"Everything okay?" her caretaker asked her.

Vanessa stretched before answering. "Yeah, everything is fine. Where are we headed next?"

"You have an 11 o'clock train leaving Bethesda which will take you to your next stop. They'll take care of you from there," her caretaker replied.

"Oh wow…" Vanessa replied.

"I got you something to eat and a couple bottles of water," she handed Vanessa a wallet. "This is the identification that you will use once you get to your next stop. You'll go by the name Carmen. Start reciting "My name is Carmen" over and over in your head so you get used to it in the event you are ever stopped. Inside of the envelope is a birth certificate, social security card, and a driver's license."

"What a minute… a name change? My identity is changing?" Vanessa asked frantically. "Why?"

"We take what we do very seriously. Countless women die every year by the hands of their abusers. The goal is not only to protect you, but to protect the women who have helped you travel through from stop to stop because in the event that your spouse is dangerous and decides to come looking for you, we put our lives on the line and we could be in danger as well. Which is why we do not allow contact to your past life," her caretaker explained. Vanessa turned away and looked out the car window. She then looked in the wallet and took out the ID. It was a Georgia issued ID. She wasn't even sure when the picture they used was taken. But it looked legit. *"Carmen Thompson"*, she said herself. *"My name is Carmen Thompson…"* she began reciting that in her head again and

Yani

again before closing her eyes and taking the ride to the train station with her caretaker.

7

Eric had driven around for almost two hours trying to find where Vanessa had gone. He didn't even realize that for three blocks, he was driving behind the car that she was in. Had he not been so impatient with how slow they were driving and sped around them as a light was turning from green to red, he would have seen Vanessa when she got out of the car to go into the first safe house.

"Oh my God! That's him!" Vanessa exclaimed in the back of the Acura with the tinted windows.

"That's who?" Marcella asked.

"Eric, the man that's been beating me for almost two years! That's his car! I know that's his car!" she panicked.

"Okay, calm down sweetheart. Just calm down. He can't see you because the windows are tinted and judging by the way he is driving, he seems to be preoccupied with something else." Marcella told her.

"I'm gonna be sick…" Vanessa said in a breathless voice before puking in the back of the car.

Yani

Eric was ready to say fuck Vanessa, and let her go wherever the hell it was that she was going. He told himself that he was getting tired of looking at her and was ready to move onto someone else. But when he got back home that night, the sight of the trashcan that he previously kicked over along with the trash on the floor infuriated him all over again. He was going to wait until the morning to clean it up until he remembered that it was trash day the next day. He wanted to choke the life out of Vanessa.

Eric grabbed the broom and the dust pan and began picking the trash up when he saw part of the pregnancy test box amidst the trash pile that he was about to dump back inside of the can. He picked it up and looked at it for a moment.

"What the hell…?" he said out loud. He began to sift through the trash looking to see if the pregnancy test was in there. He found the first one and looked at the results and then looked at the box to see what the results on the test meant. He then looked for the other pregnancy test when he saw that there were two boxes in the trash and looked at both of them just as Vanessa had done earlier that day.

"Well, I'll be damned. She's pregnant. She had the nerve to leave knowing she's carrying my baby!" He threw the tests to the floor and grabbed his phone. He had called Vanessa's phone numerous times while he was out driving around looking for her, but there was no answer. He dialed her again and felt stupid when he heard the faint ringing of her phone coming from the upstairs bedroom. He went upstairs to the room thinking Vanessa had come back. When he saw that it was only her phone and not her, he became even more pissed. He picked her phone up and silenced it.

Eric was tempted to smash her phone against the wall but figured he better go through her call log and her texts to see who she was in contact with last. The only name that popped up was his name in calls and texts. Nothing from her friends and nothing from her mother.

"Unless her ass deleted her phone activity…" he mused out loud. He went to her Facebook page to see if she had any updates but couldn't locate her. "She deactivated her Facebook…" Eric then saw that she had done the same with her twitter account and her Instagram.

"I bet that bitch Arianna knows where she is. But I ain't asking her shit."

Yani

Eric ordered Chinese food and sat on the side of his bed picking at it more than eating it. *"Who the fuck told you you could leave me? Huh, bitch? And while pregnant with my child at that? Who's helping you?"* Eric mused as he picked through his food. He wasn't going to let her get away with this shit. He was beginning to wish he had killed her ass months ago when the thought first crossed his mind to do so.

"See Ricky, I told you to get a better handle on these little young gals. You gotta knock the sass right outta 'em because once they start thinking they have the upper hand on you, you're never gonna be able to get 'em to fall in line," Eric heard his father's voice in his head. He closed his eyes as his mind began to wander.

Eric sat huddled in a corner with his knees pulled into his chest and his arms wrapped around them tightly with his head bowed. He rocked himself back and forth as he tried to block out the noises coming from his parents' room.

"Please, Kevin! Please, stop!" he heard his mother begging his father. It had become a regular occurrence in their home for his father to beat on his mother and terrorize him.

Kevin cocked his fist back and smashed it into his wife's face before grabbing her by the hair and throwing her onto the bed. "You yelling in my house, gal! I told you before about that shit! I'ma learn you today. I'ma learn you right hard and right now!" he said in a drunken, southern drawl.

Eric could hear the struggle from his room and closed his eyes tightly before putting his hands to his ears to try to block out his mother's pleas for his father to have mercy on her. But her cries fell on deaf ears and Kevin continued to unleash his wrath on her.

He rocked himself faster and harder now joining in with his mother, begging God to spare her. He began to think that God could not hear him or her.

Eric's bedroom door opened and he jerked his head up. He trembled at the site of his father who was a tall, intimidating man standing at six feet and six inches. He weighed a little over 300 pounds and was dark as night. He was what the White folks in the south would consider to be a "burley nigra" or a "mandingo", strong, and made for hard, physical labor. While Kevin had a job, it was one he hated; working in a meat packing factory. Eric remembered how his father always came home with a bottle of Absolut Vodka, smelling of blood and meat. Eric looked up at his father wearing his usual dingy white, tight undershirt that was stained from sweat and his navy blue trousers. His thick belly peeped out from beneath the undershirt and hung over top of the black leather belt that held his pants up. The stench of his musky body odor, blood and meat from that day's work, along with the bottle of vodka that was in his hands, filtered into the room making Eric feel sick to his stomach.

"Get up, boy!" Kevin said to his son in a loud and intimidating voice.

Eric scrambled to his feet. "Yessir?" he answered, timidly.

"Get your little scrawny ass over here. I wanna have a lil' chat with ya about these sassafrass damn womens, running 'round here like they don't know their place."

Eric hunched his shoulders and sulked slowly towards his father. Kevin felt the boy wasn't moving fast enough and snatched him by the scruff of his neck, yanking him closer.

"Boy, when I say get here, I mean get here right quick!" Kevin piped.

Eric whimpered, already putting his hands up, expecting his father to strike him just as he had done his mother moments before.

"Put your arms down, boy. I ain't finna touch you. Come in this room and have a look at your momma. I want you to see a no good, low down dirty, disrespectful whore in living color."

"Kevin, please… not in front of our son… not in…" Eric's mother began to plead as she tried to hide the bruises in her face. She was cut off by Kevin's strong hand as he slapped her back onto the bed. He stood over top of her, strong and intimidating, shaking his

finger at her like a man would chastise a dog who had just pissed on the floor.

"You shut your goddamn mouth unless I ask you to speak, understand me!" Kevin bellowed. He looked at his wife Diane for a moment longer to make sure she didn't try to challenge him, and then turned his attention to his son. He snarled in disgust as he saw the tears running down his face. "Cut out that damn sissy crying and act how a man is 'spose to act. None of that pussy-boy crying 'round here!"

Eric sniffed and wiped his face as he stole a quick and terrified glance at his mother before looking back at his father. "Yes, daddy."

"Now there's some womens in this world who knows they place and knows to do as a man says without question. And then there are whores like ya momma here, who got to learn the hard way. A gal like that, you 'pose to knock 'round when she step outta line 'cause that's the only way to get her back in line, ya understand me, boy?"

"Yessir," Eric replied.

"Don't you get you no uppity gal thinking she can say and do what she wanna 'cause them bitches are the root of all evil. You get yourself a good wholesome girl, untouched, quiet and well behaved. Mark my words boy, anything other than that and you'll have more trouble on your hands than needed, understand me, boy?"

Yani

"Yessir..." Eric replied again.

"But ya didn't listen to me..." Eric heard his father's voice in his head again.

"Get out of my head, you old bastard," Eric mumbled to himself.

"You should have listened to me and none of this woulda happened to ya. Now you done fucked around and let that little gal get the upper hand. More than likely she got a man helping her and that man finna raise your youngin' like his own. They probably laughing at you right now, boy."

Eric threw his food at the wall out of frustration. "Shut up! Shut up, shut up, SHUT THE FUCK UP!" Eric yelled. Before he knew it, he had slid to the floor with his back against the bed, his knees pulled to his chest and his arms wrapped around them, rocking back and forth just as he had done when he was a child. It took him a moment to calm himself and realize what he was doing.

"I'm not about to let that man fuck with me..." Eric mumbled aloud. But the sound of his father's words continued to echo in his mind, and the idea of Vanessa being with another man, lying in his arms while he assumed a father-role position over *his* child nagged at him.

"Fuck this shit!" he growled. He snatched up his cell-phone and called a close friend of his that was a private investigator.

"Hey, Tony. How's everything going?" he spoke into the phone as he began to pace back and forth in his bedroom.

"Hey, Eric! Everything is going good over this end. How about you?" Tony replied as he kicked back in his chair.

"That's what I'm calling about. Listen, I got another job for you."

Tony sat up at attention. Whenever Eric said he had a job for him that meant there was going to be some serious money coming his way. "I'm all ears, bro. Tell me what you need."

"I need you to track somebody down. Remember the young lady that I've been seeing for almost two years?"

"Yeah, yeah. The cute little honey from La Salle that you had been scoping for a while before you finally got with her at the mall that day. What about her?"

"Well, she ran off with another dude and I just found out that she's pregnant. I'm positive the baby is mine, I just want to catch up with her to make sure she doesn't do anything stupid," Eric lied as he continued to pace.

Tony was silent for a moment. They had been down a similar road almost three years prior with another young lady that Eric had been dealing with. He happily obliged when Eric asked for his help that time, thinking he was simply "tracking a person down". Until Regina was found dead in the woods near Belfield Avenue, wrapped in a sheet after being raped and strangled to death. He suspected it was his good friend Eric, but he had a motto: If the money was there, he did not care.

"Tony, you still there, bro?" Eric asked as he stopped pacing.

"Yeah… I was just thinking about the last girl you asked me to track down…" Tony trailed off.

It was Eric who fell silent this time. He waited to see if Tony was going to finish his thought. When he saw that he wasn't, he cleared his throat. "Yeah… I thought I was never going to get over what happened to her. If only I had followed my first thought and went to see her instead of waiting…"

"Yeah… I know," Tony replied quietly. "Well hey, V-Dot ran off with this other guy, maybe the baby isn't yours and she wanted to spare you the pain of thinking that it is only to find out that it ain't, ya know?" While he had his motto, Tony didn't want any more blood on his hands.

"Nah, I know this baby is mine, trust me," Eric replied adamantly.

Tony put his hands to his head knowing there was no way he could deter Eric from his plans. "So who's the guy?" he asked.

Eric hesitated, "I'm not sure. Things happened kinda suddenly."

"Okay… how do you know she's pregnant?"

"Because I knocked over a trash can by accident and two pregnancy tests came out. Both of them were positive. Come on, Tony. I thought we were better than this. What's with all the questions? Don't I pay you well?"

"Yeah but…" Tony started.

"But what? Have you forgotten about that little coke incident I took care of for you. When the cops were on you, I took care of that. I risked my career adjusting that paper work to make your side money look legit," Eric reminded him.

Yani

"I know, I know. I didn't forget," Tony shook his head. He hated when Eric reminded him of the helping hand he extended to him.

"I'll tell you what. I'll pay you double your fee. If you're able to track her down sooner than later, I'll add an additional bonus to your fee as well," Eric said. He knew Tony was a money hungry bastard and definitely wouldn't refuse him at that point.

Tony didn't need to think long. He reminded himself of his motto once again. *"If the money is there, I do not care. After all, it's not my hands that are actually getting the blood on them. All I'm doing is locating the bitch. What happens to her afterwards is not my problem,"* he thought to himself.

"Alright, give me 48 hours to access all camera footage in the area to see if I can get facial recognition or any footage on her. If she took the bus or a cab or got a ride, I'll be able to look into where she went from any cameras in the area. Our best bet are traffic cameras if she was in a car or traveling on foot. The minute I have something for you, I'll call you and let you know," Tony told him.

"My man, Tony. Good looking. I'll send your fee to the usual account tonight. Thanks a lot."

"No problem," Tony replied before hanging up. He got a bad feeling in the pit of his stomach as though something was warning him against completing this job for Eric. But then he thought about the amount of money he was going to make from it and shook the feeling off before getting to work.

8

Two months after Eric hired Tony to help him locate Vanessa, he received a much awaited phone call. He was lying in bed with a new young lady that he had met a month before Vanessa left him. Though he was planning on replacing Vanessa with this new young lady, the split was supposed to be on his terms and not hers. In his mind, he was the only one allowed to move on with another person. Many times he contemplated keeping them both as there were some things that Vanessa was good at that his new companion was not. He had a second apartment in the Chestnut Hill section of the city that he normally spent time with his new friend while Vanessa stayed at home. He knew that Vanessa was none the wiser of his cheating ways. And he also knew the new young lady Clarissa wasn't too much worried either, considering he kept her blessed with the finer things in life. Eric knew that she wanted to keep living that good life and would keep her mouth closed and play her part. Otherwise, it would be back to the three bedroom Section 8 house with her mother and five brothers and sisters all crammed together with the roaches and mice practically sitting at the dinner table with them.

"Hello," Eric said into the phone quietly.

"Hey Eric, this is Tony. Sorry to call so early in the morning…"

"I hope this isn't another bullshit update, Tony. I paid you double your fee and was expecting results two days after you'd been hired. It's been two months. Do I need to hire somebody else?" Eric said in an aggravated voice.

"Hey now, easy tiger. No need to go off the deep end. I have something this morning," Tony replied.

Eric sat up in his bed. "You found her?" he asked eagerly. Clarissa stirred in the bed next to him but did not wake up.

"Not exactly. But remember when we both said it was odd that she wasn't contacting her mother or the friend Arianna at all?"

"Yeah, yeah, what about it?"

Yani

"Well, she finally made contact this morning. She called her friend Arianna. She called from some type of burner phone. No information came up on it yet, I'm still running a scan and trace to see if I can get a beat on the phone's network. That way I can hack into the phone's GPS. Now if the GPS was off while she made the call, I can hack into the phone's camera and hopefully get a clear enough pic of where she was when she made the call."

"Okay, that's a start. So you think it's possible that Vanessa told Arianna where she was?" Eric asked eagerly.

"Well, unless they were talking in codes, no. She didn't say specifically where she was. All she said was to tell her mother that she was okay and to let her know that she was going to be a grandmother. You were right, E-money. She is pregnant and judging by the conversation, the baby is yours," Tony confirmed.

"What do you mean? What else did she say?"

"Not too much. Arianna just told her congratulations and said that she was happy for her even if she was carrying the spawn of the devil… or something like that."

"Bitch," Eric mumbled.

"Say what?" Tony asked, unable to hear what Eric said.

"Nothing, nothing. Let me ask you this, if Arianna called the number back, would you be able to trace the location that way?"

"I might be able to do it a little faster since the call is going out to Vanessa's phone versus coming in from the phone. But Vanessa told her not to call the number back so I don't think that angle is going to work."

"You don't worry about that. I'll take care of that part."

Tony hesitated for a moment not having a good feeling. "Well… if you turn up with something that I couldn't get, I'll work with that and see what else I can come up with."

"Okay, no problem. Thanks Tony. I'll be in touch." Eric hung up the phone and continued to sit on the bed. He was hoping to have found Vanessa by now. He knew she was getting help but from whom? He decided he would have a talk with Arianna and persuade her to tell him what she knew about Vanessa's whereabouts. And if she refused, he would learn her. He would learn her hard.

"That's what ya gotta do, Ricky. Ya gotta learn these dames. Let them know who really runs the bingo. Stop letting them think they can outsmart a man, teach 'em their place and do what needs to

be done to make sure they stay in it." Eric heard his father's voice in his head again. He shook his head as if to clear it even though a part of him believed his father was right.

Eric knew he couldn't approach Arianna because there would be a cold day in hell before she told him anything he wanted to know when it came to Vanessa. He decided to call Tony back and get him to assist him with another task…

Tony was able to find out where Arianna worked easily. For three days he followed her around to get an idea of her routine when she got off of work. Once he knew her route, he gave it to Eric.

Instead of following behind Tony as he tailed Arianna, he decided to ride in the car with him, grateful that he had tinted windows.

"So what's the plan?" Tony asked as they followed behind Arianna one night.

"Just keep tailing her and wait for my orders," Eric said. His adrenaline was going at a rate so high that he began to get an erection. He breathed deeply as they followed behind her car. When they got to an intersection that was practically deserted that humid, summer evening, Eric decided to put his plan into action.

"Hit the back of her car. Not hard, but just enough for her to feel it," Eric said. Being that close to acting out his intentions made his erection even more intense.

"You want me to what? Man, this is a Cadillac! Who's going to pay for the damages?" Tony piped.

"Put it on my tab. Hurry up and do it before the light turns green or someone else comes," Eric said hastily.

"Man, this is some bullshit. This better not fuck up my car, man. I just got this shit detailed," Tony grumbled. He lightly stepped on the gas causing his car to slowly roll behind Arianna until it hit the back of her car causing her to jerk forward.

"Muthafucka!" Arianna piped. She reached for the volume button to her radio and turned the music down. She had been jamming so hard in her car, happy about a promotion she had just earned after only being on her job for five months that she never noticed the black Cadillac CTS following behind her. She practically ripped her seatbelt off and put her car in "park". "You've gotta be muthafucking KIDDING me!" she screeched.

"Get out the car," Eric told Tony. "Get out the car and apologize. Keep her back to the car like you're looking at the damages."

"Wha…?" Tony asked.

"Hurry up, she's getting out of the car."

Tony huffed as he got out of his car. "Oh Miss, I'm so sorry. I can't believe I did that. This is completely my fault…" Tony rambled as he walked over to Arianna.

"Damn right it's your fault! How the hell did you hit me like that? Did you not see the damn red light? Did you not see me sitting at the damn red light not moving? Like seriously, bruh!" Arianna snapped.

"Come on, Tony. Get her to turn around," Eric said as his hand was on the door ready to open it. His erection was so utterly intense that he could feel pre-cum leaking out. His palms began to sweat and his leg shook as he anticipated his next move. He watched as Tony finally got her to turn around so they could look at the damage to the back of her 2012 Impala. There was a dent that wasn't major but still visible.

Eric quickly got out of the car and hurried over to Arianna.

"Yo, bitch!" he said with a grimace. Arianna turned around but was caught off guard and unable to protect herself from the punch Eric threw. It connected with her face, busting her lip and making her nose bleed. Her scream was cut off abruptly as Eric grabbed her by her throat from behind and put his hand over her mouth before dragging her to Tony's car.

"What the fuck, Eric!?" Tony yelled, frightened. He ran back to his car just as Eric rammed Arianna's head into the door knocking the fight out of her. He then threw her in the back seat and climbed in with her.

"Drive!" Eric yelled. "Hurry the fuck up before somebody comes this way!"

"What about her car?" Tony asked in a panic induced state.

"Fuck that car, nigga! Let's go!"

Tony jumped in the car and sped off as he closed his driver door, tires screeching as he swerved around Arianna's car.

"I don't believe this, man! I don't fucking… if I had known this is what you were going to do…" Tony stammered as he tried his best to drive rationally to avoid being pulled over.

"You would have what? WHAT!?" Eric asked, raising his voice. He knew he had the upper hand on Tony with all of the trouble he had helped him to avoid over the years. In his mind, he believed Tony knew better than to cross him.

Tony huffed as he held onto the steering wheel tightly. His palms were sweating as his mind and heart raced. He thought back to the gut feeling he had gotten when Eric first wanted to hire him for a "job" and how he ignored that tiny voice advising him not to get involved. *Me and my stupid fucking motto. If the money is there… fuck!*" he thought to himself.

"Make a right, right here," Eric instructed him. "And slow down before you have the cops on our ass."

Tony made a speedy right, almost jumping the curb.

"Ay, what the fuck did I say, man!?" Eric bellowed as he peeped out of the window to make sure there weren't any cops sitting idly by in a squad car.

"My bad, man. I'm just… never mind." Tony murmured. "Where are we going?"

"Just keep driving…" Eric replied as he peered down at Arianna, who went unconscious after having her head slammed into the car. "Yeah bitch, you ain't so tough without that fucking knife now, are you?" he smirked.

They arrived at what appeared to be an abandoned house in the Kensington section of Philadelphia. Eric instructed Tony to keep watch while he carried Arianna inside. The house was semi dark and dusty, with trash scattered about. Tony came in a few moments after Eric and threw his hand over his mouth to suppress a cough. He gagged over the dank stench as he gazed around.

"What in three fucking hells is this shit?" he thought to himself. He dipped back as though he was dodging a punch when he saw a cockroach scaling a nearby wall. "Oh shit!" he yelped.

"Chill out man, don't act like you never saw a roach before," Eric replied casually. He had Arianna lying on a dusty couch. He leaned over top of her and slapped her face with the back of his hand. "Wake up, bitch. Wake the fuck up."

Arianna stirred before opening her eyes with a wince. When she realized it was Eric standing over top of her she began swinging and kicking. Eric grabbed both of her tiny wrists with one of his hands and grabbed her throat with the other. He then straddled her, putting much of his weight on her to make her stop fighting. He smiled devilishly at the way her face turned red and her eyes began to tear up.

Yani

"Calm the fuck down or I'll snap your neck like a chicken-bone," he threatened her as he leaned close to her face.

Arianna was terrified and knew there was only one reason why she could be in this situation. She tried to calm down as best as she could while making sure she kept her eyes on Eric.

When he was sure that she wasn't going to fight him any longer, he slowly got off of her and moved his hand from around her throat while letting her wrists go. Arianna turned to her side and began coughing and gagging as she struggled to get in air to breathe.

"If you don't need me here, I have a few errands I need to run…" Tony said nervously from behind Eric. But the look that Eric gave him let him know to sit in a corner somewhere and shut the fuck up. He preferred to stand.

"It seems Vanessa's been a bad girl," Eric started as he paced around her.

"I don't know where she is," Arianna said as she rubbed her throat.

"You think I'm stupid, don't you?" Eric asked as he looked down at her.

Arianna snickered. *"Think?"* she replied sarcastically. "Oh no, baby. I *know* you are."

Eric hauled off and slapped Arianna ferociously across the face, almost making her fall off the couch. She hollered out in pain. "Your mouth should have gotten you a check your ass can't cash a long time ago."

Arianna giggled. "That's what I love about weak little pussies who beat on women like you; always got some slick shit to say out of your mouth."

Eric swung at Arianna again and she managed to block it. She used the palm of her hand to strike him in the face, causing his nose to bleed. When he staggered back, she jumped up to run but Tony grabbed her.

"Get off of me!" Arianna screamed as she struggled against the much stronger and taller Tony.

Eric touched his nose tentatively and looked at his fingers and the blood that covered their tips. He stormed over to Arianna, snatching her by her hair. She clawed at Tony, scratching him as Eric slung her across the room. She hit her head on the hard, wooden banister to the staircase and slumped to the floor, lying still.

"You spick-ass-bitch, get the fuck up!" Eric barked at her. Tony placed his hand to his neck where Arianna scratched him and winced as Eric walked over to where Arianna was laying. He peered at her on the floor and suddenly had a feeling that she wasn't getting up. "Looks like she ain't so tough after all. Knocked the fight right outta her ass," Eric smirked as he nudged her with his foot.

Tony came over to her, getting a closer look and saw the blood spilling from her head. "Oh shit, Eric…" he said as he frowned. He nudged her with his foot but she didn't move. "I think you did a little more than knock the fight out of her."

"Why you say that?" Eric asked as he took a look at her from Tony's angle. "Oh…" he replied, sounding like a child saying *"Oops"* after spilling juice on the new carpet. They stared at her for a moment. "Check her pulse," Eric said to Tony, elbowing him.

"Hell naw, nigga! You check her pulse!" Tony frowned.

Instead of checking her pulse, Eric checked her pockets and was elated that her cell-phone was inside. Arianna had not done as Vanessa instructed her to do. She never deleted the number figuring she would hold on to it in the event that something important happened and she needed to get in touch with her best friend.

"Find the number in the phone," Eric instructed Tony as he passed him the phone. Tony couldn't take his eyes off of Arianna. *What if she's dead? Now I'ma be an accessory to murder fucking with this crazy nigga!*

"Hey! Snap the fuck out of it and check her phone for the number Vanessa called her from," Eric said louder.

Tony took the phone with a shaky hand and began scrolling through Arianna's call log. He was tempted to say the number wasn't in there just so he could get the hell out of dodge but he didn't think Eric would believe him.

"This is the number. You want me to call it now?" Tony asked as he peeked at Arianna again. She was still laying on the floor not moving. He stared harder than he meant to and was positive that he didn't see her breathing either.

"No, wait until you get back to your spot. I want the call traced. I wanna know exactly where she is," Eric replied as he made his way over to the door.

"Wait… you're leaving? You're going to leave her here like this?" Tony asked frantically.

Eric looked at his friend as though he were stupid. "Well, the bitch ain't talking so…" he trailed off.

Yani

"Shouldn't we call the cops or something?" Tony thought to himself. He decided it might not be wise to vocalize his thoughts and followed Eric as he left out of the raggedy house. He took one glance back at Arianna before Eric closed and locked the door.

9

Red and blue police lights flashed outside of the small house in Kensington. Cops questioned people in the neighborhood while other cops worked inside of the abandoned home trying to gather as much evidence as they could to determine what happened to the young lady who was left for dead inside.

Arianna was brought out on a stretcher and paramedics worked feverishly on her to keep her alive. En-route to the hospital, she coded on them twice, but they were able to bring her back around. Her head injury was extensive and she was going to need surgery. The doctors tried to stabilize her enough to get a CT scan to see the extent of her injuries.

"Ms. Stone, the doctors are going to do everything they can to save your life. We're going to need your help to get the bastards that did this to you, okay? Just stay with us, please," One of the cops said as he moved down the hallway alongside her stretcher.

Yani

Arianna was unable to form her words due to her head injury but she held her hand up to the cop. He reached out to hold it and she shook her head.

"It's okay, ma'am. I'm right here. I'm not going anywhere," the cop assured her sympathetically.

"No, you idiot! Check under my nails! I scratched that bastard and I know it should be something under my nails to ID him. Please, God, let them check my nails…" Arianna thought to herself. She took a self-defense class after she learned of what Vanessa was going through and one of the first things that she was taught was in a struggle, to do her best to get one of her attackers DNA on her through either scratching or biting. Arianna had Eric and Tony's DNA on her; Eric's from when she hit him and made his nose bleed and Tony's from when she scratched him. She didn't think of Eric's blood on her hands, but she hoped like hell they checked her nails.

"Of all the times for me to lose my ability to speak, why did this have to be one of those times? I don't want to die… not like this… not so soon… please…" Arianna thought to herself. She struggled to fight off the darkness that threatened to take over. She could hear the machines that she was hooked to going off. And then silence.

"Time of death… 11:46pm." One of the doctors said as he pulled his gloves off. He walked out of the room Arianna was in shaking his head at the cop who promised to be there with her.

"She bled into the frontal lobe and the swelling of her brain was just too much. If she had gotten here just an hour sooner, we might have been able to save her life," the doctor said to the officer.

"Got damn it…" the cop said sorrowfully. "Was she raped? Were there any fluids found on her?" he asked the doctor.

"Well, we didn't get around to the rape kit because we wanted to take care of that head injury right away. But we'll do one anyway just to see."

"Okay, good. Also, she kept reaching her hand out to me like she was showing me something. Maybe she fought with her attackers. Check her hands also; under her nails and make sure the blood on her is her blood and not anyone else's," the cop requested.

"Absolutely. We'll give her a thorough exam once we do the autopsy."

The cop gave him his business card and walked away to work his investigation. He decided to start with the anonymous caller who tipped them off about hearing a struggle inside of the house.

10

Tony raced down the street, unable to drive like a normal person. He wanted desperately to get Eric back to his car and get as far away from him as humanly possible.

"Pass me that phone," Eric said casually as though nothing had happened moments before. "And watch your speeding."

Tony reached in his leather arm rest and pulled the phone out. He handed it to Eric as he made a left turn.

Eric took the phone and started going through it, looking at the phone number that Tony said Vanessa had called from. He couldn't wait to hear her voice. Better yet, he couldn't wait to see the look on her face when he showed up at her door step or wherever she was. He half-way grinned to himself as he imagined the look of fear in her face. He had seen that look with her many times when he had to correct her or get her back in line.

Yani

Tony pulled up in front of Eric's home, double parking. He wanted his friend to get out so he could speed off with the hopes of never looking back.

"What are you doing?" Eric asked him. Tony looked at him as though he didn't know what he was talking about. "Man, park the damn car and bring your scary ass in the house. I want this number traced. I need to know where Vanessa is…" Eric hesitated for a moment. "I need to make sure my baby is okay and she didn't do anything stupid." He really wanted to ring her damn neck for having the nerve to walk out on him while carrying his child.

"Oh, like you didn't just do something stupid back there," Tony thought to himself. Instead of speaking his thoughts, he parked the car and they both got out with Tony following behind Eric. Once inside, Eric poured himself a drink before offering Tony one. Tony quickly declined. He was nervous as hell and peering at Eric with extreme caution. He paced back and forth, stopping a few times to peek out of the window, almost positive that the cops were going to show up any minute and arrest the both of them. Now Tony watched Eric and frowned.

"Can you do a trace on the number from my laptop?" Eric asked his friend.

"I… I don't know," Tony said, nervously. "Maybe you should let this go, Eric. I mean, look on the bright side, at least you don't have to worry about being tied down with no brat. And I highly doubt Vanessa is going to come after you about some child support since she left without even telling you about the baby."

"Nah, fuck that! I'm not going to be denied the chance of being in my child's life. And I'm sure as hell not about to let another nigga play daddy to my child either," Eric replied before taking a sip from his glass.

"Is this even really about the baby or are you sore that Vanessa left you?" Tony asked.

Eric looked at Tony with fire in his eyes for a space of heartbeats. He didn't like what Tony was implying; that he was acting like a nut over some pussy that didn't want to be bothered with him anymore. "What the fuck are you saying?"

"I mean, no disrespect Eric, but if you did anything to her like what you did to the little honey back there in Kensington, it's no wonder she walked out on you."

Eric sat his drink down and before Tony knew it, Eric had him hemmed up against a wall with his collar in a grip. "Who the fuck do you think you're talking to? Huh?!" Eric seethed through clinched teeth. "I paid you to do a muthafucking job, right?"

"Yeah but..."

"Ain't no buts, bitch. Don't ask any questions. Don't think. Because that ain't what the fuck I paid you for. Do what the fuck I paid you for and we won't have any problems." He let Tony go with a jerk, partially knocking him into the wall.

"You didn't pay me to commit murder..." Tony said quietly.

"No, I didn't. But who says the bitch is dead?" They were quiet for a moment as Eric poured himself another drink. "I didn't pay you to go to jail either. But if I get caught, you get caught. Capisce?" he replied as he swirled his finger around in his drink. He then peered up at Tony with a look on his face that was so cold, Tony caught a chill. "Trace the call."

Tony sulked over to Eric's laptop and plugged Arianna's phone in with a USB cable. Eric leaned into his table as Tony typed. Tony held the phone out to Eric.

"Oh no, I want you to call her. If she answers and recognizes my voice, she'll hang up before I have a chance to get her to tell me where she is and then she'll probably change the number and I'll never have the chance to find her. You call her."

"What the hell am I supposed to say to her?" Tony frowned.

"Be creative," Eric replied in a menacing tone.

Tony wished like hell he never took this job. He took the phone from Eric thinking if he just did what he was told so he could leave, then he wouldn't have to worry about much. He dialed the number and nervously waited as it rang.

"No one is answering," Tony said after the third ring.

"Wait for the voicemail," Eric replied. He was beginning to feel the same intense anticipation he felt when they were driving behind Arianna.

After the fifth ring, Tony shook his head. "No voicemail, it's just…" he stopped speaking when he heard someone pick up. He held his hand up to Eric. "Hello…?" he said when he didn't hear anyone speak.

"Who is this?" a female said into the phone.

"Someone called me from this number a few weeks ago and I'm trying to get in touch with them. Is this Vanessa?"

Yani

"You have the wrong number," the woman said into the phone and hung up abruptly. Tony looked at the phone.

"Was it her? Was it Vanessa?" Eric asked.

"It didn't sound like her. She said I had the wrong number," Tony replied as he looked at the phone number that he dialed.

"Give me the phone," Eric said before taking it out of Tony's hand. He pressed redial on the phone and waited for an answer. He wanted to hear the woman's voice to see if it was Vanessa.

"Maybe it was the wrong number, I mean we're calling from her best friend's phone. If it weren't the wrong number, she wouldn't have said that."

"Dumb-ass, we're calling from her best friend's phone but we're not her best friend. Of course she's going to say we have the wrong number," Eric sneered.

"Which begs the question; why is she ducking you so hard?" Tony mused. He kept his thought to himself.

No one answered and there was no voicemail when Eric called, so he dialed the number again. This time, the phone was answered after the second ring.

"Hello?" the woman answered.

"Vanessa?" Eric said quickly. "Vanessa, if this is you, all you have to do is tell me where you are. I'm not mad, just tell me where you are."

"Sir, I've already told you, you have the wrong number. There is no Vanessa at this number, I'm sorry," the woman said patiently.

"She called me from the number," Eric said.

"Okay, listen…"

"No bitch, you listen. You… hello… hello?!" Eric looked at the phone and slammed it on the desk. "BITCH!"

Tony leaned into the desk pretending to be occupied with picking dirt from under his nails. If he had any second thoughts about Eric's ill intentions should he ever get his hands on Vanessa, they were out the window. He was positive that if Eric didn't do it himself, he had someone kill Regina, who was the last young lady he was hired to track down. He knew without a shadow of a doubt that if he helped Eric any further in finding Vanessa, he was going to do more harm than good.

"Can you put a tap on that number?" Eric asked hastily.

"Yeah but…" Tony started.

Yani

"No buts. Tap that phone, monitor the calls. Anything coming in or going out about Vanessa, from Vanessa or to Vanessa, I wanna know about it. If that bitch orders a sausage, egg and cheese sandwich from a diner, I wanna know if she got a coke on the side with the shit. You understand me?" Eric barked as he poured himself another drink.

"I can do it from here since the phone is already attached to the laptop. Her calls will be attached to a recording software and they can be listened to at any time," Tony said nervously as he leaned over the laptop and began typing.

"Good, show me how to listen to the calls so I don't have to wait."

Tony waved Eric over to the laptop and explained how the program worked. He showed him what to do if he wanted to listen to a live call or if he wanted to listen to a call that had already been recorded. Just as he was done showing Eric, a green flashing light went off.

"What's that?" Eric asked.

"Someone is making a call from the number we dialed." Tony replied as he grabbed his set of *Beats* headphones so he could listen.

"Hello," a woman's voice was heard on the line.

"Ms. Marcella, I think we may have a problem with one of our packages," another woman said.

"A problem like what?" Marcella asked.

"I just received a call from someone looking for Vanessa. They said she called them from my number."

"Got damn it, Crystal! How many times have I constantly spoke of the importance of not leaving phones around when any of our packages are traveling through the network? How many times have I stressed the importance of that?" Marcella scolded the young woman.

"I'm sorry Ms. Marcella. I normally always take my phone with me and I never let any of the women use it for any reason. It must've been the day that I went to Walmart before I dropped her off at the train station." Crystal said as she thought back to that day.

"Jesus, Crystal. That was almost three weeks ago! The minute you realized you left your phone in the car with her, you should have notified me so that phone could be dumped and another one could be provided to you. Even if you don't see them using the phone, assume that they have!" Marcella shook her head before taking a puff from her cigarette.

"What should I do if they call back?" Crystal asked feeling horrible over her misstep.

Yani

"Nothing because immediately after we hang up, your phone will be deactivated and another one will be issued to you. Do not let this happen again Crystal, or you will be removed from the program permanently. Understood?" Marcella said firmly.

"Yes, Ms. Marcella."

The call disconnected. Tony took the headphones off and frowned.

"What did they say?" Eric asked.

"It seemed like they were talking in codes about a package and a network. But Vanessa was definitely associated with this number."

"They said her name?" Eric asked.

"Yeah…" Tony said softly as his mind began to race.

"What did they say? Did they say where she was or can you tell where the chick was that answered the phone?"

Tony toggled a few screens on the laptop. "A small suburb outside of Baltimore, Maryland."

"Wait, what? What the fuck is she doing all the way the fuck out there?" Eric asked with a frown on his face. Tony shook his head as he shrugged his shoulders. And then something clicked. He didn't need to listen to the recording again to understand the conversation even with them talking in partial codes. He knew exactly what was going on. Vanessa had not run off with another man. She was trying to get away from Eric and used the help of some women or some program for battered women to get away. He realized Eric was more than likely beating the hell out of Vanessa and whatever network she was traveling through, she compromised it by calling Arianna and he had possibly did even more damage.

Tony looked at his watch. "Oh shit, I've gotta go. I have another job to handle," he stammered as he grabbed his jacket and began to put it on.

"Another job like what?" Eric asked.

Tony hesitated. "It's for a VP of a corporation. He suspects there's been some embezzlement going on and hired me to check on some things and some people. Some real uh… tedious things I have to do but, we're supposed to skype tonight and uh… I'm running late." Tony was lying through his teeth. While he did have that particular job to handle, he had already done the bulk of the necessary research. He mostly wanted to get the hell away from Eric.

"Alright man, well get back to me soon so we can close this thing out," Eric replied as he gave Tony a firm handshake.

"No doubt," Tony replied, avoiding eye contact. He checked to make sure he had everything and then headed out the door to his car. In case Eric was watching him, he pretended to make a call as he walked down the drive-way and talked loudly. "Hey, yeah man… I'm running a little late, I got caught up with some work at the office. Give me about twenty minutes…" he spoke to no one on his phone. He got in his car and kept up with the charade for a few more seconds before driving away. When he got a few blocks up the street, he turned a corner and pulled over. He then put on a pair of rubber gloves and pulled his own burner phone from his pocket before dialing 9-1-1. "Yes, I want to report a domestic dispute… yes… I think I heard a woman screaming a lot and it sounded like a struggle." Tony gave the address to the dispatcher and then disconnected the call. He then drove over to Spencer Arms apartment off of 10th and Spencer and threw the phone in the dumpster before driving to his house.

10

Tony paced back and forth in his home's office unable to shake the evening's events from his mind. He couldn't believe the side of Eric that he had seen that night; heartless, cruel and cold. He suspected the last time he helped Eric out and things went badly that he was behind the young lady's murder but to ease his conscience, he told himself that it was just an odd coincidence that the same girl he was contracted to locate for Eric turned up dead not even a week after he gave her location to him.

Tony could still see Arianna laying on the floor as blood spilled from her head when he closed his eyes. He beat his fists against his head as he paced some more trying his damndest to shake that image from his mind. But it would not go away and was already beginning to haunt him.

Tony's phone went off and he saw that it was Eric. No way was he answering his phone call. He didn't give a shit what he hung over his head, he was going to try his best to get as far away from Eric as humanly possible. Right after the ringing stopped, his phone alerted him to a voicemail that Eric left and then a text message populated on his phone telling Tony to call him as soon as he could.

"Nah, fuck that… We ain't got nothing…" Tony was cut off when he happened to glance at the TV and saw Arianna's photo pop up on a split screen next to the house in Kensington which was lit up with lights from police cruisers and TV news stations interviewing people and filming the scene.

"Tonight, police were alerted by an anonymous caller of a struggle in this house behind us. When police arrived, they found a woman who was severely beaten in the home. She was rushed to Frankford hospital where she died moments ago. She was identified as 23 year old Arianna Stone. At this time, outside of the anonymous caller, police have no leads, suspects or a motive…"

Tony stared blankly at the TV screen unable to hear anything else that the news broadcaster was saying. The ringing in his ears drowned out everything else including his phone which was ringing again.

"We killed her…" he mumbled to himself. "I knew I never should have tried to help him find Vanessa. Fuck…!" Tony panicked. He began moving through his house, grabbing a few of his items to throw in a duffle bag along with some money that he had stashed. If Eric had seen the news and heard of the anonymous caller, he knew that Eric would immediately suspect him. And while they were both professionals in what they did, he knew the consequences of snitching. Tony definitely knew that he had to get away as soon as possible.

Tony was rushing to his front door when he saw the flashing red and blue police lights in the front of his home.

"Oh shit…" Tony said as he stopped dead in his tracks. He wondered why the cops would be at his home when he called from a burner phone that he always kept handy. After he made the call, he took the battery and sim card out and tossed it in separate trash cans, blocks away from one another. He then had a thought that maybe Eric flipped on him.

He heard the three rapid and loud knocks on his front door before a loud and intimidating voice spoke from the other side with tremendous base.

"Mr. Antonio Vasquez, open the door. We have a few questions for you," the officer said.

Tony turned from left to the right trying to decide where to put his bag. He didn't want them to see that he was preparing to leave because that would surely make him appear guilty. He quickly pulled the clothes from the bag and threw them in a closet and tossed the money back in his safe.

"Just a minute…" he called back to the officer, stalling for more time to get himself together.

He straightened his clothes and took a deep breath to calm himself before opening the door. "How can I help you?"

"We would like you to come down to the station with us to answer a few questions," the officer said to him.

"A few questions about what?" Tony asked calmly.

"Sir, it would be a lot better if we have this conversation at the police station," the officer replied.

"Am I under arrest for something?"

"All things considered sir, we could arrest you right now since we have probable cause. But if you come willingly, and answer some questions, that might help you out in the long run."

Tony weighed his options as he looked the cop over, noticing that his hand rested loosely by the butt of his service revolver. He knew he had no wins up against the four police officers who were outside of his home. He sighed deeply and stepped outside, closing his front door behind him and followed the officers to the police car.

Yani

11

The sweetest sound ever heard by Vanessa's ears rang out inside of the delivery room. It was the sound of her precious baby girl crying after entering into a new world and taking her first breath. Vanessa cried tears of joy as her heart filled with more love than she ever knew she was capable of having for another person. Arianna held the small bundle of joy with a broad smile on her face as she made crooning noises at the precious little one. She passed the baby to Vanessa and her heart felt as though it would melt once she laid eyes on the baby.

"My God, if I didn't just go through all of that pain pushing her out, I would have sworn she was your baby!" Vanessa joked in a light voice.

Arianna planted a lingering kiss on her forehead. "That's just God's way of making sure I'm always with you," she said in return. But her voice sounded as though she were a million miles away.

"Wha… what do you mean?" Vanessa asked. She looked up and Arianna was gone. In a blink of an eye, the doctors were gone as well. She looked around frantically and jumped when she heard slow hand claps coming from the doorway. She struggled to sit up.

"Who's there?" she asked hesitantly.

Eric stepped forward from the shadows scaring the living hell out of her. She scooted back on her hospital bed and held the baby closer to her.

"You did good, V-Dot," Eric said to her as he walked over to her slowly.

"No," Vanessa said in a soft voice. She then said it louder. "No! You can't have her! You stay away from her! You stay away from me, you sonuva bitch!"

"Carmen! Carmen!" a woman said as she shook Vanessa lightly, waking her from her sleep. Vanessa jumped after opening her eyes, looking as though she was going to knock the fire out of someone. She breathed heavily as she looked around and then lightly touched her stomach which held a very small bulge. She closed her eyes as she tried to shake the bad feeling that the dream had left her with.

"Are you okay?" the woman asked her.

Vanessa shook her head feeling groggy. She hated the nightmares that she periodically had about Eric. They all scared the hell out of her. But that one, the way Arianna seemed so far away and what she said, left a knot in her stomach and she felt the need to cry.

"I'm okay…" she mumbled.

"You sure? You were talking in your sleep again. Would you like for me to schedule you an earlier session with Dr. Reynolds?" the woman asked her as she looked her over with genuine concern.

Vanessa shook her head as she sat up. "No, I'm fine. It was just a dream."

The woman looked after her for a moment longer and then went back to what she was doing.

Vanessa's words hung in the air a little longer. *"It was just a dream…"* But the dream left a bad taste in her mouth and a longing feeling for her best friend. Though she understood the importance of not contacting people from her past life in order to keep the program and the people within the network safe, she wanted more than anything to pick up the phone and call her best friend. She just wanted to hear her voice and share a few laughs. The pregnancy and the journey that she was on right now would go a lot smoother, in her mind, if Arianna was there with her to hold her hand and tell her she would be okay. But it wouldn't be some sentimental bullshit.

"Man the fuck up, V-Dot. Brickyard ain't raise no nut-bitches. Tough cookies don't crumble and no matter how fucked up

shit gets, look at life like a good poker hand and never fold. You got this sis. And I got you. Cradle to the grave…"

Vanessa smiled as she heard those words in her head said by her best friend. "Cradle to the grave…" she said softly.

It was now going on three months since she made her great escape from Eric, and though she missed her home, family and the few friends that Eric had not completely isolated her from, she was grateful for the second chance she was given. She thanked Tremaine and his wife every morning when she woke up and every night before she went to bed. Vanessa viewed them as her guardian angels that God had sent to her to give her the courage to take the necessary steps to reclaim her life. They, along with Marcella, had given her a fresh start, a do over, and she vowed to make the best of it not only for herself, but for the sake of her unborn child.

Vanessa looked down at her stomach and touched it lovingly. "How's about some yummy pancakes? You want some pancakes? Mmm, that sounds delicious, doesn't it? Let's grub!" she said to her unborn child.

Vanessa lived in a safe house for battered women that was more-so like a mini apartment complex. At the moment, she only had a room and shared a kitchen with two other ladies. While she was always polite and friendly, she mostly kept to herself. She didn't want to get too attached to anyone in the event that she had to move again.

Luckily, most of the women were already at work and the section of the complex that she lived in was pretty much empty. She flipped through the CDs that were with the stereo in the kitchen and grabbed Usher's *Confessions* album. The album's groovy tunes put her in an upbeat mood and she began to dance around as she made her breakfast of pancakes, scrambled eggs and turkey sausages. She jammed as she listened to *Caught Up* not noticing the guy standing in the doorway watching her. He grinned as he sipped his coffee while watching her bop and sing along with the song.

Vanessa turned to put her eggs in a bowl and whip them up and was startled by the man's presence. She jumped, dropping two of the eggs on the floor.

"Oh, Miss, I'm sorry. I didn't mean to startle you," he replied as he sat his mug on the counter and grabbed the roll of paper towels.

"It's okay…" Vanessa said in a soft and nervous voice. She held her hand out to get the paper towels from the stranger, but instead he bent over and cleaned up the eggy mess from the floor. "Oh… I was going to clean that up."

"No, that was my fault. I should've said something instead of standing there lurking like that. You probably think I'm a whole creep now," he chuckled as he threw the paper towels in the trash.

Vanessa remained quiet not wanting to respond one way or another. She looked at the floor instead.

The silence became awkward so the stranger went over to the refrigerator and got her two more eggs. "Here's your eggs," he said to her.

"Thank you," Vanessa replied softly. She went back to the frying pan and flipped her hot cakes before moving her sausages around with her fork.

"I'm Derek by the way…" Derek replied. He was hoping to spark up a conversation with the young lady but noticed how tentative she was to interact with him.

"Nice to meet you, Derek." Vanessa replied in her same quiet tone. She continued to move her sausages around even though there was no need to do so.

Derek smiled, "And your name…?"

"Why?" Vanessa asked as she peered at him.

Derek felt taken aback. He paused for a moment and then shrugged his shoulders. "Why not?"

Vanessa cracked open one of the eggs and then shook her head. "My name is Carmen."

"Nice to meet you, Carmen. So are you new here? I work at the property manager's office and don't recall seeing you before."

"You ask a lot of questions," Vanessa replied as she looked up at him suspiciously.

"I'm inquisitive," Derek told her. They stared at each other for a moment. Vanessa felt like he was studying her and it made her uncomfortable. She was not ready to interact with men on any level and really wanted this Derek character to let her cook and eat her breakfast in peace.

"I'm sorry… I'm not being rude I'm just not much of a people person. I guess I'm a bit of an introvert," she replied as she began to whip her eggs.

"I can respect that. I've always been an extrovert. I like meeting new people. Especially beautiful ones." Derek cracked a charming smile but Vanessa was unmoved.

When he saw that he was getting nowhere with her, Derek retrieved his mug of coffee from off of the counter. "Well it was nice meeting you, Carmen. Enjoy your breakfast."

"Thank you," Vanessa replied softly. She sprinkled salt and pepper into her bowl of egg yolk and whipped it a little more with her fork. She peered up to see if Derek was gone and then let out a sigh of relief.

"*You've got to chill, girly. He seemed like a really nice and friendly young man,*" the voice in her head said to her.

"Yeah, Eric was a nice and friendly man too, at first. But everybody ain't what they seem," Vanessa mumbled.

"*Not every man is out to hurt you. And you keep thinking that way and you'll be alone for the rest of your life,*" the voice said in return.

"Rather be alone than beaten and broken..." Vanessa shook her head becoming angry at herself. More and more she was finding herself answering the voice in her head. She was thankful that she only did it when she was alone but she was beginning to think she was going crazy; talking to herself and answering voices in her head. Having conversations with herself.

"*Sometimes the best conversations are the ones we have with ourselves. Helps us to think more clearly...*" she heard the voice in her head again. But this time, it sounded more like Arianna. She shook her head again and finished fixing her breakfast.

As she was eating, a young lady tapped her on the shoulder. "Are you Carmen?" she asked politely.

"Yes," Vanessa replied.

"Vera needs to see you in her office when you're finished your food. She said it's urgent," the young lady said to her.

Vanessa swallowed down some of her food. "Okay…" She began to think that she was in trouble and out of habit, after everything she had been through with Eric, she began to obsess over everything she had done, wondering if she had broken a rule or left a mess behind somewhere. She hurried up and finished her food and washed the dishes she used before putting them away. She then made her way over to Vera's office. Vanessa knocked on the door.

"Come in," Vera replied as she looked through some of her documents.

"Hi, Miss Vera. I was told that you wanted to see me," Vanessa said timidly as she came into the office.

"You must be Carmen?" Vera replied as she looked Vanessa over.

"Yes, ma'am."

"Close the door and have a seat."

Vanessa shut the door behind her and then sat across from Vera.

"I received a phone call from a very upset Marcella this morning. It appears some time ago before you came here, you reached out to someone using your transporter's cell phone. Is that true?" Vera asked as she peered at Vanessa over the rim of her eye glasses.

Vanessa bit her bottom lip and looked down at her hands. "Yes ma'am," she said as she nodded her head.

Vera removed her glasses and folded her hands on her desk. She waited a moment before saying anything. "I understand that this journey is difficult and because of your current circumstances, it's even more difficult for you. But there are reasons we forbid any communication with people from your past life. Such communications could jeopardize our entire network. It could not only put you in danger, but your baby and the lives of all of the people who've helped you to get to where you are now should your abuser decide to come looking for you. Do you understand the severity of what you did?"

Vanessa's lip trembled. Being with Eric had made her incredibly sensitive. At that moment, she felt like a five year old being scolded for scribbling on the wall. Vanessa felt small, weak, submissive and even worse, stupid. Her eyes stung from the tears that threatened to fall. She quickly wiped them away.

"I'm sorry, Miss Vera. I didn't intend to cause any trouble. I just wanted to let my best friend know that I was okay. And I wanted her to let my mother know I was okay because I was sure they both were worried sick about me. And I was scared and just needed to hear a familiar voice…" Vanessa rambled. Vera put her hand up to silence her.

"Again, I understand. We've all been through this. It's very difficult to just pick up and leave everything and everyone behind. But all it takes is a ten second phone call and everything could be compromised. Who did you call?"

"Her name is Arianna. But I swear, she would never tell a soul or give the number to anyone."

"Well according to Marcella, someone got the number and they called your transporter last night looking for you. They didn't give a name, but she said it was a man and he asked for you specifically," Vera replied.

Vanessa froze. She thought back to the dream that she had with Arianna holding the baby and kissing her on the forehead. Did Eric get to her? She knew Arianna would never tell him where she was. More importantly, she never told Arianna where she was. And she knew that Arianna would protect her with her last breath…

"Carmen?" Vera said, snapping Vanessa out of her thoughts. Vanessa shook her head as though she was clearing it and looked at Vera.

"You said it was a man?" she asked.

"Yes," Vera told her. Vanessa became quiet again. "Your transporter's phone has already been dumped and hopefully, the call was not traced. Hopefully, whoever that was won't try to locate you."

"It was Eric…" Vanessa said. "I'm positive. Oh my God, I hope he didn't do anything to her. Please let Arianna be okay," Vanessa said. She suddenly felt overwhelmed with guilt and sorrow. *If he got that number from her, he didn't get it willingly.*

"Eric is your abuser?" Vera asked.

"Yes!" Vanessa replied before bursting into tears. Vera handed her a tissue. "I only wanted her to know that I was okay."

"I understand, Carmen. Just calm down. Everything is going to work out fine. We just need you to understand that things like this cannot happen. Is that understood?" Vera asked as she came around the desk and put her arm around Vanessa. Vanessa nodded her head as she sniffed.

"I know that I'm not allowed to reach out to anyone from my past. But if Eric got the number I called Arianna from, my gut is telling me he didn't get it in a peaceful manner, you know? They hated each other. Arianna pulled a knife on him once to protect me," Vanessa rambled.

"Sounds like a very good friend," Vera replied.

"She is. Arianna has always been there for me through so much." Vanessa hesitated, almost afraid to make her request. "If it's not too much trouble, is it possible that someone can make sure she is okay. I need to know he didn't hurt her." Vanessa looked up at Vera with tear drenched eyes. "Please," she pleaded.

"Well, just because he got the phone number that you called her from doesn't mean that he interacted with her in order to get it. It's quite possible that he put a tap on her and anyone else he thought you might make contact with and got it that way," Vera suggested.

Vanessa shook her head. "Trust me, Eric thrives off of physical contact. And considering she pulled a knife on him, if he could pay her back for that while getting information on my whereabouts, he wouldn't hesitate to kill those two birds with one stone. I hear what you're saying and I wish I could believe that he didn't make contact with her in order to get that number, but my gut is telling me otherwise."

Vera sighed and gave in. "Okay. But only this one time. I have a friend who is a private detective. Give me her full name, last known address and date of birth and I'll get back to you with whatever turns up."

"Thank you so much," Vanessa said gratefully as Vera slid a piece of paper and a pen over to her. She hurriedly scribbled down Arianna's information and gave it back to Vera.

"That's all for now. But in the event that you are feeling home-sick, or lonely and need someone to talk to, stop by my office. If I can't get a session arranged for you, my door is always open and my ears are always listening. You can talk to me anytime. Understand?"

"Yes, Miss Vera. I understand." Vera gave her a friendly smile before Vanessa excused herself from her office. She walked down the hallway with her mind racing and thinking the absolute worst. She always knew in the back of her mind that Eric was not going to let her walk away that easily. She only hoped that nothing happened to Arianna, but the abuse she suffered for almost two years had caused her to be a paranoid pessimist and thinking otherwise.

12

Tony was being questioned by the police officers. Because he did not anticipate Eric's ill intentions, he did not do a complete surveillance of the area Arianna traveled in while coming home from work. A camera at a nearby coffee shop caught the altercation on film. And while Eric's face was not shown on the footage, Tony's license plate was in plain view giving the police probable cause to question him.

They were wearing Tony down with their questions. His guilt over his participation in the events that led to Arianna's murder was already eating away at him. But he knew the consequences of snitching, and while he may have been granted a lighter sentence or even walked away from this with no jail time, he knew the likelihood of him staying alive if he gave up Eric was slim. Tony was not prepared to go to prison for something he didn't do, though. He was trying hard to think up a story before he requested his lawyer. He prayed that there was a way for him to get out of this situation without implicating Eric, but if he had to, he knew he'd better run for his life afterwards.

They played the footage of the altercation between him, Arianna and Eric. Tony watched with a straight face not wanting to give them the impression that he was scared shitless. But seeing the way Eric hit Arianna with that right-hand-cross made him reflect back to the deadly blow inside of the house. He looked away from the TV screen not wanting to see Eric drag Arianna to his car as the guilt washed over him.

The first officer paused the footage just as Tony's car was swerving around Arianna's.

"So Mr. Vasquez, you want to explain to me exactly what happened on that video?"

Tony looked over at him with a straight face. "You just watched the same video I watched. I think you have a pretty good idea what you just saw."

The officer chuckled. "You really don't want to leave this up to my interpretation, wise guy. Right now, you're an accessory to murder. We can add kidnapping charges in there, assault…"

"Right now, the lab is running tests on the blood found under Ms. Stone's finger nails. It's already been established that you have a prior record. All we have to do is match your DNA with the evidence under her nails and we can bust your ass for murder," the second officer said coldly.

Reflex almost caused Tony to place his hand on the part of his neck that Arianna scratched when they struggled inside of the house, but he intertwined his fingers instead.

"I think I better wait for my lawyer to come before I answer any more of these questions," Tony replied nervously.

The first cop smirked and shook his head at Tony in disgust. He knew in his heart that Tony was guilty of Arianna's murder and he was not going to stop until he got to the bottom of it all.

They left Tony alone in the interrogation room to wait for his attorney. His mind was racing everywhere. One thing he did decide on was that he was not going to jail for something he didn't do. He was not going to take the fall for something Eric did. It was bad enough that the guilt was eating away at him.

Yani

For some reason, Tony began to think back to the young woman Regina that Eric hired him to look for. He still remembered the news segment on television that showed her wrapped in a sheet on the side of Belfield Avenue by the park. *"An unidentified woman was found earlier today near Belfield Avenue. She had been raped, beaten and strangled to death. No suspects…"* Tony folded his arms on the metal table and rested his head on top of them.

"Hey, Tony my man. How's everything?" Eric said when Tony answered the phone.

"Hey, Eric. Everything is fine on this end. What's going on?" Tony replied.

"Listen, I've got a job for you bro. I need you to locate someone for me. I think she might be in trouble…"

Eric proceeded to tell Tony about a young lady he had been helping out of a rough patch. Her name was Regina and she had fallen down on hard times. Eric was letting her stay with him until she found a job and had gotten back on her feet. He told Tony that he was worried that she might have done something to hurt herself and insisted that if he was able to locate her, instead of approaching her, to just give him her location and he would try to reason with her.

And so Tony did as he was hired to do without asking any questions. If the money was there, he did not care and to him, the story sounded legit. Regina wasn't that hard to find either because she was still using her credit card to stay at a motel. The first red flag was she walked around in sun glasses with a scarf on her head even at night. She appeared paranoid, constantly looking over her shoulder as though she suspected someone was either following her or looking for her. If only Tony had gone with his gut feeling and listened to the little voice inside telling him something was not quite right with what Eric told him…

"Hey Eric, I located the girl Regina," Tony said on the phone a few days after initially talking to him.

Eric swirled around in his chair and scooted closer to his desk. He grabbed a pen so he could write down whatever information was given to him. "Damn, that was quick. I like how you do business." His leg moved back and forth as anticipation began to build up inside of him. Tony read off the address to where he located Regina. "You didn't approach her did you?" Eric asked.

"No, I just watched her from a distance. She looked a little… off." Tony replied with hesitation. He waited to see what Eric was going to say.

Eric hesitated also but then said with a sigh, "Well… it's like I said; I'm worried that she might try to hurt herself. She's been going through a lot of shit lately, so she's probably…" Eric trailed off not knowing what he should say. "You know…"

Yani

Tony hesitated again but then shrugged his shoulders. He did what he was being paid to do and decided not to ask any unnecessary questions. "Well, that's the address, Bro. Anything else you need from me?"

"No, buddy. Thanks again. I'll send your payment and a little something extra to the usual account," Eric replied as he stood from his desk and grabbed his coat.

"Alright, peace."

Three nights after Tony had that conversation with Eric, Regina's body was located on the side of the road on Belfield Avenue wrapped in a sheet. *"Beaten, raped and strangled…"* And now almost three years later, dealing with that bastard again had him sitting in an interrogation room facing possible criminal charges for a crime he didn't commit.

His attorney came into the room. "Mr. Vasquez?"

Tony looked up and felt relieved to see his face. "Man, am I glad to see you," he said with a sigh of relief as he shook the lawyer's hand.

"After that little coke incident, I didn't think I'd see you again. You wanna tell me what the hell is going on here?" The lawyer sat his briefcase on the table and took a seat across from his client.

Tony blew out air as he put his hands on his head. He didn't know where to begin so he gave him a short version of the story about him hitting the back of Arianna's car and Eric grabbing her and putting her in the back of his car.

The lawyer periodically jotted down notes as Tony talked. When he finished, he rubbed the hairs on his chin. "Okay, let me make sure I understand you. You hit the back of the woman's car. Was it by an accident?"

"Well… yeah," Tony stammered.

"Did you know this woman?"

"No… not really."

The lawyer looked at Tony suspiciously feeling like something wasn't adding up with the story. "Come on Vasquez, don't bullshit me. We've been down this road before and you know how I get down. While I enjoy getting this money to defend your black ass, I will not sit in a court room looking like a complete dickhead because you didn't give me the whole story. So this is what I'm going to do before the cops come back in here and start drilling you with questions again…" Tony's lawyer ripped up the paper he was jotting notes on and sat it to the side.

Yani

"Start from the top and don't leave anything out. What the fuck happened?"

Tony shook his leg nervously knowing his ass was about to be in some deep shit. Actually, he was already in some deep shit that was pulling him in like quicksand, and the shit was about to get deeper. "Okay, okay, okay. A buddy of mine named Eric contacted me for a PI gig…" he started.

"A buddy of yours?" his lawyer asked.

"Well…yeah. We've known each other for a while. He helped me out of a situation a few times and found out I do PI work on the side so he hired me to look into a situation for him," Tony explained quickly.

"What was the gig?"

"He asked me to locate his girlfriend. Said that she was pregnant by him and she ran off with some guy and he was worried that she was going to do something stupid," Tony replied.

"Has he ever hired you for a job like this before?" the lawyer asked. Tony fell silent not knowing how he should respond. "Tony?"

"Rob, attorney client privilege means you can't say anything to anyone about anything I tell you. Even if I suspect that someone else might have done something crazy, right?" Tony asked with a raised eyebrow.

"Anything you say to me stays between me and you, you know that, Tony." Rob looked at his client as though he should have known better.

Tony waited a moment before telling his lawyer about Regina. "He hired me for a job similar to this almost three years ago and well… you remember a young lady named Regina Smalls who went missing and then a few days after she was reported missing, they found her body on Belfield Ave wrapped in a sheet?"

"I remember the story. She was a young college student from University of Penn. The press was all over it. Wait a minute, you think this guy had something to do with it and you were stupid enough to do another job for him? What kind of special-stupid are you?" Rob asked with a disgusted look on his face.

"Hey, I don't need this from you, alright." Tony stood up from his seat and began to pace in the room.

"Okay, no judgments. Just finish telling me."

"So I tried locating this girl through the normal channels. No charges on her debit or credit cards. No activity on her bank accounts, no cell phone, nothing! It's almost like the bitch vanished like Batman. I got a real bad feeling man, real bad feeling. I mean when a person disappears like that it's either because they're dead or because they don't want to be found."

"Alright, so what happened after that?"

"I tried to get Eric to leave the situation alone, tried to convince him that maybe the baby wasn't his if she was really pregnant and suggested that maybe he should walk away. But he insisted on finding this girl. So I tapped the phones of her best friend and her mom and waited to see if she would make contact. She called the best friend," Tony finished in a low tone.

"And let me guess, the best friend is the dead girl, Arianna?" Rob asked. Tony nodded his head.

Rob shook his head and tapped his pen as he thought for a moment. "This isn't good, Tony. I might be able to work some angles for you, get them to lessen the charges to accessory…"

Rob was interrupted by the two officers who came back into the interrogation room.

"Sorry Tony, but there won't be any deal for you. DNA under the victim nails matches yours. We're busting your ass for 1st degree murder," the first cop said as he pulled his handcuffs.

Tony backed away becoming frightened. His heart raced as he faced the possibility of going to jail for 25 years for murder. "No! Wait, there has to be something. I didn't kill that girl, I swear to God!" Tony said frantically.

"Tell it to the judge and your lawyer can try to explain how your DNA got under her nails," the second cop said.

"Tony, if you know something, now is the time for you to speak up. It's not much I can do for you with your DNA under her nails man, especially with your prior record," Rob said to him quietly. Tony looked at him terrified. He knew the consequences of snitching but it was his ass on the line. Would Eric be so quick to take the fall for him if the tables had been turned or would he throw his ass under the bus and play Mr. Innocent? Common sense told him that a man of Eric's caliber wouldn't go to jail for any man or bitch. Tony also had another philosophy that he lived by- self-preservation and all that shit.

"Shit man, I'm fucked either way," Tony said as he shook his head.

"Tell us something, Tony."

Yani

"The guy on the camera whose face you couldn't see. That's who killed Arianna," Tony said.

"That's pretty fucking convenient. We couldn't see his got damn face on the camera, how do we know you're not just trying to throw the blame on someone else."

"Hear him out," the lawyer replied. "After all, you can clearly see on the video that my client was talking to her calmly when the other party came over and attacked her. That's enough right there to get a jury to acquit on reasonable doubt."

"Give us a name and tell us what happened and even more so, you're gonna have to get us some kind of evidence to prove what you're saying. Because contrary to what you're lawyer is saying, the same way a jury might acquit off of that tiny speck of reasonable doubt, the jury may also see it as a lie that you cooked up to save your own ass," the second cop replied.

"His name is Eric Washington. He hired me to find a girl and when I couldn't find her, he had me tap Arianna's phone and the mother's phone. His girlfriend Vanessa called Arianna about three weeks ago and that's why Eric had me follow her. After he took her from the car tonight, he had me drive him to the house in

Kensington. They got into a struggle, she tried to make a run for it and I grabbed her. That's when she scratched me, trying to get away and that's how my shit got under her nails. And then Eric grabbed her and pushed her…she hit her head on the banister and then she just dropped like a ton of fucking bricks." Tony stared with a hazy gaze in his eyes as though he could see her again lying lifeless on the floor with blood pouring from her head. "It was a lot of fucking blood. But it was no big fucking deal to Eric. He took her cell phone and stepped over her like she wasn't shit…like how A.I stepped over Tyron Lu in the finals that year."

"So who called the cops with the anonymous tip?" the first cop asked.

"I did. Eric had me come back to the house but I lied and said I had another client to see. I keep a burner phone with me for when I have to make calls and I don't want people to have my number. I called in what happened and then dumped the phone in the dumpster at Spencer Arms apartments," Tony finished. The room fell silent.

"We're going to need your statement in writing and you're also going to have to testify."

"No fucking way, man. This guy's got money out the fucking ass. He'll off me before it even gets to trial!" Tony said hysterically.

"If you testify, your lawyer can argue that you didn't know what his intentions were. We can get it down to a misdemeanor and you'll only look at six months. You may not even see jail time, just probation. Not to mention if what you're saying is true and Eric has Arianna's phone, we can get him for the murder," the second officer told him.

Tony shook his head. "Mannn, y'all don't understand. The minute he's brought in, I won't be seeing shit at all!"

"Tony, we know you want to do the right thing because you made the call. This is your chance to get this bastard off the streets for good. Because if he walks free, two more lives are in danger. If what you're saying is true, there's a woman and a baby out there that he's still looking for and if anything were to happen to them, I don't think you want that on your conscience also, do you?" the first cop asked.

Tony looked at the cops and his lawyer for a moment and gave in. Either way, his fate was sealed and he was on the verge of having a serious problem on his hands by the name of Eric Washington.

13

Eric lay on his bed staring up at the ceiling with his arm under his head. He put a blunt to his lips and took a long drag, holding the smoke in before slowly blowing it upward and watched it fade away as it approached the ceiling. For some reason, Regina Smalls popped into his head also. That bitch. She had caused him a lot of unnecessary problems, running her mouth about things she had no business running her mouth about, causing trouble for him at his place of work and with his colleagues. She was exactly the kind of sassy, trouble making bitch that his father warned him about when he was younger.

"These sassy young gals gotta be taught their place. You gotta learn 'em, Ricky. You gotta learn 'em hard and you gotta learn 'em good." Eric heard his father saying.

"Shut up, you old bastard," Eric mumbled before taking another pull from his blunt. He closed his eyes and held the smoke as he did before and then let it escape towards the ceiling.

"*Regina Smalls…*" Eric thought to himself. He closed his eyes and began thinking back to the day he caught up with her after she called herself leaving him; after she dared to disrespect him and cross him by calling the cops on him. She had to be taught a long lasting lesson…

Eric pulled up to the Days Inn Motel near the airport in an old Cutlass '88. He had a baseball cap on pulled down low so you could barely see his eyes and a hooded sweatshirt on. He sat partially hunched down in the driver seat of the hoopty he was driving and watched eagerly and with patience for Regina to either leave out or go in.

Multiple times he sat up at attention thinking various women were Regina only for them to not be her. His anticipation was driving him insane as he fantasized over the expression on her face when he finally approached her. He became so sexually aroused that his erection intensified with every passing second. He reached his hand down his pants and slowly began to jerk himself off.

A young woman in a gray hooded sweatshirt and a pair of black tights crossed the street in front of Eric's hoopty. He sat up at attention when he recognized her as Regina. His heart raced in his chest and his palms began to sweat as every nerve in his body compelled him to spring from the car and grab her.

"Calm down. Not yet. Don't want to make a scene," Eric told himself. He breathed heavily as his eyes followed her like an animal stalking its prey. Watching her tight ass sway in her tights heightened his sexual excitement and he licked his lips as he watched her go inside of the motel.

Eric jumped from the car and casually jogged across the street. He stuffed his hands in his pockets and walked with his head slightly bowed so he could still keep an eye on Regina without her seeing and recognizing him. She was the only one getting on the elevator, so he pretended to talk on his cell phone while discreetly keeping an eye out for which floor the elevator stopped at.

"Third floor," he mumbled to himself. He decided to take the stairs keeping his head bowed and continuing the fake conversation on his cell phone. He got to the third floor and peeped out of the doorway. There was no one around, so he decided to walk the halls to get an idea of his surroundings.

The hallway extended at the end around a corner to another side where a small sitting room was with a vending machine and an ice machine as well. There was also a stairwell. Eric took the stairs down to see where they led and smiled once he saw that they led to a back door which was near an alley way. He checked to see if there were any "No Parking" signs to be sure he wouldn't get towed and then left out to move his car. He came back through the front and was happy to see no one was at the desk. Eric hurriedly went up the stairs and peeked out to keep watch for Regina. There were only four rooms on the third floor. He eliminated two of the rooms when he saw an Asian couple go into one room and a fat white guy come in and out of the other room a few times without a shirt on. The site of him disgusted Eric and he had to contain his urge to punch the fat bastard in the throat.

It was down to two rooms, one which was right by the stairwell that he was peeking from and the other across the hall from it. He prayed that no one took the stairs and came up behind him, catching him peeking out of the door like a creepy stalker. He then began to worry that she may not come out of the room at all. If that were the case, his next plan was to knock on both doors pretending to need a lighter or change for a dollar and when she answered…

His thoughts were interrupted when one of the doors opened. He stood statue-like still as he watched to see who came from the room.

"What if she's not alone? Or what if she's been in the room with the fat fuck or the other room all this time?" he pondered.

"Shit, they can get it, too," he mumbled.

Yani

Regina came out of the room and began walking down the hall towards the ice machine. Eric opened the door wider to see more of her but then quickly closed it back when she abruptly turned around to come back to the room as though she had forgotten something. He cracked the door open and watched her while slipping his hand into the pocket of his hoody and rubbed the plastic bag he had. She went inside of the room and then quickly came back out, leaving her door opened.

"This bitch is making this too easy," Eric mumbled with an evil grin on his face. He reached in his back pocket and pulled out a pair of plastic gloves. Regina turned the corner to go to the vending machine and the ice machine and Eric moved towards her room quick as lightening. He slipped inside and stood behind the door with the plastic bag in his hands.

Regina moved back down the hallway towards her room clueless about what was waiting for her behind her door. She was humming a tune to herself when she went in the room. She never had a chance to defend herself. Eric quickly pulled the plastic bag over her head and kicked the door shut. Regina gagged and clawed frantically at Eric's hands and then began pulling at the bag.

"Yeah bitch, having trouble talking, now? Huh? This is what happens to bitches who run off at the mouth and don't know their *fucking place!" Eric practically growled as he yanked Regina around like a rag doll.*

Regina managed to claw a hole inside of the bag and began to suck in air profusely. Eric placed a strong hand around her throat and squeezed.

"Oh no you don't, bitch," he said as he dragged her to the bed and slammed her on it. He continued to squeeze as he leaned close to her face, loving the site of her eyes and the way they were teary, the way she was losing the light in her eyes and the color in her face. "I'ma teach you what happens to bitches who snitch. I'ma learn you today. I'ma learn you hard and good…" Before he had a chance to finish what he was saying, Regina passed out. Eric snickered. "You always were a light weight."

For the next three hours, he raped and beat Regina. After breaking her jaw and seeing her face bruised and battered, she was no longer appealing to him. He turned her over on her stomach and anally raped her before taking his belt and tying it around her neck, strangling her to death.

Eric got up and casually left the room, using the stairwell to get to his hoopty. Inside was a large suitcase and a gym bag. He took them back up to the room. He carefully clipped her finger nails and dipped her hands in bleach to destroy any DNA she may have collected during her brief struggle. He did the same with her vaginal area, using an empty squirt bottle to squeeze bleach inside of her in the event that the condom broke. He then wrapped her body in a sheet, stuffed her inside of the suitcase, and left out as though nothing happened. Eric struggled to his car with the suitcase and put it in the back seat. With the help of a trusted friend who worked in law enforcement, he dumped her body on Belfield Avenue near a pile of trash and took the car to a chop shop where he paid handsomely for them to destroy it.

When her body was discovered a few days later by the trash men who were picking up the load, Eric put on a performance that should have granted him an Academy Award. And while her family suspected he had something to do with her murder, or knew more than what he led on, there was no evidence, Eric insured he had a solid alibi and he made off scot free.

"Regina Smalls," Eric thought to himself again before drifting off to sleep.

14

Vera held the phone to her ear listening to her close friend and detective give her the details surrounding Arianna's murder and the investigation. Her heart ached for Vanessa as she dreaded having to tell the young lady about her best friend's murder.

"Thank you, Jeremy. Keep me updated on the investigation. I want to know the minute they catch that bastard." She hung up the phone and stared at it for a moment. She then picked up her phone again and dialed a number. "Derek, I need you to locate a young woman named Carmen. She's in room four. Bring her to my office, please." She hung the phone back up and began to rehearse in her head how she was going to let Vanessa know that her best friend had been murdered and that more than likely her ex was responsible for it.

Derek made his way over to Carmen's room. After their first encounter, he wasn't too thrilled to see her. He

Yani

tapped on her door gently and waited patiently for her to respond.

Vanessa peeked out of her door. Though she was annoyed that it was Derek, she managed to keep a straight face. "Can I help you?" she asked flatly.

"Vera wanted me to bring you to her office," Derek replied in the same tone.

"Again? What did I do now?" she pondered. Instead of asking any questions, she came out of the room and closed the door behind her and then walked with Derek to Vera's office. Derek stole a few glances at her and immediately felt the same attraction to her that he felt when they initially crossed paths a couple of days before. Instead of trying his luck with her again, he remained silent as they walked to Vera's office.

"Come in," Vera said when she heard the knocking on her door. Derek held the door open for Vanessa and she took a seat.

"Is there anything else I can do for you, Miss. Vera?" Derek asked politely.

Vera waved him off. "No, I'm fine. Thank you." She waited for Derek to close the door behind him before beginning her conversation with Vanessa. She thought she had come up with a way to break the bad news to her about her best friend, Arianna. But with Vanessa sitting across from her, she was at a loss for words and fidgeted with a pen she had been writing with.

"Did I do something?" Vanessa asked after becoming uncomfortable amidst the awkward silence.

Vera shook her head quickly as though she had been snapped out of a daydream. "No, no you haven't done anything. I just needed to talk to you."

Vanessa let out a sigh of relief but then noticed the sad look on Vera's face.

"Carmen, I called you in here because… well…" Vera was at a loss for words. She averted her eyes unable to meet Vanessa's gaze.

"It's Arianna, isn't it?" Vanessa asked quietly.

Vera nodded her head. "I spoke to the friend I told you I would reach out to and he got back to me not too long ago. Apparently, about three nights ago there was an anonymous call to the police about a house in Kensington where there was a domestic disturbance…" Vanessa put her hands to her mouth anticipating what Vera was about to say. "They found Arianna inside of the house and rushed her to the hospital… she died before they could stabilize her and get her into surgery."

Vanessa burst into tears. She cried harder than anytime she had ever cried after being beaten by Eric. Though Vera was talking, she couldn't hear anything. Every bone in her body ached as she let out shoulder trembling, gut wrenching, soul shaking cries. Her best friend for over ten years who had been there for her through some of the best and worst moments of her life was dead and she couldn't help but feel responsible.

Vera was trying to console her, but Vanessa suddenly felt sick to her stomach. Before she had a chance to make it to the trashcan, she vomited all over the floor.

"It's all my fault!" Vanessa bellowed as she sobbed.

"No, no sweetie. Don't ever think that. Don't tell yourself that. You are not responsible for the person who was callous enough to end her life. That is not your burden to carry," Vera assured her. She grabbed some tissues and gave them to Vanessa, but it began to sound as though she was hyperventilating.

"Derek! Derek, I need you in here!" Vera called out. Derek came back into the room and saw Vanessa gasping for air as she continued to cry. He knelt in front of her and talked to her softly while Vera searched for a paper bag. When she found one, Derek helped Vanessa put it to her face and instructed her to take slow, deep breaths in between reassuring her that everything was going to be okay.

"You've gotta calm down before you make yourself sick. You have a baby to think about, now. Calm down and relax, okay?" Derek said to her softly. Vanessa continued to sob as she calmed down. She closed her eyes and rested her head on his shoulder, pulling the bag away from her face once she had her breathing under control. Derek stroked the back of her head and looked up at Vera.

"What happened?" he mouthed quietly so Vanessa could not hear him. Vera shook her head as she looked down at Vanessa sorrowfully. She felt in her gut that Vanessa's ex-boyfriend was responsible for Arianna's murder and steps would have to be taken to make sure the program along with the people who helped Vanessa along the way were not jeopardized.

After Vanessa had calmed down, Vera passed her a small cup of water. She sipped on it and then looked up at Vera with tear drenched eyes.

"No matter what you say, I know it's my fault. If I hadn't called her, he wouldn't have attacked her." She lowered her eyes. "I can't even go to her funeral to pay my respects or apologize to her family. I never should have left."

"You listen to me," Vera said as she knelt in front of Vanessa. She cupped her face in her hands and looked her in the eyes. "If you'd never left, it could be you that Arianna is paying her respects to. If you'd never left, he could have beaten you and caused you to lose your baby, disfigure you, injure you beyond healing or even worse, kill you. Is that what you want?" Vanessa shook her head as more tears flowed down her cheeks.

"Derek, take her back to her quarters please and sit with her for a little bit while I take care of some things," Vera instructed. "I will speak to the counselor to see if we can schedule an emergency session." Derek nodded and helped Vanessa stand before walking her back to her room. Vanessa stopped him after she opened her door.

"Thank you for helping me back there. But you don't have to stay with me. I'll be okay."

"Are you sure? It's really not a problem," Derek double checked.

Vanessa nodded her head and went into her room, closing the door behind her.

"You're welcome," Derek said quietly before walking away to get back to work.

15

Eric was meeting with another PI that he worked with. This was a back-up that he started using when he began to suspect that Tony might fold under pressure the night that Arianna was killed.

"Yeah, he's shown he can't be trusted. Good thing you hired me as back-up," a man said to Eric as he sat in his office.

"I had a feeling he was going to crack under pressure," Eric smirked. "Paranoid little bitch."

"So what do you want to do about him?"

Eric thought for a moment and then shrugged his shoulders. "Kill 'em. Fuck 'em," he said blandly as though he was giving an order to scramble his eggs instead of ordering a business associate to be killed. "Make it look good. A freak accident, a robbery gone wrong, a home burglary. Whatever. Just make sure you're efficient and the shit doesn't trace back to me."

The man Eric was talking to snickered as he rubbed his chin. "Yeah, I would hate for you to be having a similar conversation about me with someone else."

Eric ignored his last comment. "So what do you know about the number Vanessa called from?"

"Well, it was a burner phone and it's already been dumped. However, I was able to do a trace on the location that the call came from when the chick reached out to uh…" he hesitated as he looked through something on his phone. "…a Marcella. She was calling from Bethesda. I've got the address."

Eric grinned like the cat who had just caught the canary. "I like how you do business, Alex." He looked at the address on the phone his partner had. "And the address on Marcella?"

"Yeah I have that too," Alex replied as he pulled a paper out of his pocket and handed it to Eric.

Eric took the paper and looked at it briefly as he walked over to his desk drawer. He pulled out a thick white envelope that was folded over and handed it to Alex. "Here's the first 25k. You'll get the rest once Tony is taken care of."

"No problem, boss. I'll call you when it's final."

Yani

Alex left the house and Eric looked over the information he had for him. Knowing that he was close to locating Vanessa aroused him. Imagining what he would do to her just as he had done with Regina excited him even more.

16

Tony was cooperating with the police in the murder investigation for Arianna. He was scheduled to call Eric in a couple of days pretending to have information on Vanessa's whereabouts. In a meeting with Eric, Tony was to wear a wire and get Eric to incriminate himself in the murder of Arianna. That meeting would never happen.

He was on his way to meet up with a friend in South-West Philadelphia and was getting on the expressway off of Wissahickon Avenue. As usual, he weaved in and out of traffic wanting to hurry and get to his exit at Montgomery Drive. Just as he was coming past the City Line Exit, a car merged into his lane, suddenly. Reflex caused Tony to hit the brakes and swerve to another lane. His car didn't slow down.

"What the fuck?" Tony panicked as he kept stepping on the brakes. He swerved in another lane with cars honking, braking and swerving out of the way as well. One car didn't move out of the way in time and Tony slammed into him, setting off a chain reaction.

"Oh shit!" Tony exclaimed. And those were his last words. An 18 wheeler hit Tony sending him spinning towards the over-past. The car skidded to the over-past at almost 90mph and flipped over it, crashing down below before bursting into flames…

The Schuylkill expressway was chaotic as traffic was backed up for miles on both the east and west side. Multiple ambulances, fire trucks and police cars had the dark night lit up as they worked feverishly to get the injured to the hospital and conduct an investigation into what could have caused such a gruesome accident. There were four fatalities in all, which included Tony.

"Un-fucking-believable," Detective Felix said as he stared at the multitude of cars stuck in the traffic jam. Their head-lights and brake lights lit up the highway above them.

"This shit looks like a got-damn Greek tragedy," Detective Michaels replied. "What the hell happened out here?"

"Your guess is as good as mine," Felix replied. They continued collecting evidence and getting information on what happened as rescue wagons began to move the injured to nearby hospitals.

A uniformed officer came over to the two detectives and shook their hands.

"What do you have for us?" Michaels asked.

"Well witnesses say the guy in that Cadillac CTS swerved out the way of one car, slammed into another car and next thing you know, a bunch of other cars began crashing around them like this was Final Destination or something. Then the 18 wheeler slammed into the CTS and he went over the edge. One of our guys ran his plates. His name was uh…" the uniform hesitated as he looked at the notepad where he wrote his information down. "…Antonio Vasquez."

The two detectives looked at the uniformed officer and then looked at each other with their mouths gaping open.

"Coincidence or naw?" Michaels asked sarcastically.

"That would be a pretty big fucking coincidence. Twenty bucks says this was a set up," Felix said before stepping over some debris and heading over to where they were loading Tony's body into the coroner's truck.

Yani

"A set up? Don't you think if someone wanted to off him, they would have just put a bullet in the back of his head or something? A wreckage on the expressway that not only took him out but three other people, that's pretty fucking thin. Maybe ole' Vasquez's time was just up. Shit happens. Cased closed." Michaels said.

"That may be the case. But what if the plan wasn't to have him wipe out on the expressway but to just have him crash his car somewhere," Felix replied.

Michaels chuckled. "Come on, man. You make it sound like someone had a remote control to his car and made him steer the shit into the path of other cars and then pitched his ass over the edge."

"No, but who's to say that someone didn't tamper with the car like his brakes or steering column?" Felix stated. Michaels was quiet for a moment and then began to think maybe his partner was on to something.

"I want this car impounded and fully inspected; lights, turn signals, brakes, the whole she-bang, you understand? If there's anything wrong with it, I want it checked, double checked and then checked again. Let's go, people." Michaels said to the people who were working. "Y'all asses finna get some serious over time on this one."

Felix rubbed the hairs on his chin as he began thinking. His partner noticed the serious and focused look on his face.

"What's on your mind, partner?" Michaels asked.

"Nothing," Felix replied even though it was quite the opposite. His colleagues might not have given much thought into Vasquez's story about being hired to find some girl which led to Arianna's murder, but for Vasquez to be dead now only two weeks after sharing that information with the cops, this was more than just a car crash. He decided he would do a little digging on his own to find out what Vasquez was working on and see where that would lead him.

16

Marcella was in a hurry to get home after the long day she'd had. As a courtesy to Vanessa, she went to Arianna's funeral to pay her respects and obtain an obituary for her. She then went to countless meetings and wanted nothing more than to go home and take a hot bubble bath before relaxing for the rest of the night.

Marcella was an older woman in her late 40s standing at 5'6 with skin the color of honey and short hair that was neatly twisted in the beginner stages of locs. While she was a well off woman financially, she presented herself as "Plain Jane" dressing moderately in jeans, skippies, a shirt and blazer. She rarely ever wore make-up outside of lip balm. The only thing flashy she owned was a 2014 Mercedes Benz.

She had done well for herself as a social worker and had used money willed to her after her father's death to start a program for women against domestic abuse. The program was like a secret organization that worked the same way as the "Underground Railroad". Various safe houses across the country were put into place and women were hired to escort women who were trying to escape abusive relationships, from point A to point B. The idea for the program came into play after her daughter had been killed by her abusive boyfriend. The abuse had been going on unbeknownst to Marcella with her daughter hiding her bruises and fears very well. It wasn't until a month before her daughter Octavia was murdered that she began to suspect something was not right with the man she initially thought was perfect. On a rainy Saturday morning, the police showed up to her door to inform her that her daughter had been found dead in her car from one single gunshot wound to the head. Her boyfriend and killer was in the passenger seat also dead from a self-inflicted gunshot wound to the head. It was viewed as a text book murder-suicide. Marcella swore the day she buried her only daughter that she would do her best to provide a safe way out for any woman who needed help escaping an abusive lover. The program thrived for more than ten years with little to no interference… until Vanessa.

Yani

Marcella was half way home when she realized she didn't have important documents that she needed to sign and drop off to a client 8am the next morning. She was exhausted and tempted to just leave out a little earlier the next morning, get the papers and sign them, but decided against that, feeling like it would be seen as unprofessional. She made a U-Turn on Ridge Avenue near 29th street and headed back to the office.

The closer she got to her office, the more Marcella got a nagging feeling in the pit of her stomach that something was wrong. She ignored that feeling as she parked her car and used her key to get into the building.

The door squeaked loudly as it opened and closed slowly behind her. She twirled her keys around her finger as she made her way down the hallway. The nagging feeling in her stomach grew stronger and stronger with every step she took towards her office. Marcella stopped in front of the door with the key in her had. Something was wrong. Something was very wrong and it wasn't the nagging feeling that had her stomach in knots that led her to believe something was wrong, it was her own common sense. Every day that she left her office, she always locked the door behind her because of the sensitive information she kept in her office. But today, her office door was not only unlocked, but slightly cracked.

"Maintenance…" she thought to herself. *"They're cleaning the offices and probably haven't finished mine,"* she told herself. But when she opened the door and saw the way her office had been tossed as though someone was in there looking for something, her heart felt as though it would jump from her chest. She stepped inside and looked around with her mouth hanging open. Something inside of her told her to get the hell out of there. Just as she was backing up to run from the office and back to her car so she could dial 9-1-1, she felt a strong hand go over her mouth and another hand go around her throat. She cried out against his hand which muffled her.

"Shhhh," a male voice said. "Don't fight me, don't scream. Otherwise, I'll snap your fucking neck like a twig," he threatened.

Marcella whimpered feeling scared out of her mind. She told herself to remain calm and do whatever he required her to do to make it home alive.

Eric moved his hand from her mouth and his other hand from her throat. "I just have one question; where's Vanessa?" he asked.

Marcella played dumb. "Who?"

"Bitch, don't play with me. You don't even want to know how creative these hands can be."

"I swear I don't know anyone by that name," Marcella lied.

Eric shook his head. He then pulled a ten inch knife from out of his jacket pocket and put the tip of the blade to Marcella's throat. Her eyes became wide as her breathing became exacerbated from her fear of what he could do next. Her fear excited Eric and he stood closer to Marcella so she could feel his erection. She grimaced, squirming a little bit and feeling disgusted, only stopping when she felt Eric place the tip of the blade into her throat a little more.

"Please… please God don't hurt me," she begged.

"That all depends on you, Marcella. Where is Vanessa?" he asked again.

Marcella's eyes looked around the room as she wondered how this bastard knew her name. She decided to ask him. "How do you know my name?"

"That's the least of your worries. I'm only going to ask you one more time. Where the fuck is Vanessa?" Eric asked in a slower, menacing tone.

It then dawned on Marcella that her attacker was the ex-boyfriend of Vanessa. "Eric? Listen, you don't have to do this. Just let me…"

Marcella's words were cut off when Eric grabbed her by her throat and turned her around aggressively causing Marcella to yelp. Her feet back peddled as Eric pushed her backwards. She had never seen that look of evil in a man's eyes before and she felt more terrified than anything in the world.

"You bitches always insist on learning the hard way," Eric grimaced before shoving his blade into Marcella's stomach. She grabbed the knife as a look of pain, horror and anguish washed over her face. Eric smiled at her, always loving the way a woman's eyes became glossy when they were in pain or gasping for breath. He pushed the knife in deeper with a jerk. Marcella looked passed him as the pain quickly began to subside and she began to feel light as though she were about to slip into a sweet slumber.

"Tavi, baby? When did you get here? That dress is so beautiful on you. You look amazing." Marcella could hear herself saying that in her head though the words weren't being vocalized. She reached her hand out to the hand that was extended to her. When their fingers intertwined, Marcella felt whole again, a feeling she hadn't felt in ten

years. She smiled at Tavi as she was pulled closer to her, and Tavi smiled back…"

"Octavia…" Marcella mumbled before her eyes fluttered and began to close. Her head leaned back slowly as though she had fallen asleep. But like the heartless bastard he was, Eric tossed her to the floor like a ragdoll.

"Who the fuck is Octavia?" he asked the empty room.

"Never mind the small stuff, Ricky. The point is you shoulda been keeping these dames in line from jump street and you wouldn't have this problem on ya hands. You got to find this gal and learn her good and hard, but slow so she knows better'n to step outta 'er place again. This never woulda happened had you not been such a lil' pussy and learned from when I tried to teach you about these no good whores starting with ya momma."

Eric grimaced. He beat himself in the head with his fists hating the sound of his father's voice. Nothing he ever did satisfied him even when he did his best. If what he did wasn't something his father would have done or it wasn't done the way his father told him to do it, it got him an ass whipping. He saw himself as a child bent over in between his father's strong thighs as he rained down fiery blows from his thick, black leather belt. Eric could still hear the whistling sound the belt made as it sailed through the air before connecting with his bare back or ass.

"No!" Eric bellowed. "No, no, no, no, no, NO!!" he said again and again before sliding to the floor. He wrapped his arms around his knees hugging them to his chest as he rocked himself back and forth. He rocked and rocked and rocked until the sound of his father's voice disappeared and the visual memory of his father whipping him mercilessly as a young boy disappeared as well.

Eric got to his feet and looked down at Marcella's lifeless body. A small part of him felt remorseful as he thought how much Marcella resembled his mother and the way she would lie motionless on the kitchen, living room and sometimes, bathroom floor after taking a beating from his father. He looked away from her.

"I'm sorry…" he murmured, and then quickly and quietly left the office.

17

Vanessa lay in her bed staring up at the ceiling thinking about Arianna. She dabbed the corners of her eyes with a tissue, hurting tremendously over the loss of her best friend. She thought back to their last conversation and how brief it was, grateful that she told Arianna that she loved her one last time. For some reason, her mind wandered to Derek and how he comforted her after she'd learned of Arianna's murder. The manner in which he whispered in her ear to soothe her and stroked the back of her head as she laid on his shoulder gave her butterflies. Not meaning to, she found herself blushing. She hadn't had that feeling since the very beginning of her relationship with Eric, before everything went to hell.

Vanessa shook her head trying to clear the last thought she had of Derek. She'd just gotten through with a terrible relationship and the last thing she needed to be thinking about was another man, especially while she was pregnant… or so she told herself. Nevertheless, the butterflies continued to flutter in her stomach at the mere thought of him.

The following days, she began going to the kitchen area to fix herself breakfast, going the same time she went when she initially came in contact with Derek, hoping that she would run into him again so she could have the chance to be more cordial with him. But day after day had passed and he was nowhere to be found. She was tempted to ask a young lady that she'd recently befriended after Arianna was murdered if she had seen him around, but she didn't want to seem obvious.

"*Or like a stalker,*" the voice in her head said. She jumped as it sounded more like Eric than the usual voice she heard. "*Bitch, that nigga ain't thinking about your tired ass. What can you give him besides a baby that belongs to another nigga other than some pussy? And your shit never really was that great. You're black as shit, stupid as fuck and don't have shit going for yourself. Stop trying to find a fill-in-pop and go sit your ugly-ass down somewhere and stay out the fucking way.*"

Vanessa was in the middle of stirring a pot of grits when she heard those words in her head. Her self-esteem quickly came crashing down. Eric always knew exactly what to say to her to knock her down a peg or two. Her eyes teared up as those words echoed in her head. She blinked them away and continued stirring her grits. She was feening for a cup of coffee but knew the caffeine wasn't good for her pregnancy, so she opted for a glass of orange juice instead. Just as she was pouring herself a glass, Derek came into the kitchen area. Vanessa suddenly became overwhelmed with nervousness and spilled the orange juice on the counter.

"Here, let me help you with that," Derek offered politely. He grabbed a few paper towels and began to wipe the juice from the counter. The smell of his cologne danced her way and teased her nostrils. She had never came across a man who smelled so good that the mere scent of him took her breath away.

"How are you today?" Derek asked her as he put on a pot of coffee.

"I'm good, thank you. And yourself?" Vanessa replied politely as she began to stir her grits a little more.

Derek was shocked that she said that much to him. "I'm well, thank you." They fell silent for a moment while Derek made his coffee and Vanessa began to place her food on her plate. He took a sip from his mug. "You enjoy the rest of your day," he said with a smile.

Vanessa's heart began to race not anticipating he would be leaving so quickly. "I'm sorry, would you like something to eat?" she asked quickly. She then looked away hoping he didn't hear the desperation in her voice.

"Yeah, you damn sure did sound desperate. I see you still insist on learning the hard way," the voice in her head said again. It took every ounce of self-control that she had to keep from saying "shut up" out loud.

Derek paused for a brief moment. He was only planning on having his coffee for breakfast but was never one to turn down a meal. Especially one that smelled as good as what Vanessa was cooking.

"What are you having?" he asked her.

"Um… nothing fancy, just some grits, scrambled cheese eggs, a couple slices of ham and some crescent rolls. But if you don't eat pork, I think there's some turkey sausages in here…" she said quickly, turning back to the refrigerator to check for them.

"No, no it's fine. I don't eat pork but you don't have to fix a substitution. Thanks for offering."

Vanessa struggled to keep from blushing but failed miserably. Derek caught her and smiled to himself. He stopped her as she was about to reach in the cabinet to get another plate and cup to fix him something to eat.

"How about you have a seat and let me take care of that," he said to her before pulling out her chair. Vanessa thanked him and had a seat. Derek fixed his plate and sat across from her at the table. Vanessa was taken aback when she saw him bow his head and say his grace. She couldn't remember the last time she had done that before a meal. With Eric, if he even allowed her to eat with him, he normally just dove right into his plate without thanking her let alone God.

Derek put a spoonful of the grits in his mouth along with some of the scrambled cheese eggs. "Unh girl! Wooo, now this is some good cooking. Man, I haven't had eggs and grits this good since I lived with my momma!" he said with a smile. Vanessa chuckled.

"She didn't cook for you after you moved out?" Vanessa inquired as she ate some of her food.

Derek cocked his head to the side and then shook it. "Well, she didn't get the chance to, really. She passed away about a year after I left."

"Oh… I'm sorry to hear that," Vanessa replied solemnly.

"It's okay, I mean it was hard on me because it was so sudden. Here one day and gone the next, you know? But it taught me not to take life for granted and not to take people for granted. I would tell myself all the time I was going to go see her tomorrow, next week, the day after that and I just kept letting things distract me. Things that didn't even matter like kicking it with this homie or going to dinner with this girl or going to this event. The biggest mistake people make is thinking that tomorrow will be here for us to do all of the things that we could be or should be doing today. We take today for granted as though it's trivial. Losing my mom taught me that nothing is trivial."

They fell silent for a moment as Derek's words weighed in on Vanessa. She thought of all the times she said she would call Arianna before she left Eric. All of the times that she said she would make plans to hang with her closest friend. Now she wouldn't be able to. She blinked away the tears that threatened to fall as she stirred her food in her plate with her fork, no longer hungry. Derek noticed the look of sadness on her face.

"I'm sorry, I did mean to get all doom and gloom on you knowing you just experienced a loss of your own."

Vanessa forced a smile. "It's okay. Death is a part of life," she replied quietly.

Derek noticed there was a fly soaring near her shoulder and tried to shoo it away causing Vanessa to jump as though she was expecting to be slapped or punched. He pulled his hand away and stared at her for a moment. Feeling embarrassed, she excused herself from the kitchen and went to the bathroom.

He knew that she had been abused hence why she was at the facility. But he suspected her situation was much more unique than some of the others. He could tell that she was very young which made him pity her, knowing that depending on how severe the abuse was, she may never trust another man again or feel safe in a relationship with one.

At the risk of succumbing to the hero complex, Derek yearned to get to know her more with the hopes that he could show her that all men aren't monsters and there are still some around who honor, protect and love their women. He didn't expect anything from her, but if he could at least be a good friend to her to help mend her heart and heal her spirit, that would be good enough for him.

He tried to wait for her to return from the bathroom so they could exchange numbers but saw that it was very close to time for him to clock in and he didn't want to be late. He then suspected that maybe she was trying to wait him out because she felt uncomfortable around him. He quickly cleared their dishes and washed everything up for her. He then walked back to her room and slipped a note under her door thanking her for breakfast with his phone number on the bottom.

When Vanessa was sure that Derek was gone, she left the bathroom and made her way back to the kitchen to dump her breakfast and wash the dishes that she used. She was shocked to see that it had already been done for her and hoped that it hadn't been by a supervisor who was annoyed with the mess that was left behind. She returned to her room and saw the note left by Derek. Her first reaction was to ball the paper up and throw it in the trash but she couldn't bring herself to do it.

The loud speaker came on. *"Ladies and gentlemen, may I have your attention? At this time we are asking for those who are*

Yani

at the facility to please report to the courtyard for an emergency meeting."

Vanessa stuffed the note that Derek left her in her yoga pants pocket and made her way over to the courtyard.

"Do you know what this is about?" a young lady named Sally asked Vanessa in the hallway.

"My guess is as good as yours," Vanessa replied. She then noticed that Vera and one of the counselors were hugging each other crying.

"What is going on?" Sally asked after noticing the two women hugging and crying as well.

There were about twenty people at the facility at the time the emergency meeting was called. They stood in the courtyard all wondering what was going on and what happened. Vanessa noticed Derek was staring at her and her face flushed. She was glad when Vera came to the center of the courtyard to address the crowd.

"Good morning everyone. I know you're all wondering why I had you come out here so suddenly. I wanted to speak to as many of you at once rather than relay the same message to you individually," Vera started. She searched the faces of the crowd until she found Vanessa before she continued. "I wanted to let you all know that "Sistahs on the Move" has suffered a terrible and tremendous loss. Our founder, the woman who was like a mother to us all, who saved many of us and helped give us a second chance in life was found late last night…" Vera broke off unable to compose herself any longer. The silence in the courtyard was deafening as many of the people stared at her in disbelief. "Marcella Jackson was found late last night in her office. She had been stabbed. Her office was ransacked. We don't know who her killer is or what he or she was looking for, but we have to assume that whoever it was, they are looking for someone that passed through our program. Therefore, security at this facility will be beefed up. Unless you are a student or have a full time job, until you receive housing, no one is to travel anywhere alone. You are to take at least one buddy with you anytime you leave this facility. I know many of you became close with Marcella when you sought help from her. Counseling sessions can be set up and we will conduct a prayer circle this evening at 7pm…" Vera looked at Vanessa again before turning away from the crowd and heading back inside of the facility.

Vanessa was numb. She was positive Eric was behind this. *"Which means you better run like hell because he's coming for your ass and God help anyone in his way,"* she heard the voice say in her head.

"First Arianna, now Ms. Marcella…" Vanessa whispered.

"You say something?" Sally asked.

Vanessa shook her head, "No… I just can't believe someone would want to hurt Ms. Marcella. That's crazy!"

"Shit, it'll be just our luck if some dumb ass called her ex-husband or ex-boyfriend on some lonely shit and now his ass is coming after anybody that helped her," Sally said in a low voice.

Vanessa had no response because Sally was spot on. Apart of her hoped that Marcella's murder had been something very random. But deep down inside, she knew that it was Eric. That one phone call she made caused at least two deaths and she was feeling extremely guilty and every bit responsible as if she had been the one who committed the crimes herself.

"I'm going to head back to my room. Stop by later if you want to chat," Vanessa replied as she gave Sally a hug. She moved through the crowd to head back to her room when Derek stopped her.

"What happened to you earlier?" he asked her.

Vanessa fumbled. "Oh, I felt sick and needed to run to the bathroom," she lied.

"Oh. Are you feeling any better?"

"Yeah. I just can't believe what happened to Ms. Marcella."

"Yeah… I can't believe it either," Derek said also as he shook his head in sorrow. "Did you get the note I left for you under your door?"

"Yeah." Vanesa's face flushed again.

"Well, I have to get back to work. Ms. Vera more than likely will want to discuss new security measures that she wants to implement. Call me tonight."

Vanessa nodded her head and watched Derek as he moved through the crowd to go back to work. She then thought of Marcella and caught a chill that made her tremble.

"*1, 2, Eric's coming for you…*" a voice sang in her head. She closed her eyes trying to block out the chilling tune as it continued in her head. As much as she wanted to tell herself that it wasn't necessarily Eric who had killed Marcella, she knew it was a great possibility that it was. Instead of going to her room, she made her way over to Vera's office. She tapped on the door lightly.

Yani

"Come in," Vera said loudly.

Vanessa opened the door and peeped her head inside. "Is this a bad time?" she asked.

Vera stared at her for a moment trying very hard not to be angry. A big part of her blamed Vanessa for what was transpiring. As a victim of domestic abuse and a woman who had traveled through the network just as Vanessa and many other women had, she understood how hard it was to leave her former life behind. Many times she wanted to give up and go back to her old life figuring it would be easier to deal with what was familiar to her instead of facing the unknown, but she stayed strong with the help of Marcella and other women, and made it through.

"No, this isn't a bad time. I actually was going to send for you. Come in and have a seat," Vera said as she directed Vanessa to the chair on the other side of her desk.

Vanessa sat down. The silence made her feel uncomfortable as she wondered what Vera was thinking at the moment. She looked around the office at the many photos that Vera had of herself and other women that more than likely received the same help that she was receiving. Framed certificates, diplomas and degrees adorned the wall. She found herself enthralled with the long navy blue velvet curtains to the huge windows behind Vera's desk and the way they were wrapped with a fancy rope and pulled to the side slightly letting in a hint of sun-light. Though on that day, there was no sun-light. The gloomy clouds outside set the tone for all that had occurred; things that more than likely were occurring because of one phone call that Vanessa made.

Vanessa decided that she would be the one to break the silence. "Ms. Vera, do you think what happened to Ms. Marcella was because of me?" she asked innocently.

Vera sighed as she looked Vanessa over with a blank expression on her face. Her hand reached for a wooden case atop her desk and opened it. She pulled out a slim cigarette and then searched her drawer for her lighter. When she found it, she placed the cigarette between her lips and lit it. Vanessa watched the way her hand moved casually as though it were doing a dance. Vera softly sucked on the cigarette and closed her eyes, holding the smoke in before curving her lips to blow the smoke out of the corner of her mouth. Vanessa then noticed the large "No Smoking" sign above Vera's head.

As though she knew what Vanessa had just seen, Vera said blandly, "Yeah, I know. No smoking. But shit, an exception has to be made today." She coughed slightly and cleared her throat. Vera debated briefly whether or not she should be nice with choosing her words, but then considered the serious nature of the current situation. "Do I think what happened to Marcella is because of you?" she asked back. "Absolutely. Without a shadow of a doubt, I believe her murder is because of you."

Vanessa lowered her eyes as Vera's words stung her deeply. She suddenly felt even guiltier than she had felt when she found out that Arianna was dead. She felt lower than worm shit, a worthless moron who couldn't follow simple rules. Vera noticed the look on her face and sighed deeply.

"As I said to you before, I understand how hard this journey may be for you. I've been there. Many of us have been there. But I will not lie to you when answering your question. It won't do you any good. It doesn't do me any good or this program. And it sure as hell won't do any good for Marcella and anyone else who has been or will be effected by your actions," Vera said as her anger began to seep through.

"I understand," Vanessa replied.

"No Carmen, I don't think you do. You are now considered a liability and while I believe Marcella would never just dump you and let you find your own way, I have to consider the safety of every other person that helped you past through this network as well as the many other women who are in this facility."

Vanessa trembled as she feared what was about to be said next. "What happens to me now?"

Vera took another slow drag on her cigarette, blowing the smoke out as she'd done previously. "I don't know, Carmen. I'm going to talk it over with our security personnel after I get details on Marcella's murder investigation. Depending on what we find will determine our course of action with you. But understand something, I will not jeopardize anyone else in this network because of your mistake. Are we clear?" Vera asked with a serious expression on her face.

Vanessa nodded, unable to speak. She stood up and left the office so she could go back to her room. She began to worry about what she would do in the event that she had to leave the facility. Where would she go and who would help her.

Yani

"*1, 2, Eric's coming for you…*" the voice sang in her head again slowly.

"Shut up!" Vanessa said out loud. She looked around to see if anyone had heard her and was grateful that the hallway was clear. "Please just leave me alone, Eric. Please…"

18

While working the murder investigation of Arianna and keeping tabs on Tony Vasquez's murder investigation to see if the two of them could be tied together, Felix did further investigating outside of the work he and his partner were doing together. It wasn't that he didn't trust his partner, he just trusted his gut more than he trusted anyone else. His gut told him that what Vasquez told them about Eric Washington was true. He made copies of Tony's records, specifically of the PI work he'd done for Eric. As he was going through the files, he came across Regina Smalls' information.

"Regina Smalls?" Felix said aloud as he sat at his work desk in his apartment. "Why does that name sound familiar?" He got on his home computer and did a quick search which led him to the news story of her body being found near the park on Belfield Avenue. He breezed through the articles and became very interested when he saw Eric Washington's name mentioned.

Yani

"I'm convinced he knows more about what happened to my baby than he (Washington) is letting on," the mother of the 22 year old college student stated. "Regina was trying to leave him and now all of a sudden, she's dead? My baby didn't have any enemies and this wasn't just some random act. I believe he knows something or he had something to do with it and one way or another, the truth will come out…"

"Coincidence or naw?" Felix mumbled. He went back to Vasquez's files and thumbed through them trying to remember the name of the young lady he said he was hired by Eric to find. "What was her name? Victoria, Valerie…? Shit," Felix said as he scanned each paper. He finally came across the information. "Vanessa Lofton."

He pulled all of the papers out that Tony had on her and kicked his legs up on his desk. After reading through part of the file and seeing there wasn't much information, he then decided to use the police network to see if he could find anything on her. Felix ran into the same brick wall that Tony had run into. There was no cell phone activity, and no bank account, credit card or ATM transactions in almost four months. In under an hour he was able to access her bank records and saw that the last debit card transaction was on April 7th at ShopRite in Cheltenham

Mall. He then did a random Google search on Vanessa's name. What came up caused him to sit up in his seat. He clicked on one of the articles and became very intrigued with what he was reading. Felix began to realize at that moment it was more to Eric and Vanessa than he imagined.

"Well I'll be damned…" Felix pulled the case file on Arianna to get the date of her murder which was on June 16th. He then remembered that Tony mentioned a phone call that had been made to Arianna which led to the night of her murder. It prompted him to have her phone records pulled.

"What did you know, Arianna?" he asked the empty room. He thought back to how she kept trying to show him her hands, and the determined yet frantic look in her eyes and shook his head in frustration. Instead of going through the phone records, he decided to pull Vanessa's last known address which was where Eric lived. He didn't want to tip him off, so he decided he would speak with the neighbors instead. After all, if this was a matter of domestic violence which resulted in Vanessa leaving, he was betting that someone next door had heard something going on.

Yani

Camille was in her garden tending to her bushes when Felix pulled up in his black two-door 2012 Monte Carlo. Camille glanced up from her work and dusted her hands off as she wondered who it could be.

"How are you today ma'am?" Felix greeted her with a warm smile.

Camille looked at him suspiciously. She had noticed the flow of traffic coming in and out of Eric's house, guys that she had never seen before in the six years that he had that house as well as a few women. With Marcella's and Arianna's recent murders, she was on high alert when it came to Eric.

"Can I help you?" Camille asked timidly.

Felix noticed her paranoid manner and decided to turn his back on Eric's house in the event he was peeping out of his window and watching them. "I'm a detective working on the murder investigation of Arianna Stone and your neighbor is a person of interest. I was hoping that maybe you could tell me about a young lady who used to live here named Vanessa," he said in a low voice.

"I said he had something to do with it. I knew it, I knew it. My husband and I have been saying it for weeks ever since we saw the story on the news."

"If your husband is home and it's alright with him, can we have this conversation inside? I think you understand why that request is being made."

Camille thought for a moment and then nodded her head. She took her gardening gloves off and suddenly hugged Felix tightly before exclaiming, "Oh Junior! I'm so glad you decided to stop by! I haven't seen you since Susie Mae's wedding!"

Felix hesitated a moment but then hugged her back. "I know it's been a while, Auntie…"

Camille showed him inside of the house and called for her husband who had just gotten in from work. She closed and locked the front door while they waited for him.

"Woman, your voice is loud enough to be an alarm clock for the dead. What is it, now?" Tremaine joked as he pulled a shirt over his head while coming down the steps. He stopped when he saw Felix.

"This is a detective that's looking into the murder of Vanessa's friend. Remember we were saying how we thought Eric had something to do with it because of the strange people that kept coming in and out the house since Vanessa left? Well, Felix says he's a person of interest and wants our help," Camille explained. She was more enthused than her husband who still looked at Felix suspiciously.

"Can I see a badge or something? Pardon my suspicion, but it's been a lot of weird stuff going on lately," Tremaine asked.

"Absolutely, I completely understand. I would have shown your wife outside but if Eric were watching from his window, I didn't want him to know you were talking to cops," Felix explained.

"Yeah, cause you don't much look like a cop, honestly," Tremaine replied as he looked over the badge. When he was satisfied, he shook Felix's hand and offered him a seat. Camille went to the kitchen and put on a pot of coffee and grabbed some blueberry muffins that she had just baked earlier as well. "How can we help you?"

"Well, this is just a hunch that I'm going off of. The department is playing this too straight and narrow. I was the detective on the scene when we discovered Ms. Stone and I was really hoping that she pulled through and could give us some information as to who hurt her. The first suspect that we came across from a video in the area where

Ms. Stone was taken from her car is who led us to Eric," Felix explained.

"How so?" Tremaine asked.

"Well, he told me he had been hired by Eric to locate a young woman named Vanessa. During his search, he stated that Vanessa contacted Arianna but didn't say where she was. So Tony began trailing her at Eric's suggestion and that's what led to the night of her murder."

"Wait, Vanessa called Arianna? When?" Camille asked as she brought the tray in with the muffins and coffee along with cream and sugar. The aroma teased Felix's nose and awakened a hunger inside of him.

"Thanks," he said as he reached for a muffin. "I haven't had a chance to go through Arianna's phone records to get an idea of when Vanessa called her but I'm betting it was about a week or two before the murder."

"Damn it, I told her and I'm sure Marcella told her that under no circumstances could she contact anyone. This is the very reason why they stress the "no contact" rule!" Camille said. She became emotional as she sat down at the table with Felix and Tremaine. Marcella had been a good friend of hers for almost twenty years. She was there for her when "Sistahs on the Move" was first started after the murder of her daughter, Octavia. Blood couldn't make them any closer.

"Wait, you knew Marcella Jackson as well?" Felix asked.

"Yes, yes we did," Camille replied as she wiped the tears from her eyes. Her husband held her hand.

"It looks like I came to the right place, then. Connect the dots for me, please. I need to put this thing together more than anything right now. The look in Arianna's eyes when she was showing me her hands haunts me every night. I have to do something," Felix said. Tremaine could see the sorrow in his eyes and nodded at his wife, giving her the okay to talk.

Camille began to tell everything about what they heard and the things they saw over at Eric's house with Vanessa; her loud screams when Eric would beat her, the yelling and cursing from him, how Vanessa would try to hide her bruises behind make-up and sun-glasses.

"Finally one night back in April, I just couldn't take it anymore. He beat the hell out of her. I don't know why, not that it would matter if I did. But I just couldn't stand to see her endure anymore of his abuse. After talking it over with my husband and getting him to agree with me, we decided to talk with her and put her in contact with Marcella with the hopes of getting her some help while getting her away from Eric."

"So he was beating her?" Felix double checked.

"He was beating the hell out of that girl," Tremaine said.

"Yes he was. Anyways, she was leery about talking to Tre', I'm guessing she was afraid of what Eric would do to her if he caught them talking. So my husband suggested I try. That's when I told her about Marcella and convinced her to leave Eric. But I told her she could not make contact. She didn't listen and now Arianna and Marcy are dead."

Tremaine put his arm around his wife to console her. "I don't know if that will be enough or if what we told you will be of any help. But beyond what we heard through the walls and being the ones that helped her get away from him through Marcella, there's not much more we can tell you. I will ask though, seeing as though people are being killed, we'd like to stay out of this. We don't want our names or anything to be a part of this investigation. Because before I let that bastard bring harm to me and my wife, I'll put that sonuva bitch down like the rabid dog he is."

Felix could tell by the look on Tremaine's face that he was dead serious. "You have my word, sir. As I said, this is just a little digging that I'm doing on my own to see if the murders of Arianna, Marcella and Tony can be tied together."

"Tony?" Tremaine asked. "You mean the little Rican looking guy? He's dead, too?"

"You knew him?" Felix asked.

"Well not personally, but I've seen him around. He was around a lot after Vanessa left. I never knew what the deal was with him, he just always seemed iffy, like he had a coke problem in the past or something," Tremaine replied as he shook his head.

"He was in an accident on I-76. His car went over the over-pass, crashed and he was killed."

"You're talking about that big accident that happened last month! That was him!" Camille exclaimed. Felix nodded his head.

"By the way you were talking, I understand the importance of discretion with the program that Vanessa entered. But if Eric is tracking her and if he is the one behind these murders all so he can find her, it would be in her best interest if we found her before he does. Do you know where she is?" Felix asked them.

They both shook their heads. "Marcella had seven different destination sites with at least twenty pit-stops in between. She could be as close as D.C or as far as California. We really don't know. The only thing I can suggest is to track her through the call she made to Arianna. That's more than likely what Eric is doing," Camille told him.

Felix thought about what she said and made a mental note to check Arianna's phone records when he got back home. He stood up and shook both of their hands. "Thank you for your time and your help. I really appreciate it. Hopefully I can solve this and put Mr. Washington where he belongs. The muffin was delicious, by the way."

"You're very welcome," Tremaine replied as he and his wife walked Felix to the door.

Felix thought of something and stopped. "Have you ever heard of or remember Eric dating a woman named Regina Smalls?" he asked.

"We would probably need to see a picture of her. He's had so many different women coming in and out of that house. Vanessa and maybe one other woman three years ago were the only long term relationships we can recall him having," Camille told Felix.

"Yeah, she was dating him about three years ago and just like Vanessa, Tony was hired to find her when she left him. Then her body was found near Belfield Avenue."

"Jesus," Tremaine mumbled.

"Why can't you just arrest this bastard now?" Camille asked. "That's at least four dead people by his hand. You can't arrest him?"

"Everything is circumstantial, ma'am. We have no proof. Only the word of a known felon who is now dead, and a lot of coincidences. We can't tie him to the video we have of Arianna's abduction, we can't tie him to Regina Smalls' murder because he had an air tight alibi. This guy is good. But I promise you, I will do everything in my power to make sure he doesn't get to Vanessa or hurt anyone else. You have my word on that."

Tremaine opened the front door and Felix stepped out. Coming up the walk-way to his own house was Eric. He briefly looked at Felix but didn't pay him any mind. He waved to Tremaine and Camille casually and went inside of his house.

"That was him," Camille said in a low voice.

Felix smiled and gave her the same warm embrace that he had given her earlier. "Good seeing you, Auntie." He then shook Tremaine's hand and gave him a strong hug. "Good seeing you, too Unk."

Tremaine looked at him confused at first but decided to play along. "Yeah, you gotta come watch an Eagles' game with me in my man cave. Let Camille whip up some of her famous Jambalaya and Louisiana home fried chicken. Woo-Wee!" he said with a chuckle.

"I definitely will, Unk. I definitely will." Felix walked over to his car and drove away. Eric watched from his window for a little bit and then closed his blinds.

19

Every night since the day Derek had given Vanessa his phone number, they talked on the phone for hours. Most of the conversations were funny with Derek telling Vanessa stories of his child-hood and the kinds of trouble he would get into with his friends. Vanessa hadn't laughed so hard in a long time. But whenever the conversations would shift to her and her childhood, Vanessa would find a reason to get off the phone abruptly, or change the subject. Derek liked Vanessa a lot and was becoming drawn to her more and more every day. But she was not making it easy for him to get to know her.

Vanessa was standing in front of her mirror admiring her "baby bump" one morning. She'd just passed the sixth month milestone and was preparing for the homestretch, glowing all the while. She turned from one side to the other staring at her belly in a loving manner. Though she wanted the sex to be kept a secret until she delivered the baby, she had already picked out names. If she were to be blessed with a girl, Vanessa was going to name her after Arianna. Should it be a boy, she was going to name him after her father, Darryl Malik Lofton. Thinking of her father put her in a solemn mood. She was only fortunate enough to have him in her life until the age of sixteen. Vanessa had never learned the full story behind his death. She only knew that he was shot and killed outside of his car while coming home from work one night.

Her father had been the first man to tell her he loved her, the only man to have tattooed her name across his chest, and the first man to show her how beautiful she was inside and out. Thinking of the day he stood behind her while she sat at her vanity in her bedroom trying on make-up that Arianna bought for her birthday, she could still hear his voice as he schooled her on her natural beauty.

"Vanna, you have the kind of beauty that most women would kill for; pure, natural, undeniable. Why cover your beauty with make-up that's only going to dull a light that already shines so bright without it. Love yourself as you are or no one else will. You're already beautiful. You don't need anything more than your smile." And with those words, he kissed Vanessa on the top of her head and rubbed her neck gently.

Yani

"I miss you, Daddy…" Vanessa said softly. She heard a knock at her door and jumped. "Who is it?" she asked.

"Good morning, Carmen. It's Derek. I was about to head out to Verna's Diner for some breakfast. Would you like to join me?"

Vanessa looked at herself in the mirror and suddenly felt insecure about her appearance. Her hair wasn't done, and she was wearing a pair of sweat pants with a tank-top and Adidas flip flops. She couldn't possibly let him see the way she looked.

Derek knocked again. "Carmen, is this a bad time?"

"Um… just a second!" She fumbled around, picking at her curly bush and then frowned. "Aww man…!" she whined. She sulked over to the door and cracked it open. "Hi Derek," she managed a smile. "Verna's sounds great but I look a mess right now. I was too lazy to twist my hair last night and I'm not even dressed. Maybe some other time," she said quickly.

Derek looked her over. "You look beautiful to me. Your hair's perfect and you look comfortable. That's all that matters. Honestly, you could look like you just finished dumpster diving. Just being in your company is enough," he said with a charming smile.

Vanessa tried to suppress her blushing but was unsuccessful and that made Derek smile even more. She opened the door for him. "At least let me put some sneakers on instead of these flip flops. I'll be ready in a minute."

Derek came in and stood by her desk. "Take your time." Vanessa went into her bedroom and kicked off her flip-flops. She grabbed her New Balances from the small closet she had and slipped them on quickly. She then frowned at her appearance in the mirror and took the sneakers back off. She quickly pulled off her sweat pants and snatched a pair of faded blue jeans from her closet along with a peach and white colored top that fell from one shoulder.

"Any plans for your day off?" she asked from her bedroom as she changed her clothes.

"Nothing too special. Just enjoying the weather and seeing what the day brings me. What about you?" Derek asked back.

Vanessa quickly slipped on a pair of hooped ear-rings and dabbed on a little perfume. "No, nothing planned. Was just going to get a good book to read and maybe watch a movie or something."

Yani

"Yeah? What are you reading?"

"I was thinking of reading either *Native Son, Black Boy,* or *The Spook Who Sat by the Door.* I don't know yet."

"I love Richard Wright's work. He was very raw and authentic. Didn't hold any punches either..." Derek trailed off when Vanessa came from her bedroom. Every thought that he had been thinking vanished as he stared at her. He had not come across a woman whose beauty was breath-taking in all of his life. He thought back to when he told himself that he would be satisfied being good friends with her and knew at that moment that merely being friends would not be enough. Derek wanted Vanessa as his woman, the number one priority in his life, and he was willing to do whatever was necessary to make that happen.

Vanessa caught the way that Derek stared at her and looked away as the butterflies invaded her stomach. She tried to tell herself that it was the baby kicking and moving around, but a voice that sounded very much like Arianna told her otherwise.

"Don't fight it, Vanna. It's been a while since a man genuinely looked at you with that kind of gaze. Embrace it. Don't punish him for what Eric did to you. Let him in!"

Vanessa grabbed her purse from the table with Derek's gaze never leaving her. "I'm ready. Let me just grab my keys."

"You look beautiful," Derek told her.

Vanessa blushed again as she snatched her keys from the counter. "Thank you," she smiled.

Derek shook his head as though he was being snapped out of a trance. "I have the movie *The Spook Who Sat by the Door*. Have you ever seen it?"

"No, but I wanted to. I remember my father telling me about it but we never got a chance to watch it together," Vanessa replied as they left her small living quarters.

"Why not?" Derek asked.

Vanessa hesitated, still not sure if she wanted to talk about her past. She then shrugged her shoulders, "He was killed before we had the chance. I never really thought of watching it after that. But I was browsing some books on a website the other day and I saw it and thought of him, so I bought it on Kindle."

"Oh, damn. I'm sorry to hear that," Derek replied as he tweaked the alarm to his silver 2014 Nissan Pathfinder. He opened the door for her so she could get in and then jogged around to the other side. "Well, how about this; if you're not doing anything later outside of enjoying a good book, do you like Shrimp Alfredo?"

Vanessa smiled. "I love Shrimp Alfredo."

"Okay, well, you made me breakfast. How about I whip some up, bring it over with the movie, and we can watch it and buss a grub?"

"You can cook?" Vanessa looked at him with a smirk.

"Oh yes, a brother can burn. My momma taught me well."

"Okay, we'll see. Don't be bringing me no Chef Boy R Dee mess with some extra seasonings on it. I ain't slow," Vanessa joked. They laughed together.

"Aww, she's trying to play me. Nah, seriously. I can burn. You'll see tonight," Derek told her as he started the car and pulled out of his parking spot.

"Okay, it's a date," Vanessa smiled again. And this time she was sure that it wasn't just the baby moving around. The butterflies in her stomach danced to the beat of an unheard, melodious tune and Vanessa embraced the good feelings they left her with. She placed her hand on her stomach and smiled as she stared out of the window while Derek drove to Verna's Diner.

They talked and laughed while eating big breakfast platters of French toast, scrambled cheese eggs, home fries, sliced ham, coffee and orange juice. Vanessa had not been this comfortable in the company of a man in a long time. Talking to Derek was as easy as breathing. Vanessa was enjoying her time with him so much that she never noticed the man sitting two tables behind them watching her and discreetly taking pictures with his phone.

After they were done eating, Derek cleared everything off of the table and paid for their meal. They began walking back to his car still engrossed in their conversation when a young woman walked over to them.

"Excuse me, Vanessa?" the young woman asked.

Vanessa froze as she stared at the woman, not recognizing her as someone she knew from back home. She shook her head and smiled nervously. "Excuse me?"

"Your name is Vanessa, right?" the young lady asked in a matter of fact tone.

"No, I'm sorry, you have me mistaken for someone else," Vanessa replied as her heart raced.

"No I don't. Here," she said as she put a small, manila envelope in Vanessa's hand. "I was told to give this to you." And as quickly as the woman approached her, she was gone.

"That was odd. Did you know her?" Derek asked.

"I have no idea who she was," Vanessa mumbled as she peeked inside of the envelope. She froze as a lump of fear formed in her throat. Inside of the envelope was a photo of her standing near Derek at the diner and another photo of her sitting at the table, laughing. On the photo was a caption that read in red letters: *See You Soon, V-Dot.*

"He found me…" she thought to herself.

"1, 2… Eric's coming for you…" the voice sang in her head.

As hard as Vanessa was trying to keep a straight face, fear shook her body to the core. Derek noticed the sudden change in her.

"What's up, Carmen? You good?" he asked as he searched her face.

"I need to get back to my room," Vanessa said in a shaky voice as she looked around frantically. At that moment, everyone looked suspicious. Either Eric was there, or he had someone watching her. Vanessa was so frightened she wasn't sure if she was going to wet herself or shit her pants, but the fear washed over her body and left her feeling mortified. "Take me back to my room, please. Take me back."

"Okay, calm down, Carmen. Just tell me what's wrong."

"No, you don't understand. I have to get out of here. I… I…" Vanessa put a hand to her mouth unable to keep herself from crying. She shook in terror as she lost control of her breathing and began to hyperventilate. She leaned into Derek as she struggled to catch her breath, Derek held onto her with one arm as he grabbed his phone from his pocket to dial 9-1-1.

A bystander handed Derek a paper bag and just as he had done for her in Vera's office when she learned of Arianna's murder, he coached Vanessa through breathing with the paper bag and spoke to her in a soft voice to soothe her and calm her down. The world was spinning and Vanessa felt hot and dizzy as though she may vomit. Too many voices in her head, taunting, teasing, threatening, scaring her, warning her, chastising her. The world spun as though she were on a sadistic merry-go-round. As much as she wanted to focus on Derek's voice and let the smell of his cologne help to calm her, her fear that Eric was close enough to get a picture of her and then give it to her through a messenger was too terrifying for her to focus on anything else. She gasped for breath, each one making her chest feel tighter and tighter, suddenly thinking back to some of the many times Eric choked her until she passed out. Those images flashed through her mind like a slideshow. She also thought of the time he put a pillow over her face while he ravaged her and she was positive, like during some of the many times he had choked her, that she was going to die. Everything around her began to go dark and she thought of the Looney Tunes cartoon where everything was swallowed up by a dark circle.

"*A blee, a blee, a blee, that's all, folks!*" she heard Porky Pig say as her eyes fluttered. Before they shut, she was positive she saw Eric in the crowd of people that had begun to gather around, and then everything went black.

20

Felix was in a great mood. He was able to locate the woman in Maryland whose phone was used to make the phone call to Arianna, and was prepared to take a short vacation to go down there to meet with her so she could lead him to Vanessa. He decided to keep the information that he was coming across to himself until he was sure he could gather concrete evidence to not only have Eric arrested, but get him convicted as well.

Felix was not happy with the way the investigation was going with Antonio Vasquez. It was taking far too long for information to come back on his car to determine if it had been tampered with or if it just so happened to be a freak accident at a time when he was in a position to help solve Arianna's murder. Every time he called the lab for an update, he was told that they were backed up and hadn't gotten any conclusive information back yet. He decided he would reach out to a good friend of his that went to high-school with him and worked in forensics, figuring maybe he could get the information, if there was any, faster by going through her.

He was whistling as he twirled his keys around his finger while walking past his Lieutenant's office when his name was called.

"Felix," his lieutenant called to him. He waved Felix into his office.

"Yes, Lieutenant O'Neil."

The lieutenant grabbed a file that was on the desk and tossed it at Felix. "When you're assigned a case, you work the case with your partner, following protocol, and any and all information that leads to a break in the case of any kind should be reported to me. Isn't that typically how things operate around here?" the lieutenant asked.

Felix could tell by the expression on O'Neil's face that he was not pleased. "Yes, pretty much that's…"

O'Neil cut him off and raised his voice, "Not pretty much, very much, Felix. I don't like my officers tip-toeing around behind my back, going off on solo missions like some got damn vigilante. There are no awards, promotions or accolades given to cops who disregard the protocols put in place when working an investigation. Are we clear?"

"Crystal-clear," Felix replied. His jaw tightened as he struggled hard to bite his tongue.

"Now, Antonio Vasquez's death is being seen as an accident. There is no case with that. The only connection that accident has to the murder investigation with Arianna Stone is the fact that he is more than likely the responsible party for her murder. Therefore, the case is closed." O'Neil took the case file back from Felix and sat it on another table behind him.

"Wait a minute, what?" Felix asked with wide eyes. "What do you mean cased closed? We don't know for sure if Vasquez was behind Arianna's murder. Didn't you see the tape? There's another party involved."

"We have the word of a repeated offender who has a history of shady business dealings. His blood was under her nails. Regardless what the tape shows, forensic shows she had a struggle with Vasquez and as a result of that struggle, a young woman is dead."

"But what about what he mentioned as far as being hired to locate Vanessa Lofton. I checked on some of the things he had in his file and spoke with some people who verified that Vanessa made contact with Arianna after she was helped by Marcella Jackson. They also confirmed that this young lady was being abused by Eric Washington. Now Arianna and Marcella Jackson are dead? Come on, Lieutenant! No way can you look at that as a big coincidence. Not to mention another woman, Regina Smalls was also killed. Did you know Vasquez was hired three years ago by Washington to locate her as well? She was killed three days after Vasquez gave her location to him."

"Okay, let's say it's not a coincidence. Who are your sources outside of some files that Vasquez could have cooked up to save his own ass? What valid proof do you have that can bring life back to this case?" O'Neil asked as he played with a pen in his hand.

Felix hesitated for a moment. "They requested to not be included in this investigation, so as of now, they're just anonymous sourced that I have. But seeing the body trail, can you too much blame them?"

"Unless you can get them to come forward with any and all information that they have, I'm afraid there's nothing more I can do other than close this case."

"But Lieutenant," Felix tried to protest.

"You've been reassigned to the Jeweler's Row robberies. All the information that you need is in your inbox. I suggest you get caught up."

"What about Marcella Jackson's murder investigation? Can I at least work on that?"

"We have enough men on that case," O'Neil replied blandly as he began going through another file. "You're excused."

Felix stared down at his lieutenant for a moment feeling nothing but contempt. He believed he was being stone-walled and while his gut told him exactly why he was being stone-walled, he didn't want to believe it. But no matter what, he always trusted his gut over anything else.

He left the office feeling somewhat defeated and went back to his desk. He began looking through the file for the new case he had been assigned to but was unable to focus, his mind still occupied with everything he had discovered with Arianna's murder investigation. He knew he was on to something and there was no way he could just give up.

"If I walk away from this and I'm right, he's going to find Vanessa and he's going to kill her... just like he did Regina Smalls." He then thought back to Arianna and the frantic

manner in which she tried showing him her hands. Felix closed his eyes, still seeing the look in hers. But then he saw her hands, and it was as though that was all he could see. Not only did she have blood under her nails but she had some on the heel of her palm.

"Sleeping on the job?" Felix heard someone say. His eyes jerked open and he saw his partner standing near his desk smiling at him.

"No, I was just in deep thought, that's all. What's up?"

"I heard what happened with Ms. Stone's case. You should've let me know what you were doing, man. I would have backed you 100 percent, you know that," Michaels said in a low voice.

"Yeah, I was just going on a hunch, all the good it did," Felix replied as he stood from his desk and grabbed his file folders.

"Did you find anything that can maybe bring this case back to life? Any witnesses that we can interview or re-interview?"

Felix hesitated, "Nothing concrete. Just a hunch. It doesn't matter now, anyways. I've been assigned this bullshit Jeweler's Row crime spree. That shit will surely have me sleeping at the desk. Who gives a fuck about some stolen diamonds out here when women are getting murdered left and right, you know?" Felix said with disdain. He walked over to the elevator with Michaels in tow.

"Yeah, how about that? Well listen, I got some family stuff going on, so I'll be taking a leave of absence for two weeks and then right after that, I got that trip to Barbados for two weeks, so I'ma be gone for a month," Michaels said as he held the elevator door open.

"Oh, yeah I remember you telling me about that trip. Well, I hope they don't assign me a bullshit temp partner. Just let me work solo while you're gone, I ain't trying to fuck with these newbies. Fuck around and get me shot out here with their scary asses." They chuckled together. "Take care of your fam and have fun, bro."

"I will. Holla at you when I touch down," Michaels replied. He saluted Felix as the elevator doors were closing.

"Twenty bucks says Vasquez blood wasn't the only blood on Arianna's hands," Felix mumbled out-loud. His friend in forensics wasn't at work that day which meant he would have to make a house visit. He decided to stop home first.

Felix rode the elevator up to the floor his apartment was on still thinking about Arianna and the way she tried showing him her hands. His thoughts were interrupted by a nagging feeling in his stomach. The closer he got to his apartment, the stronger the feeling got and his gut told him that something was off. His keys were already in his hands when he got to his door, but he could tell by the marks near his lock that his keys were not needed. He backed away from his door as he stuffed his keys in his back pocket and pulled his gun instead. He checked behind him and then gently pushed his door in with one hand while aiming his gun with the other. His heart was racing a mile a minute and he was positive that he could hear its beat along with a loud buzzing noise. Felix managed to control his breathing as he swallowed past a knot of fear.

Just as Marcella's office had been tossed and ransacked, so was his apartment. His room was a mess, the mattress was partially off of its frame and the drawers to his dresser were opened, clothes strewn about, and his living room was even worse. Once he was able to clear his bedroom and the bathroom and make sure no one was in the kitchen or living room, his desk where his computer sat caught his eye. He went over to it and saw where someone had tried their damndest to hack his computer and access whatever files he might have had. Felix thanked his computer tech guy who placed security measures on his computer that not even the savviest computer geek could break through.

Felix stood up and looked around. While he was pissed off that someone broke into his apartment, he knew that he had to have been onto something with the case he was working on. He was grateful that he followed his first mind and opened a safety deposit box which is where he placed his thumb drives containing any information that he gathered for all of the cases he worked on as well as printed documents. He reached in his back pocket and called in the break-in and then called his tech guy.

"Hey George, I need you to look at my computer for me," Felix said into the phone as he looked around.

"Hey, bro. How's it going? What's up with the computer?"

"Someone broke into my apartment. Nothing was stolen, as far as I can tell. I think whoever broke in was looking for something and I want to make sure they didn't plant a virus on my computer," Felix explained.

"No prob. Holy shit, someone broke into your place? If they didn't steal anything, what the hell they were looking for?" George asked. The excitement could be heard in his voice. He always loved hearing a good cop story coming from Felix. He was a baby genius, only 19 years old with an IQ that would make Einstein jealous. Anything dealing with computers, math and science, he knew it and had created software that could rival anything created by Bill Gates and Steve Jobs. He was also a damn good hack but kept his talents low key as that would easily have the Feds on his ass to either acquire his talents or neutralize them to make sure he didn't pose a threat to "national security".

"More than likely it has to do with a case I was working on. I can't say too much. Give me a couple of hours. The cops are on their way to take a report."

"Wow! Well, be safe bro. If they're ransacking your place for whatever information they think you have or know and weren't able to find it, you already know what's next," George warned him.

Felix hesitated. "Yeah… I know. See you in a bit." He disconnected the call.

George was right on the money with his last comment and Felix knew it. This made him even more determined to solve the murders of Arianna, Tony and Marcella. He was positive that Eric was involved in the break-in, whether directly or indirectly. There was no way he could walk away from the case now after this. He needed to move fast and push his time table up. He decided to start with the woman Crystal, whose phone was used to call Arianna.

21

After hearing about the murder of Marcella, Crystal stepped up tremendously with transporting women who were traveling through the network to escape abusive spouses. She continued to organize the various routes that the women would travel as well as host support group meetings. She was one of many who did not initially associate Marcella's murder with the phone call Vanessa made from her burner device. Because of that, it left her open for Eric's assault.

Early one afternoon she received a phone call from Felix. She had only spoken with him once briefly about Vanessa and was eager to help, seeing that it was her negligence that allowed Vanessa to make the phone call which was setting everything in motion. She did not believe she was in danger, but was sure to carry her .22 pistol with her as well as her mace and pepper spray.

"Hello, Felix. How are you today?" Crystal said into the phone as she gathered up the things that she needed to get her day started.

"I'm doing well, Crystal. Thank you for asking. I was wondering if I could still meet with you to discuss Vanessa and her whereabouts. I remember you saying that you would send me over some information, but due to a recent incident, I think it would be better if we met in person and not spoke too much over the phone."

"Well, my schedule has been very hectic since Ms. Jackson's passing. I sent everything I had to the email address that you gave me. Beyond that, I'm not sure what more I can tell you about her," Crystal replied.

"Unfortunately, I think it's possible my email may have been compromised. I had a break-in earlier today and I'm almost positive that it's attributed to the case I'm working that may possibly involve her."

Crystal fell silent for a moment. She was conflicted knowing that the whereabouts of a package weren't to be shared with anyone, but she also wanted to make sure that if Vanessa's ex was trying to track her down, that he could be caught before the network was compromised.

Yani

"How soon can you get to Maryland?" she asked after giving in.

"I can drive down tonight and maybe we can link up in the morning over breakfast or coffee," Felix replied as he grabbed some of his items to prepare for the trip.

"Alright. Give me a call when you check into your hotel room and we'll go from there."

"Thanks, Crystal. Have a good day."

"You do the same," Crystal said before disconnecting the call. She headed over to the facility to get her day started.

Crystal was exhausted at the end of her work day. She transported three women to their next destination, hosted a seminar on domestic violence, and conducted two support group meetings. She never noticed the man who attended each of the events she participated in. There was no need to physically follow her, as a tracking device had been placed underneath her car to learn of her every move.

She walked over to her car and got inside, plotting in her head on the roast pork, string beans and mashed potatoes that she had at home from the night before. She was exhausted but felt good inside after being able to help many of the women that she came in contact with during the day. She wanted to try her best to continue Marcella's great work.

Her thoughts were interrupted as she was about to put the key in the ignition when she heard a click behind her, as though someone had chambered a round in a gun. She adjusted her rear-view mirror and a small scream escaped from her when she saw a sinister looking man looking at her with a gun pointing in her direction.

"Shhh," the man said. "We can do this the easy way, or the hard way. That all depends on you."

Crystal's heart was racing a mile a minute as she felt terror from her head to her toes.

"Please, don't hurt me. If it's money you want, my wallet is in my purse. Take whatever you want. If it's something else… please God, wear a condom, you can have that too, just please don't hurt me," Crystal begged as a tear slid out of her eye.

The sinister man laughed and shook his head. "You don't have enough money for me to want to rob you. And I get pussy thrown at me 24-7. You're cute. But not that cute," he said coldly.

"Then what…?" Crystal asked confused.

Yani

"Drive," he instructed. "Go where I tell you to go, answer a couple of questions to my satisfaction, and you live to fight another day. Try anything slick, or decide to play dumb, and your family can bury you wherever the fuck they bury you. Understand?"

Crystal sniffed as she fumbled with her keys, her hands shaking from fear as she tried to get it into the ignition. Once she got the car started, the sinister man behind her moved his gun from her head to the back of her chair while threatening her with the very real possibility of having a whole blown through her back if she tried anything slick.

He directed her to a deserted rode that was extremely dark and had her park as well as turn off her lights.

"Throw the keys," he said to her in a low voice.

Without hesitation, Crystal rolled her window down and tossed the keys, making sure she followed them with her eyes to see where they landed. She then rolled the window back up and waited to see what was going to happen next. She trembled as she breathed trying to remember a time when she had been this frightened, but could not. Periodically she glanced in her rear view hoping to steal as much of what the man in her back seat looked like so she could ID him later on… if she lived through this.

"Now, all I have is one very simple question, Crystal. Answer it correctly, and I get out of your car, I walk away, and you never hear from me or see me again. Bullshit me, and you won't be seeing anything ever again in this life, understand?" the sinister man asked in a voice too calm for Crystal's liking.

"Yes…" Crystal replied.

"Before I even give you the opportunity to lie, I want you to know that we already know you helped a young lady by the name of Vanessa Lofton. She used your phone to contact her friend Arianna, which is how we found you. All I want to know is, where is she now?"

Crystal's eyes looked around wildly as everything started to become clear. That is why the detective wanted to meet with her. Vanessa's phone call had set off a chain reaction that caused Marcella's death and God knows how many others.

"All I did was drop her off at a train station in Bethesda. Where her next destination was, I don't know. We're never given that information."

Yani

The sinister man sighed and shook his head. "That was not the answer I was looking for Crystal," he said as he put the gun back to her head. Crystal closed her eyes tightly and began to cry as she begged for her life. "You better tell me something, Crystal. You have about five seconds to tell me something worthwhile or I'ma splatter your pretty little brains all over this fucking windshield. Who's more important? A measly little bitch that you gave a ride to the train station, or you? Whose life, Crystal? Five… Four…

"They changed her identity!" Crystal said loudly in between sobs. "Please, please don't kill me."

"What do you mean?"

"She isn't going by Vanessa Lofton anymore. Her name is Carmen Thompson. There were two southbound trains leaving at 7:25am on June 2nd. One was headed to North Carolina, the other was headed to Georgia."

"Which one did she get on?" the sinister man asked.

"I don't know. I didn't stay. All I know is she took the escalator to the southbound platform. Please, please God don't kill me," Crystal pleaded as she continued to sniff and cry.

The sinister man stared at her for a moment and then took the gun away from her head. He put the safety back on and tucked it inside of its holster.

"Good job, Crystal. That wasn't so hard, now was it?" he said to her in the calm voice that was really beginning to creep her out. He ran his fingers through her hair, shushing her and telling her to calm down. Before Crystal could make another attempt to beg for her life, she felt the sting from a needle enter her shoulder. She opened her mouth to holler out in pain but was unable to make any noise. Her body shook as the contents of the syringe surged through her veins. Her eyes fluttered before closing and the sinister man gently laid her head against the steering wheel so that she appeared to be sleeping. He then exited her car while whistling a tune to himself and walked over to another car that was a few feet ahead of Crystal's. He got inside and did a search for train stations in Bethesda. When he found what he was looking for, he casually started his car and drove away as though nothing had happened.

22

Vanessa stirred in a hospital bed, feeling groggy. She opened her eyes partially but the bright lights in the room she was in compelled her to close them. She heard voices that for once weren't inside of her head and listened. She could tell one was Derek's but wasn't sure who the woman was.

"What the hell happened, Derek?" Vanessa could hear the woman asking.

"She was fine until a woman walked up to her and asked her if her name was Vanessa. Then she handed her an envelope and when Carmen looked inside, that's when she lost it," Derek explained.

"What was in the envelope?" the woman asked.

"I didn't get a chance to look because she collapsed, but I put it in my back pocket." Derek reached for the envelope and Vera took it from him. When she looked inside, he noticed that she got the same expression on her face that Carmen had gotten earlier. "What? What the hell is going on? Carmen had the same damn look on her face when she looked in the envelope."

Vera tucked the photo back inside of the envelope and then put the envelope in her pocket-book. Instead of answering his questions, she began grilling him about fraternizing with the women in the facility. "You know that is strongly frowned upon, Derek. These women are here to heal and get help with transitioning from their previous abusive relationships into a better life. They don't need any distractions."

"I'm not distracting Carmen and all we did was have breakfast, that's all."

"She's a young woman who is clearly not in the position mentally or emotionally to start a new relationship, not to mention, she's pregnant."

"Who said anything about getting into a relationship? It was just breakfast, Ms. Vera. It's not that deep."

"It is that deep, Derek. You have no idea who this woman is. You have no idea how damaged she is nor are you fully aware of the problems she's brought to this program. If it weren't for her…" Vera caught herself and stopped. She took a deep breath to calm herself.

"If it weren't for her what?" Derek asked.

Yani

"Nothing. Just watch yourself with her. A lot of the things that are going on right now are transpiring because of her. She's going to have to be removed from the facility to make sure no one else is jeopardized."

"You're kidding me? So because of a mistake she may have made, you're just going to throw her to the wolves? Then what? Whatever happens to her is whatever happens to her? That's not something Marcella would stand for and you know it," Derek said angrily.

"Maybe if Marcella were still alive, we could decide what course of action to take. I will check with two of the other facilities to see if they have any space for her. If they do, I will put in a request for an emergency transfer," Vera replied.

"And if they don't?"

Vera shook her head before shrugging her shoulders. "I don't know. My frustrated hands are tied." She walked away from him and headed over to the elevators.

Vanessa closed her eyes and pretended to be sleep before Derek turned towards her. He came back inside of her room and sat in a chair next to her trying to think of what he could do to help her. But how could he help her when as Vera said to him moments before, he knew nothing about her? They had spent countless hours on the phone talking and laughing, but outside of her favorite color, favorite food, books and movies that she liked, he really didn't know that much about her. He decided at that moment that he would get to know her and he would start with asking her who was Vanessa.

Derek ran his fingers through the soft curls to her bush, waking her up. He smiled down at her. "Hey, Sleepy Head. You gave me a scare earlier. Are you feeling any better?"

Vanessa stretched in the hospital bed and nodded her head. "Yes, I'm okay. I wasn't expecting you to still be here. Thanks for sticking around. Sorry for scaring you."

"It's cool. As long as you're okay now, that's all that matters." They fell silent for a moment as Derek pondered over how he was going to approach the subject of who Vanessa was. Finally, he decided not to beat around the bush with his questions.

"Carmen isn't your real name, is it… Vanessa?"

Vanessa looked at him startled for a moment. "I don't know what you're talking about.

"Please don't lie to me, Carmen. I understand how the program works. I understand for various reasons that certain things have to be done to insure the safety of the women who come to the facility to receive help and I'm not mad at you for not telling me your real name, especially if changing it was a condition of the program. But in case you haven't noticed, I like you, Carmen. I like you a lot. You're a beautiful woman, inside and out. You're smart, you're funny and I can tell before whatever happened to you that brought you to this facility, you were ambitious. I can't tell you when the last time I came across a woman that I was attracted to this strongly. I'm nervous like a teenage boy telling you this stuff. But I want you to know how I feel about you and I want you to know I'm here for you. But it's not much I can do to help you if you don't tell me what's up," Derek said to her.

Vanessa eyes teared up and she took a deep breath before shaking her head. "You can't help me," she replied.

"Why? Because whoever your ex was scares you that badly that you think nothing and no one can protect you?"

Vanessa covered her face and cried quietly. The only thing that let Derek know she was crying was the occasional sniffs in between each breath she took. He tried to pull her arms away from her face but she resisted him.

Finally he sat on the edge of her hospital bed and pulled her close to him.

"Ms. Vera is looking to have you transferred someplace else and I don't want to not have you in my life. Tell me who Vanessa is. Let me help you," Derek said to her softly.

"Tell him Vanna! Stop letting what Eric did to you keep you living in constant fear and unable to trust anyone who genuinely cares about your well-being. Let him in. He's not like Eric. He cares about you and he wants to help you. Let him in!" Vanessa could hear the voice in her head which sounded very much like Arianna. Her heart ached for her best friend and she wished she had listened to Camille and Marcella and not made contact. Now Eric had possibly found her and it would only be a matter of time before he caught her someplace by herself and learned her... learned her real good and real hard.

Vanessa took a deep breath and decided to heed the words of her best friend as they sounded off in her mind. She began to twirl her finger around the string to Derek's hooded sweat shirt as she told him all about Vanessa and Eric; the match made in hell.

Yani

Derek listened intently as Vanessa told him how she met Eric and how everything went from being blissful and sweet to a hellish nightmare. She never thought she would be able to tell anyone about the things he did to her; the beatings, the verbal assaults, the sexual abuse, being locked in the house for days at a time without food or a ways to contact anyone; the time he locked her in the basement, choked her and smothered her while raping her. All of the different ways he abused her to maintain his power and control over her, she told Derek. Lastly, she told him about Camille and Tre' who were kind enough to put her in contact with Marcella and how that was what led to her leaving Eric and making her way to the facility.

"So now you know who Vanessa was."

Derek swallowed past a knot of anger inside of him. Listening to the things that Vanessa told him not only made him angry, but they made him sick to his stomach. He had never met Eric before, but he swore if he'd ever crossed paths with him, he would give him the ass whipping of the century. He wanted to beat the bullshit out of him for being such a cowardly woman beater.

"Did you know the woman that stopped you earlier?" he asked Vanessa.

Vanessa shook her head. "I had never seen her before a day in my life."

"What was in the envelope? Vera looked at it and got the same expression on her face that you did."

"It was a picture of me laughing while I was having breakfast with you," Vanessa replied. "Either Eric took the picture himself and had the girl give it to me, or he has someone following me. Either way, he knows where I am. Arianna's dead, Marcella is dead. God knows who else or who might be next. And it's my fault. It's all on me. Maybe sending me somewhere else would be what's best," Vanessa said solemnly.

"Don't ever let me hear you say that again," Derek replied. "What happened to your best friend and Marcella is not your fault. That's all on him. But you can't keep running from him, Carmen. He needs to be put away. He needs to be stopped." He stroked the side of her face softly with his finger tips and then a thought came to him. "Does he know you're pregnant?"

Vanessa shook her head. "No. I had just found out the day I left. That's mostly why I left him because I didn't want to take a chance that he would hit me one day and cause me to lose the baby, or worse."

"Are you sure you didn't leave anything behind that might have tipped him off about you being pregnant?"

"Well, I took a home pregnancy test but I stuffed everything in the bottom of the trash can underneath a bunch of other trash."

"Assume he knows," Derek said quickly. "Assume he knows and that's the reason he's looking for you. If he is controlling like you say he is, he will not like the idea of you keeping him from his child, especially if it turns out to be a boy, his name sake, his prodigy. And God forbid if there is another man in that child's life playing the daddy role."

A doctor came into the room and Vanessa sat up.

"Okay Ms. Thompson. We just wanted to monitor you to make sure everything was okay. Your blood pressure was up when you were first brought in but it seems to have gone back down to normal. You may want to take it easy, put your feet up." The doctor then looked at Derek and smiled. "Are you the husband?"

Derek looked at Vanessa and then looked back at the doctor. "No, we're not married, but I'll make sure she's taken good care of." He then rubbed her stomach and kissed her forehead. Vanessa smiled nervously.

"Well, the nurse will be in with your discharge papers and you can head on home. Nice meeting you." The doctor shook Derek's hand. "Congratulations to you both and have a great evening."

Vanessa waved to the doctor and then sat up so she could put her shoes on. "Guess I better get ready to face the music with Ms. Vera."

"Come home with me," Derek said nervously.

Vanessa stopped what she was doing and looked up at Derek. "Huh?"

"I want you to come stay with me. If you want to, no pressure. I just want to make sure you're safe until this is over with," he replied quickly.

"You don't have to do this."

"I want to."

Vanessa thought for a moment. She believed she should have declined the offer and go back to the facility, but she kept hearing Arianna saying for her to let him in. She shook her head giving in and said, "Okay. I'll stay with you. You won't get into trouble will you?"

"No, I don't think so. We'll see though, won't we?" Derek replied as he shrugged his shoulders. The nurse came in and went over Vanessa's discharge instructions.

She signed everything and then Derek took her down to his car. He drove her to the facility first to get as many of her things that she could carry. Derek talked to Vera while Vanessa bagged up her belongings.

"This is not a good idea, Derek." Vera said to him.

"No disrespect Ms. Vera, but y'all were ready to throw a pregnant woman who is the victim of domestic abuse out into the streets because of one mistake she made instead of trying to come up with a contingency plan to put in place should it actually be her ex that's coming after her. What I'm doing might be a bad idea to you, but compared to what y'all were going to do, it seems like a great idea to me," Derek stood his ground firm, undeterred in his plans to look after Vanessa until everything was over.

He went over to Vanessa's living quarters after his conversation with Vera and saw that Vanessa was waiting for him. He took the big, green bag that she had her belongings in and they walked to his car in silence.

"Are you hungry?" Derek asked her.

Vanessa chuckled. "You're asking the fat pregnant girl if she's hungry."

Derek chuckled with her. "You're not fat, though. You're carrying your pregnancy weight really well. I've seen chicks blow up into real cows."

Vanessa burst out laughing. "Lucky me, I guess. But no, I'm not really hungry. Just got a lot on my mind."

"You wanna talk?"

She shook her head as she put her seatbelt on. "Not yet. I just need to sort out some of what's going on in my head." *"You mean you want to know which voice you should listen to? How fast do you think Derek will drop your dumb ass when he realizes you're nutty as a damn fruit cake? And if you think for one minute this nigga just wants to keep you safe, no strings attached, you really are dumber than I originally thought. Pregnant pussy is the safest pussy. He can hit that shit raw and not have to worry about you getting knocked up because you already are. Damn, you're gullible as fuck…"*

"Oh my God, man!" Vanessa hissed out loud.

"What, what's wrong?" Derek asked as he glanced at her.

Vanessa leaned forward in her seat and put her hands to her face, praying silently to herself that the voice in her head would shut up. She dug her nails into her hands hoping that would help. After a moment of feeling the painful, sharp sting of her nails digging into her hands, she sat back up and shook her head. "Nothing," she replied flatly.

"You sure?" Derek checked as he glanced at her again.

Vanessa nodded her head without saying anything else.

"*1, 2… Eric's coming for you…*" Vanessa heard the voice in her head singing in a creepy, slow manner. She closed her eyes and leaned her head back against the seat, praying that he wasn't coming for her. She prayed that the voices in her head would stop. She prayed for peace and most importantly, she prayed that nothing happened to anyone else, especially Derek.

23

Felix had the locks to his apartment changed and had a dead bolt lock added as well, to make it harder for anyone else to break in. He put in a request for some time off, using the break in as an excuse. After his request was approved, he took his computer over to his technician friend and made a call to another friend in forensics. She didn't answer so he left her a voicemail.

"Hey Tamika, this is Felix. I wanted to know if you were ever able to check the lab results on the DNA collected from Arianna Stone. I also wanted to know if you were able to get any information from Antonio Vasquez's car wreck. I'm heading to Maryland to take care of some personal matters. Give me a call when you get this. Alright, Mami. Peace."

"You were right, Felix." George said as Felix was disconnecting his call. "Someone planted a sonuva blip of a virus on this baby. The only way to get rid of this jawn is to wipe your entire drive. I hope you don't have anything on here that you want or need."

"Nah," Felix said as he shook his head. "Just some skin flicks I made with a big booty cutie I knew, but I can always make another one later." George looked at Felix wide-eyed and Felix cracked a grin. "I'm just fucking with you. Ain't nothing on there. Wipe that shit."

"You're a funny guy," George laughed. "How soon do you need this back?"

"Take your time, no rush. Everything I need is on a thumb drive some place safe." Felix's phone rang and he was happy to see that it was Tamika from forensics. "Hey Mami, you get my message?"

"Yeah Papi, I got it. You haven't talked to your partner?"

"Yeah, I ran into Michaels on my way from the precinct earlier. He left for vacation."

"It must've slipped his mind. I gave the reports to him. The first time DNA was pulled from Ms. Stones' person, they found two different blood types; neither of them were hers. The first one was Antonio Vasquez' and the second one we couldn't determine. We're still running it through the system in hopes that something will come up. But I gave it all to Michaels and he told me he would make sure you got everything."

Felix fell silent as his heart raced in his chest. Why wouldn't his partner give the information to him especially seeing that the case was being closed? "What about Vasquez's car. Do you have anything on that?" he asked calmly.

"I gave it all to Michaels. He told me to give him the copies too so he could get them over to you and to the Lieutenant," Tamika replied.

"Alright, thanks Mami."

"Maybe he left them on your desk before he left," Tamika suggested.

"Maybe, I'ma holla at you later." Felix disconnected the phone and called over to a friend of his at the precinct that he knew was at work. "Yo Bill, what's up?"

"Ahh nothing much. Just in here doing a bunch of dumb-ass paperwork. They still got me on desk duty because of my shoulder. Bullshit if you ask me," Bill replied.

"Yeah, how about that. Listen, do me a favor. Check my desk and see if anything from forensics was left on there." Felix waited patiently for Bill to come back to the phone. He didn't want to believe he had a dirty partner. They had been partners for more than five years and Felix trusted him with his life. He prayed the file was on his desk and Michaels had been so preoccupied with going on vacation that he forgot to tell him. Bill came back to the phone.

"Nope, nothing from forensics, buddy. Was somebody supposed to leave you something?"

"No, I guess I got my wires crossed. Thanks." Felix hung up the phone. "Sonuva bitch," he mumbled.

"What's wrong?" George asked.

Felix didn't respond as his mind was racing over the recent turn of events. How could he have had this partner for so long and missed the signs of him being a dirty cop.

'Maybe he's not a dirty cop but knows Eric from somewhere and is just trying to cover for him while he gets to the bottom of it… he could be working separate angles just like me…" Felix thought to himself. But the smarter part of him knew better. Giving Michaels that kind of benefit of the doubt could cause him to make a critical mistake that could cost him his life, and he was not about to let that happen.

"Wipe that drive," he instructed George as he pointed at him with his phone while moving towards the door. "This shit just got real. Is it any way you can trace that virus to see where the information would have gone if it had been obtained? Does that make sense?" Felix frowned as he had a thought that maybe he was hanging around George too much.

"I understand what you're asking. I could try. But the virus is kinda like "God's Eye" from the movie *Furious 7*. I mean, they can't see you wherever you are in the world, but every key stroke you make, every icon you clink on, every site you visit, every email you open, it's opening some-where else and someone can see what you're seeing," George explained.

"So you could track it?" Felix asked.

"I could try. But chances are, the virus is so intricate that it will intercept any counter attacks against it, freeze your system and force you to keep starting over. The time it would take me to hack that virus, flip it and track it back to whoever it's linked to, you'll be wishing me a happy new year," George smirked.

"Fuck... I ain't got that kinda time. Alright, wipe the shit. I've gotta go. Call me if you come up with anything." Felix walked over to George's door and then stopped. He then backed up and pulled his keys out of his pocket. "If anything happens to me, you take this key and unlock my safety deposit box at Wells Fargo bank up on Germantown Avenue. Take everything in there to the 22nd district and ask for Jamal Williams and Dante Smith. Give everything to them."

"You don't want me to give it to your lieutenant or captain?" George asked as he took the key.

"No. Only those two."

"What do I tell them?" George asked.

Felix hesitated for a moment. "If I don't want you to give it to my lieutenant or captain and I'm trusting you with this key over my partner, I'm sure you'll figure it out."

George frowned as he thought over what Felix said and then his eyes became wide once he realized why the request was being made. Felix shook his hand firmly and then left so he could make his way to Maryland, hoping that he wasn't too late.

24

Vanessa laid on the couch half-asleep after eating a batch of Derek's shrimp Alfredo with buttered rolls and string beans. It was the best home-cooked meal that she had outside of her own cooking since the last time she had dinner with her mother more than a year prior. If Derek had not been in her site, she was tempted to run her finger across the plate and lick the sauce. She offered to wash the dishes since he had done all of the cooking and wouldn't let her help, but he insisted she have a seat and relax after the long day she'd had.

As she drifted off into a deeper sleep, she began to think of her father. Her dream began as a memory of the two of them at Temple University's track running laps. Her father, Darryl, was training her for the upcoming track season at Central High School. They were taking a break, talking and laughing when Darryl noticed someone standing by his car.

Yani

"Vanna, I want you to jog down the straight away until you get to the curve and then I want you to sprint. Do the same on the next straight away and then sprint around the last curve. Walk a lap to get your breathing back and then I want you to do it again except this time jog the curves, sprint the straight away. I need to talk to someone real quick, I'll be right back," he said to his daughter.

"You're not going to run with me?" Vanessa asked with big, sad eyes.

"I will in a bit. I just need to have a talk with a very distraught young man who just lost his parents. Give me a few minutes, I'll be right back." Darryl stood there a moment as Vanessa began to run the way he instructed her to. He then walked over to his car.

"What are you doing here?" Darryl asked, trying to mask his annoyance with the individual.

"You told me if I needed to talk, I could come to you anytime. So here I am," the young man responded.

"During office hours. I'm out here with my daughter. You don't just show up…"

"It's a public place. I was actually considering running some laps myself and noticed you out here as well and figured maybe we could talk. You have a beautiful daughter," the young man said with a slight smirk on his face.

Darryl looked at him with cold eyes. *"I will be back at my office tomorrow. If you need to talk then, I will have my secretary pencil you in around 12 and we can talk through lunch. But not here, not today. Understand?"* he then stood closer to the young man. *"If you ever come near me while I'm with my daughter again, I won't see you as a patient. I will see you as a nigga on the street and treat you accordingly, you got that?"*

"I noticed you said daughter and not family as though your wife isn't included in this. Does either of them know you were fucking my mom? Was that apart of your little therapy sessions?"

Darryl grabbed the young man by his collar and pushed him up against the car. *"You have no idea what you're talking about. I suggest you get the hell out of here or…"*

"Or what?" the individual smirked again. He looked behind Darryl. *"Your daughter is watching us."*

Darryl looked over his shoulders and noticed his daughter was standing in the entry way of the track field. The young man yanked away from him and chuckled. He then waved to Vanessa.

"How you doing, sweetheart?" he spoke sweetly.

Darryl gave him a slight shove. *"Get your ass out of here, now."* He then turned to his daughter. *"Go back onto the track field baby-girl, I'll be right there."*

Yani

Vanessa hesitated as her heart raced, wondering what was going on between her father and the other person. She looked at them a moment longer and then went back inside as her father instructed when she saw the other person walking down the street.

Darryl looked at him for a moment longer and shook his head. He hoped like hell his daughter didn't hear any of the conversation between the two of them. He went back over to his daughter and knelt down to adjust his shoes strings.

"Dad, who was that? Why'd you two look like you were going to fight?" Vanessa asked her father.

Darryl hesitated for a moment before answering her. "Usually I don't share patient information with outsiders because it's against the law. But he's not really a patient so…" He blew out air and shook his head. "This young man just recently lost both his mother and father in a murder suicide and he blames everyone except who was directly responsible for what happened," Darryl explained.

Vanessa's heart pounded in her chest. "Oh no, someone killed his mom and dad and then killed themselves?" she asked with wide eyes.

"No baby, his father killed his mother and then turned the gun on himself. She tried to leave him because he was abusive. The young man found them both when they wouldn't answer the house phone."

"Aw man, that's crazy! What do you have to do with anything? It's not like you pulled the trigger?"

"You're right. But, his mother was coming to me for therapy and guidance. I helped her gather the courage and the strength to leave her abusive husband. So I guess that's why that young man is putting the blame on me."

"Well then he's dumb. If he should blame anybody, he should blame his dad for not knowing how to keep his hands off of a woman. His dad was a coward even to his end so, he needs to just get over it."

Darryl smiled slightly and hugged his daughter close to him. "I love that you're such a head strong young lady. It's make me proud to see that I've been doing my job as a man and as a father, and am raising you right. Just make sure that you never let a man come in and try to stomp that strength and make you weak. Any man who tries to do that isn't a man. He's a coward, just like you said," her father schooled her.

"I won't, daddy. And even if he tries, I'll just get you to beat him up." Vanessa looked up at her father and winked at him making him laugh.

"And you know damn well I will, too." He patted her on the arm and took off running. "Too slow!" he yelled at her. Vanessa took off running behind him and they finished doing their training

that afternoon before getting strawberry and banana smoothies and vegan burgers afterwards.

Less than a week later, Vanessa remembered she had just gotten out of the shower and had put her night clothes on. She reached in the stand that contained many DVDs and pulled "The Spook Who Sat by the Door," a movie that she and her father discussed watching when he came home from work. Their doorbell rang and just like she always did, she stood at the top of the steps and looked down to see who it was. She was baffled when she saw that it was two policemen. She couldn't hear what was said but she could tell that whatever it was had her mother upset.

"My daughter is 16. Can she stay here while I come with you, I mean I won't get into any trouble with social services, will I? If it is him, I don't want my daughter to see. I'd rather just tell her in my own words," Karen said as she tried to keep her composure.

"She's old enough to stay home ma'am and if you would like, we'll keep a unit outside of the home until you are brought back."

"Yes, please." Karen fumbled as she grabbed her jacket from the coat stand by the door. She called up to Vanessa but was startled when she saw that her daughter was near the bottom of the steps behind her.

"Mom, what's going on?" Vanessa asked as she looked from her mother to the two officers behind her.

"Nothing sweetie, I just need to do something real quick and I'll be right back," Karen said to her daughter.

"But mom…" Vanessa said.

"I'll be right back," Karen closed the door before she could say anything else. Vanessa ran to the door and looked out the window. She watched her mother get into the cop car and they drove her away.

It was two long hours before Vanessa's mother returned. Vanessa was on the couch and had begun to nod off when she heard her come in. She was confused as to why her father wasn't with her.

"Mom… where's dad?" she asked as she looked her mother over and could immediately tell that something was wrong.

Karen opened her mouth to speak but couldn't find the words. She snatched her daughter close to her and burst out in tears, sobbing loudly.

"Mom, what happened? Where's my dad? What happened, mom?! What happened?!" Vanessa practically yelled as she tried to pull away from her mother.

"They killed him, baby! They killed him on his way home from work. Someone shot him and he's dead!"

"What… no… that can't be! Mom…" Vanessa said back almost in hysterics. She screamed for her father, demanding that God send him back to her because he obviously made a mistake. Of all *the horrible people in the world that he could have easily taken, why would he take her father?*

It was that night that she lost her faith in God feeling as though if there was one, he didn't know how to really be a God when the good were dying or getting killed at a young age while all of the bad people got to live and enjoy life.

"Daddy…" Vanessa mumbled in her sleep as tears slid out of her eyes. "Why…? Why daddy…?"

Derek heard her and tapped her on her shoulder trying to wake her. He tapped her a little harder and she jumped up startling him.

"Carmen… are you okay?"

Vanessa frowned as she clutched her chest. The dream made her miss her father terribly. She could still see his face so clearly from the dream, and hear his voice. She could even smell his cologne. She burst out in tears feeling the loss due to him being murdered all over again. Derek sat next to her and put his arms around her.

"What's wrong?" Derek asked as he wiped her face. "Were you dreaming about your dad or something?"

Vanessa nodded her head. "I wish he was here. None of this would have ever happened if he was still here," she said as she became choked up.

"You wanna talk about it?" Derek asked. He knew how leery she was to talk about her past but hoped that after what happened today and after she was able to share her abusive past with him earlier that she would be able to open up more to him.

"They never found the person who killed him. They questioned people and had a suspect, but nothing ever panned out from it," Vanessa said with a sniff.

"Do you know what happened to him?"

"All I know is what my mother told me. She said he was on his way to his car when someone tried to rob him and they shot him. He died on the way to the hospital."

"Damn…" was all that Derek could think to say. "Did you ever look into it, like try to find information about his murder on your own?"

A flash from the dream came back to Vanessa of the young man her father was arguing with. He looked familiar but Vanessa wasn't sure. Derek noticed the confused look on her face.

"Carmen?" he called to her.

"No… I was so mad after it happened, I just threw myself into my school work. I quit the track team and I just… I don't know. But I never thought to look anything up. I guess I was always scared that my father would have gotten a small little paragraph on the side of a page in the newspaper and that was it."

Derek rubbed her back as she rested her head on his shoulder. He wasn't sure if he should push the issue or let her decide what she wanted to do, so he asked her. "What do you wanna do?"

Vanessa thought for a moment and then looked up at him. "Do you have a laptop?"

"I got a MacBook. Hold up a second." Vanessa sat up while Derek went down the hall to his bedroom to get his MacBook. He came back and sat on the couch next to her. Vanessa's heart raced with anticipation as he opened up a browser. "Alright. Let's start by doing a general search on his name to see what comes up."

"Darryl Malik Lofton," Vanessa replied.

"You didn't have his last name?" Derek asked. He then remembered that she had her name changed. "Never mind."

He typed the name in and the results came up. The small practice that he shared with two other people along with the clinic that he did group sessions in twice a night came up in the search. They scrolled down and saw that there was a memorial page for him on Facebook. Derek clicked on it and they browsed the photos, many of which included Vanessa and her mother. Vanessa shared brief memories of the photos they looked at and for once, Derek was getting the chance to get to know the woman he had become fond of and was starting love.

"You look just like him," he told her.

"That's what everybody used to say. They would tease my mom and tell her I looked like my father spit me out and my mom had no parts of my creation." She laughed out loud and shook her head. They scrolled down a little further and was able to find a link that led to a news story about her father's murder. She was shocked that it was more than just the tiny paragraph she was expecting him to have.

Derek and Vanessa read through the article on Darryl Lofton and followed links that went to other stories about his murder. It was the last link that had Vanessa feeling like she might lay down and die from a heart attack.

"35 year old Darryl Lofton dedicated his life to doing what he loved most- helping people. But was it his love and passion for helping others that cost him his life in the end? His secretary, Donna Stewart speaks with us exclusively in a tell all interview sharing what she

believes is what led to the fateful night where Lofton's life tragically ended just a few feet from his place of work"

"Mr. Lofton was an extraordinary man," 29 year old Stewart spoke candidly of her former boss. "He had a gift for helping people, for getting them to turn their lives around and make the right choices for their own benefit. But one of the last women that he helped, I think he became too close to her, too personal."

They skimmed through the article that told of a woman Darryl was helping by the name of Diane Washington, who was in a terribly violent and abusive marriage to Kevin Washington. Vanessa's heart raced as she read through the article, her dream coming back to her more and more.

"There was suspicion that Mr. Lofton was having an affair with Diane because of the amount of time he was dedicating to her. Sometimes he would reschedule other clients so he could have private sessions with her. We didn't want to believe he would ever cheat on his wife because he was very openly devoted to her and his daughter. But the relationship he shared with Diane seemed a little more personal than professional."

"That bitch is lying," Vanessa hissed angrily. Derek looked at her wide-eyed unable to ever recall a time where she used profanity. "My father wasn't a cheater. He never would've touched another woman, he loved my mother!"

"Let's see what else the article says first, Carmen. Don't trip yet. You know people always doing shit for their 15 seconds of fame," Derek replied.

They continued to read on. *"We began to dismiss the idea of them having an affair once Mr. Lofton began adhering to his schedule like he normally would. However, he seemed overly pleased that Mrs. Washington was leaving her husband. Not too long after she made that decision, Mr. Lofton learned that she had been killed and her abusive husband killed himself as well."*

The room swam as Vanessa thought of her dream and the young man that her father said blamed him for the death of his parents. The last name Washington made her gasp.

"Oh my God…" she said.

"What?" Derek asked her. Vanessa didn't respond. She pulled the MacBook into her lap and exited out of the article. She then typed in Kevin Washington and Diane Washington. She scrolled through the results that came up in the search engine until she got to a news story link.

"Murder-Suicide claims the lives of a married couple and rocks a South Philly Neighborhood," she read aloud. She skimmed

through the opening paragraph as butterflies filled her stomach and her heart raced. *"What neighbors are saying was an unsettling but not surprising end have police busy tonight as they investigate what appears to be a murder suicide in the 2500 block of South 25th and Montrose Streets. The body of 42 year old Diane Washington was found in her kitchen, dead from multiple gunshot wounds, and her husband 47 year old Kevin Washington was found upstairs in the bathroom with an apparent self-inflicted gun-shot wound to the head. The bodies were discovered by their only son, Eric Washington who decided to come home after calling both of their cell phones numerous times but unable to reach either of them…"*

"Oh…my… GOD!!" Vanessa practically screamed.

"What?" Derek asked. Vanessa jumped up and began to pace as her mind raced, briefly showing flashes from her dream of the young man her father was in the heated discussion with all the while hearing a jumbled combination of her father explaining why the young man was upset with him, the words from the interview with Donna Stewart, and the words from the article about the murder-suicide.

"The world can't be this small. The world can't be this fucking small!" Vanessa said as she paced back and forth. "Oh my God…! That… that motherfucker killed my father!" Hearing herself say it out loud made her sick to her stomach. But the rage boiling inside of her prevented her from vomiting up her dinner. "All this time… all this fucking time he's been right there in my face. That sick fucking… that fucking…" Vanessa stopped dead in her tracks when everything became clear.

"Carmen, talk to me. What are you talking about?" Derek asked. "Sit down before you make yourself sick." He took her by the hand and brought her back over to the couch. Her eyes looked around wildly as she replayed the memory from her dream and tried to gather her thoughts so she could explain everything to Derek.

"Okay, I had a dream about my father. But it was more like a memory. We were at Temple University's track field back in Philly and he was helping me train. All of a sudden, he sent me to run without him so he could go talk to this guy that was standing by his car. I noticed that the conversation didn't look too friendly, so me being nosey, I went over to the opening gate to the track and watched. After the guy left, my dad told me what the deal was, that basically the young man blamed him for his father killing his mother and then killing himself," Vanessa explained.

Yani

"So the guy that you saw talking to your dad is the guy from the article? You think he killed your dad?" Derek asked her.

"I know he did," Vanessa said in a matter of fact tone.

"Wait, how do you know?" Derek asked.

"I don't believe in coincidences. He blamed my father for the murder of his parents and then not even a week later, my father is dead?"

"Stranger things have happened," Derek replied.

"And this does get stranger. Because that bastard is my damn ex. The one I'm pregnant by. The one who had me living in fear for almost two years! The one who beat the hell out of me. The one who pretended to love me so much when in all actuality, he knew who I was all that time. It's like he purposely selected me! Like killing my father wasn't enough, he had to finish me off also."

"Wait, wait, wait… you mean to tell me this nigga waited until you were old enough, and then swooped in like Casanova, got you to fall in love with him only to beat on you the way his father beat on his mother? All because he blamed your father for what happened to his parents? That's crazy," Derek said with a frown.

"Yeah, because he's crazy," Vanessa said as she sat back on the couch next to him. "He's not just coming after me because I'm pregnant and he doesn't want to be kept from his child," she said after a moment.

Derek shook his head. "If what you're saying is right, no he's not. He's coming to kill you."

"And anybody in his way which means I need to leave," Vanessa said solemnly. She was about to get up from the couch but Derek stopped her.

"Stop running from him, Carmen. Fuck that nigga! You think if you keep running, he's going to stop looking for you? Hell no! That man wants you dead. The only way to stop a muthafucka like that is to catch him or kill him. And they haven't caught him yet so you know what that means," Derek said to her.

"But I don't want anything to happen to you because of me. Look what's he's done to my best friend and Ms. Marcella, and God knows who else! I don't want you to suffer because of me."

"You don't worry about me, okay? I got this. And I got you. If he comes, he better be about that life because I got goons all over ATL that will put them thangs on him. You give me a pic of that nigga and I'll have all of ATL looking for that nigga. Trust me, he don't want Derek Jordan as a fucking problem." He pulled Vanessa close to him and kissed her forehead. For the first time since before her father was killed, Vanessa felt safe and truly protected. The realization that Eric was more than just a handsome gentleman that she met in Saks Fifth Avenue and turned into a nightmare was still very unsettling for her.

Vanessa looked up at him. "Thank you," she said quietly. Derek kissed her softly and gently on her lips, shocking her. She hesitated before kissing him back.

"I got this," he said to her again. "I got you."

25

Eric checked into his hotel suite at the Hilton Savannah DeSoto. He had just gotten off of his long, delayed flight and wanted nothing more than to take a hot shower and get down to business. The PI that he was now working with was able to determine which southbound train Vanessa had gotten on and began tracking her from there. It wasn't long before he located her at Verna's Soul Food breakfast diner, stumbling across her accidentally when he stopped in to get himself some breakfast. He discreetly took photos of her and sent them to Eric to verify that it was her. He took a chance running to a nearby Walgreen's and printed the photo out before paying a young woman $50 to deliver the envelope to Vanessa.

Eric got out of the shower and sat on the side of the king size bed in his hotel room. He looked at the photos that his PI sent to him and felt fury bubbling and rising inside of him. He could see the glow that the pregnancy was leaving her with. But what burned him up inside more was seeing her in the company of another man, smiling and appearing happy. He wanted to get his hands on her more than anything in the world. He wanted to learn her slow, and hard, again and again to remind her who the fucking boss was.

His phone rung and he tossed the pictures to the side as he answered it. "Hey, what's good? Anything new?" he asked when he saw that it was his PI calling him.

"Well, she had some kind of attack at the diner I located her at. They rushed her to Emory University Hospital. The guy that she was with name is Derek Jordan. He's a 29 year old in charge of security detail at the Sistahs on the Move facility. He took her back there," the PI explained. He gave Eric the address.

"Is she still there?" Eric asked.

"She left with him carrying a large green bag. I tried to tail them but there was some kind of construction going on and I was stopped before I had a chance to pass through and continue tailing them. So I don't know if she went with him somewhere and stayed or if he brought her back to the facility."

"Okay. I want his address also just in case he wants to play super save-a-hoe and has her at his place. Try to stay outside the facility to see if she comes back."

"Alright, give me a second." Eric waited while his PI did a search. "When will people learn to keep themselves from being listed? He's located at Heights at Midtown apartments, 507 Bishop St. NW."

Eric wrote it down quickly. "Alright, call me if you get something else." He hung up the phone and then ordered room service as he plotted on his next move against Vanessa.

"You can change your name bitch, but it won't mean a damn thing once I get my hands on you," he said to himself as he looked at one of the photos his PI took of her.

Yani

26

Felix checked into his hotel room in Bethesda, Maryland, ordered himself some room service and then called Crystal so they could meet up. When she didn't answer, he left her a voicemail. "Hey Crystal, this is Felix. I just wanted to let you know that I made it to Bethesda. When you get a chance, give me a call so we can link up. Peace." He disconnected the call and hoped that she didn't get cold feet and backed out.

An hour had gone by and he had finished the food that had been sent to his room. He still had not heard from Crystal so he called her again. This time a man answered.

"I'm sorry, I think I might have dialed the wrong number," Felix said before glancing at his phone quickly.

"You may not have. Are you looking for Crystal Dubois?" the man asked.

"Yes, actually I am. But if she's busy, I can give her a call back…"

"Crystal is in the hospital in serious condition. Are you her spouse or boyfriend because we have been having a hard time locating next of kin?"

"Wait a minute… next of kin? What happened to her?" Felix asked as he stood up and grabbed his jacket.

"She was found in her car on a side rode unconscious. We found a deadly drug cocktail in her and have been working diligently to flush it from her system. We were able to stabilize her and have sedated her."

"You can't be serious. I'm a detective from Philly and was supposed to meet with her in the morning because she had some information for me. What hospital is she in? Is there any way I can see her tonight?" Felix asked.

"She's at Holy Cross Hospital on Forest Glen RD room 418," the doctor said to Felix.

"Okay, I'm on my way." Felix disconnected the call and rushed from his hotel room. He then hopped in his car and drove over to the hospital that Crystal was in. He flashed his badge and was directed to her hospital room. When he got to her, he shook his head in sorrow as he looked at her laying in the hospital bed. He pulled a chair beside her and sat in silence not knowing what to say.

Yani

"I'm not much of a praying man. Religion has never really been my thing, I guess. But man, I can't help but feel the need to pray for you because you're another victim caught up in this mess. And it feels like it's nothing I can do about it. I feel like I'm a step behind everything that's going on and all I want to do is catch this bastard and stop him before he hurts anyone else," Felix said to her quietly. He put his hands to his face and pondered over what he could possibly do next. With Crystal hospitalized, he had no idea what his next course of action should be. He knew he couldn't give up because a young woman and her unborn child's life depended on him closing out this investigation the right way. But what was he going to do, now?

Felix jumped when he felt a hand touch his elbow. Crystal had awaken.

"We were not supposed to meet this way," Felix said as he shook his head. "My name is Felix. I tried calling you to let you know I made it to Bethesda and a doctor answered your phone letting me know you were here. I came as soon as I could," he fell silent for a moment. "How are you? Do you know who did this to you?" Crystal shook her head no and made a slight movement with her hand.

"It's all kinda fuzzy," she struggled to say slowly. "He was in the back of my car when I got in and made me drive somewhere. He wanted to know where Vanessa was and threatened to kill me if I didn't tell him. I don't remember much of what happened after that or how I got here… I think he stuck me with something."

Felix waited a moment trying to piece together what she had said since her words were broken from her hoarse voice and slurred speech. "You said he was in the back of your car when you got in? Did you get a look at him?" he asked her.

Crystal waved her hand back and forth. Felix reached in his jacket pocket and pulled out his cell phone. He then pulled up a picture he had of Eric and showed it to her. "Can you tell or remember at all if this was the man in the back of your car?" He hoped that she told him yes. Crystal looked at the photo really hard and then closed her eyes as though she was trying to remember the small glances she stole of him while she drove the car where he told her to drive. "You don't have to be afraid," Felix said to her. "I promise, I will do everything in my power to keep you safe. Is this the man?"

Crystal looked at the photo a little longer and then shook her head. "No, that's not him."

"Are you sure?" Felix asked her.

Crystal nodded her head. "Yes, I'm sure."

"Damn it," Felix cursed under his breath. He sat for another moment.

"Can I see your phone?" she asked him. Felix passed her the phone and her hands shook as she fiddled with it. She then passed it back to Felix. "That's where Vanessa is. But she isn't going by the name Vanessa Lofton anymore. She's going by Carmen Thompson. Find her before he does. Please..."

Felix looked at the address that she'd given him. Finally, a break that he had been waiting for. He grabbed Crystal's hand and held it tightly. "Thank you. I'll do everything in my power to make sure he doesn't get to her. You take care of yourself. I'll be back to check on you, Crystal."

Crystal smiled and nodded her head. Felix hurried from the room.

"Shit, it's at least a nine hour drive from here to where Vanessa is and if Crystal gave up her location already, I'm already five hours behind," Felix said to himself as he hurried to his car. He checked online to see if there were any flights leaving Maryland for Atlanta anytime soon. Sadly, one wasn't leaving until 6:55am the next morning. He grimaced at how much it was going to cost to book that last minute flight and then went back to his hotel room to get some sleep before he had to head out the next morning. Thankfully, the flight would put him in ATL by 9am. He prayed he wasn't too late.

• • •

Felix got back to his hotel room and checked in with George to let him know he was okay. He thought he wouldn't be able to get any sleep as he was pumped up on adrenaline, excited that he may possibly be able to solve this case once he got to Vanessa. But as soon as his head hit his pillow, he was out like a light.

He woke up the next morning on time and drove himself to the airport. His flight ended up being delayed for two hours. Disappointed, he grabbed himself some breakfast to waste time until he was able to board his flight. He didn't touch down in ATL until almost 12 noon. He immediately checked in with George to let him know he was okay again, promising to check in every few hours.

Atlanta was a touch warmer than Bethesda and Philly. The sun shined brightly and the people moved about like it was the middle of July instead of late September. Felix couldn't wait to finish his business so he could go back home.

He headed over to Sistahs on the Move to speak with Vera as Crystal suggested. Felix had no luck when he arrived at the facility. The new security protocol had been implemented and without a keycard, he was unable to get inside. He buzzed numerous times and waited impatiently for someone to either answer him on the intercom, or for a person to go inside so he could go in with them. After twenty minutes of waiting outside, Felix began to feel like a stalking idiot and decided to leave. He was getting into his hunter-green Nissan Altima when he accidentally dropped his phone.

"Fuck," he mumbled to himself. He bent over to pick it up off the ground, never seeing the black Lincoln MLZ slowing down as it rolled by him. He got up, not paying the car any mind, and got inside of his rental. Felix sat for a minute, making sure his phone worked and didn't have any cracks. When he was satisfied, he started the car and drove off. A moment later, the black Lincoln, pulled off behind him.

. . .

Derek woke up before Vanessa that morning. He stared at her sleeping peacefully wondering how could any man not cherish a woman who was equally beautiful on the inside as she was on the outside. He was tempted to move one of her kinky curls from out of her face but didn't want to wake her. Instead, he slid from under the covers and went into the bathroom to take a shower. When he was done, since she was still sleeping, he threw on a pair of sweat pants and went into the kitchen to fix them both some strawberry topped pancakes, turkey bacon and home fries.

The tantalizing aroma caused Vanessa to stir in her sleep. She stretched after opening her eyes and then looked around smiling. It was the first time in a long time that she had awaken and didn't feel defeated or hopeless. It was also one of the first times she slept and didn't have any nightmares. Her stomach growled as the delicious scent of Derek's cooking filtered into the room and danced under her nostrils. She waddled from the bedroom and used the bathroom, washing her face and brushing her teeth before entering the kitchen to see what he was cooking. Her face flustered when she saw him shirtless, only wearing his gray sweatpants and a pair of white socks. She discreetly pinched herself wondering if she was still sleeping and had walked into a scene straight out of a Zane novel.

Vanessa gazed over his back which was broad and strong, smooth and flawless, and without any tattoos. She'd never imagined his body was this gorgeous nor had she ever thought of him in a sexual manner. But staring at him now as he cooked in his kitchen made her hot all over. She took a deep breath and shook her head to snap herself back to reality.

"Good morning," she said as she sat at his counter.

"Good morning," Derek spoke back with a smile. "Did you sleep good last night?"

"Yes, that was the best sleep I've had in a long time. Something smells yummy."

Derek sat a plate with a stack of strawberry topped pancakes with butter and syrup with a few slices of turkey bacon on the side in front of her and then sat a small saucer of scrambled eggs and home fries next to it. He then poured her a cup of cranberry-apple juice.

"Oh my God," Vanessa smiled. "Thank God I'm pregnant, I can blame my fatness and greed on that." She chuckled.

Derek chuckled with her. "You're not fat, Carmen. You're beautiful." He kissed her forehead and turned back to the stove so he could finish cooking.

"Vanessa…" she said hesitantly.

"What did you say?" Derek asked her as he continued to scramble his eggs.

"My name is Vanessa…" she looked down at her hands and played with her nails nervously.

Derek turned back to her. "Is that what you want me to call you now?"

Vanessa continued to fidget before shaking her head. "I don't even know. Carmen was a name given to me, what I went by because I was so terrified of Eric finding "Vanessa". You know what I mean?" she asked Derek as she looked up at him. He nodded at her. "But I'm not scared of him anymore so I don't need to hide behind "Carmen"."

"I can dig that," Derek replied with a smile. "So Vanessa, how about going to the movies tonight? I heard *The Perfect Guy* is a pretty good movie."

Vanessa hesitated in mid bite of her pancakes. "You're talking about the movie with Sanaa Lathan and Michael Ealy where his crazy self was under her bed?" Derek looked at her for a moment and was about to suggest something else until Vanessa started laughing. "The timing is so perfect. I'm with it," she smiled. She began eating her breakfast as butterflies filled her stomach. Things were starting to feel right in her life for the first time in a long time. She talked and ate breakfast with Derek, laughing and enjoying herself. She was positive everything was going to be okay.

. . .

Felix tried his luck with Sistahs on the Move's facility an hour after he left the first time. This time he was fortunate enough to run into Vera as she was heading in.

"Excuse me, I'm looking for Ms. Vera Alexander," Felix said to her as he jogged from his car to catch up to her before she went inside.

"I'm Vera Alexander. How can I help you?" Vera replied as she looked Felix over wondering who he was.

Felix flashed his badge when he saw how hesitant and on guard she was. "I'm detective Felix Montague. I was given your name by Crystal Dubois. I'm trying to locate Vanessa Lofton. I was told she is going by the name Carmen Thompson," Felix explained quickly.

"What's this about?" Vera asked.

"We have reason to believe Ms. Lofton may be in serious danger from…"

"Eric, her ex?" Vera quickly replied, cutting him off.

"Yes…"

"We're working on having her relocated. He indirectly made contact with her yesterday so we're speaking with our connections to work out a possible relocation for her."

"That's all well and good, but running is not going to help her in the long run. And how far and fast will she be able to run when she's due to have a baby in a couple of months," Felix tried to reason with Vera.

"We have it under control," Vera replied with a friendly smile.

Yani

"With all due respect, Ms. Alexander, I don't think you do. He's already killed her best friend Arianna, we suspect he killed Marcella and the other night, your associate Crystal Dubois was attacked as well. If he knows she's here or was here, how long do you think it will be before he comes after you or someone else at this facility to find where she is?" Felix stared at Vera as she stared back at him. She had no idea that Crystal had been attacked.

"Crystal… was attacked? When? Is she okay?" she asked.

"She's in serious condition. Some type of drug cocktail was injected into her. She's lucky she got help as soon as she did or she would have been another casualty in this mess," Felix rubbed his hands over his face. "I know you think you can protect her, but Eric is hell bent on finding her and has zero fucks to give about who he hurts or kills in order to get to her. Please, help me find her before he does."

Vera hesitated a moment longer and then opened the gate wider for him to come in. Once they were inside of her office, Vera dialed Derek's number. It rang a couple of times and then went straight to voicemail.

"Derek, when you get this message, I need you to call me immediately. Better yet, bring Carmen to my office at your earliest convenience." She hung up the phone and began sifting through her desk drawer in search of a cigarette. She was craving a smoke badly and the sense of urgency to get in contact with Vanessa became stronger and stronger. She finally found one and quickly flicked her lighter, letting the orange, golden flame dance around the tip before she sucked on it. She closed her eyes as the nicotine infiltrated her body and then she slowly blew the smoke out. It danced around hypnotically before fading away.

"Care for a smoke?" Vera asked Felix.

Felix waved his hand in front of his face, trying not to cough and declined her offer. He looked up just as Vanessa had weeks before and saw the same *No Smoking* sign she had seen.

"Fuck that sign," Vera replied, knowing what Felix was looking at. Felix couldn't hold in the laughter that escaped. She chuckled with him. "In all of my years working in this program, starting out as a motivational speaker, sharing my tragedies as a former victim of domestic abuse and my triumphs from when I escaped, and then moving up to a guidance counselor and now a facility leader, I've never experienced anything like this. Never. I mean, this is something out of a got damn movie." Vera took another long drag on her cigarette and blew the smoke upwards.

"Well, this guy is very determined," Felix said to her in return.

"Something tells me that he isn't this hell bent on finding her because she is pregnant by him," Vera mused out loud. She noticed the change in Felix's expression and stopped short of taking another drag on her cigarette. "What?" she asked him.

Felix shook his head, "Nothing… I just."

"Don't do that. Considering everything that is going on right now and the danger this girl, hell all of us could be in right now, don't hold back information that could possibly help Vanessa."

Felix sighed and sat quiet for a moment. "I was doing a search on Vanessa to see if I could find anything that would help me understand why Eric was so fixated on her. I wasn't getting anywhere. So then I began doing a search on Eric. The first red flag was when I read that a woman he was in a relationship with more than three years ago turned up dead. I found that out actually by looking through the files of a PI that he hired to track Vanessa down. He ended up getting killed in a car accident in Philly," Felix explained.

"How convenient?" Vera smirked sarcastically.

"Yeah, I said the same thing. It wasn't what I found in his PI's files that had my head messed up, it was what I found on my own.

"Vanessa's father was Darryl Malik Lofton. He was a counselor that helped women who were victims of domestic violence, recovering drug addicts, victims of sexual assault, things like that. Eric's mother was seeing Vanessa's father because her husband was beating the hell out of her. Apparently, she got the courage to leave her husband. One night, the husband shot her about five times and then went into the bathroom and blew his brains out. Eric was the one who found them. He was also a suspect in Vanessa's father's murder which happened about a month after his parents."

"Jesus…" Vera mumbled.

"Yeah. So I'm betting that it's no coincidence that he just happened to meet Vanessa one day and they fell in love."

"Oh hell no, of course not. That crazy bastard's been plotting on her ass for God knows how long."

"Exactly," Felix agreed. They fell silent for a moment.

"Do you think she knows?" Vera asked.

"Probably not."

Vera took another drag on her cigarette before smashing out the butt. She picked her phone up again and dialed Derek's number. It rang until it went to voicemail again. She huffed angrily before slamming the phone down. "Damn it!"

"Still no answer?" Felix asked. Vera shook her head. "Why don't you give me the address and I'll go over there? Is this guy and Vanessa in a relationship or something?"

"I honestly don't know what is going on with them. He seems to have taken a liking to her and when I expressed my concern over her being a possible liability, he insisted she stay with him until we worked out something else for her." Vera explained as she grabbed her purse. She scribbled Derek's address and phone number down on a piece of paper. "I have a few meetings to attend to. I would much rather tag along with you to make sure

Vanessa is okay. Derek is like a son to me… but with Marcella gone and all the craziness going on…"

Felix took the paper that she handed to him and looked at Derek's address. "Yes, I understand. You have an obligation to this center and the other women who need your help. I completely understand." They both stood up and Vera walked him to the door. "As soon as I get in touch with Vanessa and Derek, I will reach out to you and then we can put our heads together to figure out what the next move should be."

"That works for me. It was nice meeting you, Mr. Montague," Vera said before shaking his hand.

"Please, call me Felix," he replied with a warm smile. He hurried to his car and got inside after putting Derek's address in his GPS. Once the directions populated on his screen, he sped off towards Derek's apartment.

Vera headed back down the hallway to her office. The facility was quiet that day since most of the women were either in school, at work, or enjoying the beautiful weather. Her meeting wasn't for another hour so she decided to get some paper-work done while it was quiet.

She was engrossed in her files when she had a hunch to look up. There standing in her doorway was a man she was not familiar with. Vera was startled and felt her heart practically in her throat as she looked the individual over.

"I didn't mean to startle you," the man said with a friendly smile. "My name is Detective Alex Michaels, I'm from Philadelphia down here trying to locate a witness to a homicide. Her name is Vanessa Lofton, but she might be going by the name Carmen Thompson. Is she here by any chance?"

Vera caught a bad feeling from the man named Michaels as she continued to look him over. He didn't give off the sincerity that Felix gave off when he first approached her. She cleared her throat as she folded her hands on her desk.

"I'm sorry detective, but that young lady is no longer here," she replied, making sure she kept her voice stern and steady. Inside she was trembling with fear.

"By any chance, do you know where she went?" Michaels asked.

Vera shook her head. "My guess is that she no longer wanted the help that our facility was providing her. Yesterday, she bagged up the few things that she had here and our security escorted her to MARTA East Point train station. She didn't say where she was going." Vera's office phone rang. She reached across her desk to answer it when Michaels pulled his gun on her. She froze in terror as she looked at him.

"Be very, very mindful as to how you answer that call, Ms. Alexander," Michaels warned her in a low and cold sounding voice. He waved the gun at her slightly for her to answer it. She picked it up and cleared her throat.

"Vera Alexander's office," she said in the calmest voice she was able to muster up at that moment. She kept her eyes on Michaels and his gun.

"Hey Ms. Vera. I just got your message and was giving you a call back," Derek said into the phone.

"Is that Derek?" Michaels asked in a quiet voice. When she hesitated he put the gun closer to her. She nodded her head quickly. "Put him on hold so you can do and say exactly what I tell you to do and say."

"Derek, could you hold a minute? I have someone in my office." Before giving Derek a chance to respond, she placed his call on hold. "Please..." she murmured with tears in her eyes.

"Shhh," Michaels said as he shook his head. "Save your pleas for the next man. You have one simple task. Tell Derek that a detective is coming to see him by the name of Felix Montague. He is not to be trusted. He was hired by Eric Washington. Tell him not to let him in his apartment or anywhere near Vanessa. Make it sound good. You seem like a woman who is good at bullshitting. Go."

Vera cleared her throat again and took Derek's call off of hold. "Derek, I've been trying to call you all afternoon. Listen, there's a guy claiming to be a detective from Philly who is trying to help Vanessa. He's really a PI working for her ex and is just trying to get her to him. Whatever you do, don't let him in your apartment and don't let Vanessa anywhere near him." Vera looked at Michaels for his approval and he nodded his head.

"Is everything alright, Ms. Vera?" Derek asked.

"Right as pie," she replied. "Call me later." She quickly hung up the phone.

"Good job, Ms. Alexander. Very good job." Michaels said as he tucked his gun in the back of his pants.

"I did what you asked me to do, now please leave my office. I won't call the cops. I won't mention you ever being here," Vera said sternly, still terrified.

Quickly, like the trained marksman he was, Michaels pulled a second gun from the back of his pants that had a silencer on it and shot Vera twice. She jerked back in her leather chair and then slumped downward. He used a napkin to turn her office light off and closed the door behind him as he left.

27

Derek and Vanessa caught an early showing of *The Perfect Guy*. Vanessa couldn't remember a time where she had gone on a date and laughed while having so much fun. They walked from the theater back to his car hand in hand and drove back to his apartment that way as well.

"You look tired," Derek said to her as they came into the apartment.

Vanessa managed a smile as she sat on the couch slowly. "My back hurts. I know I only have a few more weeks left but I didn't think it would be like this." She leaned back on the couch and closed her eyes.

Derek looked at his phone and saw that he had a couple of missed calls from Vera. "You hungry?" he smiled down at Vanessa.

Vanessa giggled and looked at him. "You know I am."

Derek chuckled with her before kissing her briefly. "I'ma run to the store real quick to grab some stuff. My mom used to make these bomb-ass stuffed pasta shells with ricotta cheese and spinach and chicken parmesan. I'ma hook some up tonight. You finna be licking the plate, watch."

Vanessa burst out laughing. "You swear you're Chef Boy-R-Dee out here."

"Girl, please. Chef Boy-R-Dee ain't got nothing on me. I'll be right back. Kick your feet up, relax. There's ice-cream, juice, water, and other snacks in here. Help yourself," Derek told her before leaving out and closing the door behind him. Vanessa looked around and sighed. She felt awkward being in his apartment by herself.

"That's a sign that he trusts you, girl. Chill-ax," she heard the voice in her head tell her. It sounded like Arianna and it made her jump. It was the first time in a while since that had happened to her. She hadn't felt like she was crazy with the voices in her head in a while.

"Don't start," she mumbled to herself. She got up and made her way over to the kitchen to get a bowl of ice-cream when she caught a cramp in her stomach. "Owww," she whined while placing a hand on her belly. She took a deep breath and waited a moment before continuing into the kitchen. For some reason, the pain she felt in her stomach reminded her of one of the many punches and kicks she suffered at the hand of Eric.

"You must be outside your mind if you think I'ma let another nigga step in and play daddy to my baby, bitch. You're playing a dangerous game and about to fuck around and get you and that pussy-ass nigga bodied." This time the voice in her head sounded so much like Eric that Vanessa jumped. She dropped the bowl that she'd taken from the dish rack and it shattered after hitting the floor.

"Shut up!" she shrieked as she banged her fist on the counter. She breathed heavily in anger as she looked at the broken pieces of the bowl on the floor. Eric had terrorized her for almost two years so much so that the sound of his voice, even in her imagination, struck fear in her down to her core.

She tried to kneel down to pick up the broken pieces of the bowl but caught a sharp pain in her back that caused her to stand back up. Vanessa leaned into the counter with her hand on the lower part of her back and shook her head. She was having such a good day until the voices in her head began fucking with her again. She decided to take a hot shower hoping that would help her to relax.

. . .

Derek looked at his phone after Vera disconnected their call. A bad feeling began to settle inside of him. *"Right as pie,"* he heard her say in his head. Something inside of him told him that everything was not *right as pie* as she put it.

He was just getting in line after picking up what he needed for dinner when he decided to call Vanessa and check on her. Her phone rang, and rang until it went to voicemail. At first he told himself maybe she had gone to the bathroom and left her phone in the living room or maybe she'd fallen asleep and her phone was on vibrate. Suddenly, the line that he was in seemed to be moving slow as hell and he was getting impatient. He looked at the phone again and dialed Vanessa's number. Again it went to voicemail. He sat the food he was about to purchase on a rack near the cashier and excused himself as he squeezed pass people who were still in line. He had a nagging feeling that everything was not *right as* pie as Vera had stated, and he had a bad feeling that whatever it was, it had caught up to Vanessa. He jumped into his car and hauled ass back to his apartment.

Yani

· · ·

It took little to no effort for Eric to pick Derek's lock after gaining access to the apartment complex. He pretended to be looking for a keycard when a beautiful young woman was heading inside.

"Damn it, I did it again," he grumbled as he searched his wallet. "I left my damn keycard on the counter again."

The young woman smiled, immediately attracted to him. "It's okay, I have mine," she said in a friendly manner. "You must be new here. The same thing used to happen to me all the time when I first moved in."

"Yeah, I just moved here a couple of weeks ago and this is like the third time I've done it. I'm so used to just using my keys," Eric said in return. He gave her his charming smile nearly making her melt. After heading in, he waited for her to choose her floor first on the elevator. She chose the fifth floor and he pressed seven. They made small chit-chat in the elevator until the young lady got to her floor. Once the doors closed, he pressed two so he could go back to Derek's apartment. Michaels already had eyes on Derek and texted to let him know that he was in the market going grocery shopping.

Eric wasted no time picking the apartment lock and slipping inside before anyone noticed him. He could hear the shower water running as he quietly moved about. Being that close to Vanessa and finally being able to get his hands on her after she had the audacity to walk out on him began to arouse him. He thought back to how he caught Regina by surprise when he finally caught up with her and that intensified his erection.

"Teach her a lesson, Ricky. Learn that lil' dame hard and slow. Teach the little bitch what happens when she steps outta line. She has to learn just like your momma had to learn, Ricky. And that little nigga she's all snuggled up with, he needs to learn what happens when he tries to play super-save-a-hoe…just like her daddy." Eric heard his father's voice in his head.

"I will, Dad. I'ma learn them both. They gon' learn today…" Eric mumbled as he moved towards the bathroom.

The bathroom door was slightly ajar and Eric slipped inside quietly. It was hot and steamy from Vanessa's shower. The water beat against the glass, sliding doors heavily and he could see her curvy silhouette. His erection intensified as he imagined the look on her face when she laid eyes on him. His breath became exacerbated from being so close to her, so close that he could touch her, smell her…learn her, hard and slow.

Vanessa was completely unaware of Eric's presence in the bathroom with her at that moment. The hot, steamy shower was just what she needed to relax and soothe her tired body. The heavy water rained down on her body and she leaned her head under the water letting it hit her in the face.

Eric reached a hand out to the glass shower doors and stopped short of touching it. Instead, he used his index finger and lightly wiped a line across the glass, clearing away some of the fog. "Bitch," he mumbled. He backed away and slipped back out of the bathroom quietly as though he was never there.

"*1, 2, Eric's coming for you…*" Vanessa heard the chilling tune in her head as she was in the shower. Her eyes popped open as she felt a chill slither down her spine that even the heat from the shower could not displace. She quickly turned the water off and grabbed her towel. She wiped the water from her eyes and rung her hair out before wrapping herself in the towel and carefully stepping from the shower. The steam from the shower had already covered the finger trail that Eric left behind, but Vanessa suddenly felt like she wasn't alone.

"Derek, are you back?" she asked loudly as she stood in the middle of the bathroom floor. She waited for his answer. When he didn't respond, she opened the bathroom door wider and began walking down the hall towards the living room. Though there was no sign of him, she still felt like someone else was in the apartment with her. Vanessa decided she would call Derek while she got dressed hoping that the sound of his voice would ease her paranoia. She turned to go back down the hallway to the bedroom and almost shitted on herself when she saw Eric standing near the bedroom door.

The look on Vanessa's face excited Eric so much, that pre-cum began to leak as his erection intensified. "What, you're not happy to see me, V-Dot?" he asked with the same charming smile that once made her heart melt as it filled with love and passion. But now his smile chilled her to the bone and she was positive she was going to have a heart attack.

Yani

Vanessa stood frozen as she looked at Eric, unable to believe her eyes. The day that she feared the most and prayed never came to be was here and very real.

"We need to have a very serious talk, V-Dot. About you, me, our baby and how you thought you could just fucking walk out on me and let another nigga play daddy to my child. Why do you insist on learning shit the hard way?"

Vanessa's fear slowly began to turn to rage as she listened to Eric talk. "You are so full of shit," she said in a voice that didn't sound like her own when she spoke.

"What?" Eric asked, with his eye-brows raised.

"You know got-damn well you didn't search for me because of this baby I'm carrying. You're such a pussy, I don't know why I didn't see you for the punk-ass momma's boy you truly are."

"Oh bitch, being away from me this long gave you some fucking heart to be talking to me like you lost your muthafucking mind," Eric hissed.

"Oh please, shut up, Eric. Shut up! You murdered my father! You stalked and plotted on me for years before making your move. And for what? To prove the apple doesn't fall far from the tree and you are no different than your woman-beating, coward-ass father?!"

Eric looked at her shocked at her words. *"How the hell does she know…?"* he thought to himself. *"Never mind the small shit, Ricky. This lil girl got some serious sass in her and it's time to cut the small talk and remind her who really runs the bingo,"* he heard his father in his head.

"Bitch, you're too smart for your own good. You gon' learn today. I'ma learn you hard and slow, you bitch." He moved towards her quickly and Vanessa turned to run. Her feet were still wet from the shower and she slipped on the parquet floors. Her arms flailed outward as she tried breaking her fall and protecting her baby, but she fell hard. She cried out loudly as she turned to her side, reaching for her belly. She felt Eric's hand go around her ankle and begin to drag her backward.

"No! No, Eric! No!" she screamed out as she kicked her leg at him…

• • •

Felix pulled up to the apartment complex where Derek lived and parked his car. He hopped out and went over to the door and pulled on it. When it didn't budge, he groaned, annoyed with being stone-walled again. He dug in his pocket for his keys as he walked over to his car. He was just about to tweak his alarm when he had a feeling that someone was behind him. Before he had a chance to turn around, he felt the cold steel of a gun press against the back of his neck. His heart felt like it was in his throat and his stomach knotted up as he suddenly feared death was waiting for him right around the corner.

"You need to be more mindful of your surroundings," he heard a familiar voice say. He felt hands search his waist and then his gun was taken from him. "Letting somebody get the drop on you this easily makes me embarrassed to have had you as my partner," Michaels said as he shook his head.

"Fuck," Felix mouthed, cursing himself. He had hoped that his partner didn't turn out to be dirty. At that moment with a gun to his head, hope was dashed. He moved to turn around, but Michaels stopped him.

"Nah, stay right there, just like that," he told him.

"This is bullshit, Mike. Seriously? This is how you're going out? How long you been a fucking snake hiding behind your badge, nigga?"

Michaels laughed, "Bruh, you always had a habit of asking unnecessary questions. You should've left this shit alone like the Lieutenant said. All you had to do was keep it fucking moving, but no, here you are trying to be a hero. Heroes die every day, B." He yanked Felix by his arm and nudged him towards the back of the building. Though Felix was terrified, he managed to remain calm as he thought of a way to get himself out of this mess. It was still partially daylight and he wished like hell that the apartment complex wasn't in such of a suburban area. At least if it had been an inner city setting like North Philly, Germantown or even West Oak-lane, people would be out and someone would surely see what was happening. But the only thing that was out were scattered clouds.

They were almost to the back of the building when Michaels heard a car pull up. He took his gun away from Felix's head and put it in his back instead. He yanked his partner over by a large oak tree and waited to see who the person was that was parking. When he saw that it as Derek, he cursed under his breath.

"Could his timing be any worse?" Michaels mumbled under his breath.

Felix heard what he said and thought that it was Eric that was parking his car. When the guy got out of the car and he saw that it wasn't, he let out a sigh of relief. He knew he was just as good as dead if it had been Eric.

"My man, parking is reserved back here so, you might wanna move your car if you're parked back here because Tow Truck Bob be hawking and stalking every day around this time," Derek said as he pulled his keycard from his back pocket.

"Actually you're just the guy I was looking for, Derek. Vera spoke with you earlier about Vanessa," Michaels said, playing cop. He was trying to get Derek in perfect view so he could get a shot off that would take him out and then he could take Felix out as well.

Derek stopped dead in his tracks and looked at Felix and Michaels. *"Right as Pie"* he heard Vera say in the phone again. It was something about that saying as well as the way she said it that didn't sit well with him. "Yeah, she did…" he said as he looked at Felix and Michaels suspiciously. What bothered Derek was that he couldn't see both of Michaels' hands. He then noticed the slightly unnerved look in Felix's eyes. *"Right as pie,"* he heard Vera say again. That time he heard the saying in his head, everything clicked. He remembered sitting in on a session with Vera where she shared her experience as a battered woman. Marcella suggested she come up with a phrase to let her know if she was in trouble whenever she called. *Right as pie* stood for Reach a Policeman. The moment it became clear that her phrase was her way of letting him know she was in trouble, Felix elbowed Michaels. A shot went off, hitting the ground and Derek ducked for cover. Felix grabbed Michaels' wrist and pushed him into the oak tree, struggling to disarm him.

"Derek, run! Now Derek, GO!" Felix yelled.

Derek took off running to the complex doors. Felix saw that he was not going to get Michaels to drop the gun with the way he had him hemmed up again the tree so he head butted him. Michaels staggered back, dropping the gun but recovered quick enough to block a punch that Felix threw at him. They grabbed at each other, slinging one another around. Felix pushed with all of the strength he had and wrestled Michaels on top of Derek's car. The alarm went off. He gave Michaels a couple of rib shots, trying to knock the wind out of him, but his punches didn't have the desired effect as he'd hoped they would. Michaels brought his foot up and kicked Felix in his stomach causing him to fall back into the gate. He then reached behind his back and pulled his second gun, shooting it twice, quickly. The gunshots spun Felix around, knocking him to the ground.

Michaels spat on the ground as he breathed heavily, trying to catch his breath. His lip and his nose was bloody and his ribs were sore from the punches Felix hit him with. He took a couple of steps forward and was about to nudge Felix with his foot to see if he would move when Felix turned over quickly, holding the gun that Michaels dropped when the fight initially started. Michaels' reaction was too slow and Felix got off four shots, all of which hit Michaels in the chest. He stumbled backwards before falling into Derek's car and then hit the ground.

Felix looked at his partner laying lifeless on the ground, trembling. Though that wasn't the first time he had to discharge his weapon, it hurt him to the pit of his stomach that he had to discharge his weapon on his partner. He grabbed onto the gate to help pull himself up and winced in pain. He had on a bullet proof vest under his shirt but the second bullet hit him in his side where he was least protected by it. He placed a shaking hand where the pain was coming from and touched his side.

"Fuck," he groaned when he saw his fingertips covered in blood. He slowly limped in the direction that his partner was laying in, trying to breathe against the pain that he was feeling which was getting excruciating by the second. Michaels' eyes looked up at the sky in a lifeless manner. Felix wasn't going to make the same mistake that Michaels made. He kept his gun aimed at his partner as he kicked his gun away. He then turned towards the doors of the complex and limped towards them. He thanked God that someone was coming out as he was going in.

"Hold the door!" he managed to say loud enough for them to hear him. The right side of his body felt hot as though it was on fire but he fought against it.

"Aw man, are you alright?" the guy asked Felix.

Felix shook his head. "No, I need you to call the cops. Tell them a man has been shot out back. Tell them another man has been shot and there's a possible third man on the second floor with a gun," Felix said in a breathy voice.

"Jesus!" the guy exclaimed. He fumbled for his phone as Felix stumbled over to the elevators and pressed the button to go up.

Yani

"Please, God…" he thought to himself. *"I've come too far not to be able to save this woman. Please…"* Felix felt like he was fading but the sound of the elevator arriving at the floor snapped him back. He got on and pressed "two", and made his way up to Derek's apartment.

. . .

Derek didn't bother waiting for the elevator. He haul-assed up the stairs, skipping two at a time. He ran down the hallway to his apartment with his heart-racing. The hallway seemed longer than usual and the faster he ran, the further his apartment seemed to be as though this were a sick nightmare.

His mouth and throat were dry suddenly, and each time he swallowed, it felt like sand and dirt were in his throat. He twisted the door knob and pushed the door opened. Derek saw that Vanessa wasn't on the couch. Instead of calling out her name, he listened to determine if she was moving around. He heard noises coming from the bedroom and hesitantly walked in that direction. The closer he got to his bedroom, the tighter the knot in his stomach became. He breathed heavily as he partially feared what he was about to walk into.

"You thought you could get away from me, bitch. You thought I was just going to let that shit slide. Well, you thought wrong, you fucking cock-sucking, whore-ass bitch. I'ma learn you good, bitch. Daddy's gonna learn you real hard and real good." Derek heard a man say.

Derek walked into the bedroom. Nothing in the world could have prepared him for what he saw. The room was a mess and he could tell a small struggle ensued. But what fucked his head up more was Vanessa's naked body bent over the bed with Eric ravaging her while his belt was tied around her neck like a dog's leash. Vanessa's face was bruised and bloody and the way her body flopped around lifelessly from Eric's vigorous thrusts, he couldn't tell if she were dead or had passed out.

Eric heard movement from behind him and turned in that direction. He sucked his teeth. "Muthafucka, don't you see I'm busy right now?" he asked as he yanked on the belt around Vanessa's neck. He saw the way Derek looked from him to Vanessa while at a loss for words and smirked. "You must be the new nigga," Eric said casually. He pulled his penis out of Vanessa which was partially covered in blood and wiped himself off on the sheet. "In case you never fucked this bitch, let me just give you a heads up. She was always a boring lay." And then as though Vanessa was a piece of trash, he undid the belt from her neck and then flung her onto the bed.

Derek saw red at that moment and before he knew it he had Eric by the throat. They struggled in the corner back and forth. Derek was able to get in quite a few good punches, but it wasn't enough to knock Eric down. Eric wrestled Derek before picking him up and rushing him into the dresser. Bottles of lotion, deodorant and other items were knocked over as they fought and struggled in the room. Derek managed to hit Eric with a strong right cross, knocking him back. Eric recovered quickly and grabbed a flower vase, smashing it against Derek's head. Derek fell to the floor feeling dazed. He crawled a bit as he tried to get his bearings together.

"Yeah that's right, pussy!" Eric said before kicking him in the ribs. "Crawl, muthafucka!" he kicked him in his back making him arch it and holler out in pain. Eric grabbed the belt that he had previously put around Vanessa's neck and wrapped it around Derek's, tightening it. "You wanna be a fucking hero? Huh bitch!? Huh?" Eric practically growled as he choked Derek. Derek grabbed for the belt as well as clawed at Eric's hands trying desperately to stop him but Eric's grip did not falter. "You gon' learn today, bitch. You gon'…"

His words were cut off by the loud boom from Felix's gun. Eric was hit in the chest and fell backwards. Felix leaned into the wall for support and fired a few more times, emptying his clip. Eric lay on the floor very still, not moving.

Derek looked up at Felix as he tore the belt from around his neck. Felix slid to the floor and dropped his gun. After Derek was able to get his breathing under control, he crawled over to Felix.

"Jesus man, you're fucking bleeding everywhere!" Derek said to him.

"Don't worry about me," Felix said in a breathless voice. He managed to point a finger at Vanessa. "Check her."

Derek turned to Vanessa and scrambled over to her. She was laying on her side, still not moving. He listened closely to her mouth and could hear her breathing but barely.

Yani

"She's barely breathing!" Derek said in a panicky voice. "What do I do? What about the baby?" he asked frantically. When he didn't get an answer, he looked over at Felix. His eyes were closed and he wasn't moving. Derek pulled Vanessa in his arms and covered her body with the sheet. He used a clean part of the sheet and wiped the blood from her face. He then talked softly in her ear as he did the day she began hyperventilating when she learned that Arianna had been killed while he dialed 9-1-1 from his phone. He heard voices and what sounded like a police radio and disconnected the call. "Hang in there, babe. Hang in there, Vanessa. You're okay, okay? You're okay, just hang in there," he told her.

The first cop that came into the room pulled his gun on Derek.

"Wait!" he said frantically. "This is my apartment." He nodded in Eric's direction. "He attacked my girlfriend and then attacked me." Derek then nodded in Felix's direction. "The guy right there I think is a cop. He shot the guy that attacked us but I think he was hurt outside by another guy," Derek quickly explained.

The cop put his gun away as a few other police officers came into the room followed by paramedics. A couple of them attended to Felix as two others came to Vanessa's aid.

"How far along is she?" one of the paramedics asked

"She's 34 weeks," Derek said as he stepped out of the way. He heard a defibrillator go off and turned in that direction. They were administering CPR to Felix. He then turned back to Vanessa and watched as another paramedic came up with a portable ultrasound.

"Baby is in duress, and the mother is hemorrhaging. We've got to move them and get this baby out fast or we're going to lose them both." A female paramedic said. They loaded Vanessa onto a stretcher and put an oxygen mask over her face. Derek followed them out of the room and climbed in the back of the ambulance with her. He reached for her hand but was almost pushed to the side by one of the medics.

"She's coding!" one of them yelled. "Charge to 200!"

"Wait, what's happening?" Derek asked anxiously. He watched the way Vanessa's body jerked when the medics shocked her and became frantic.

They arrived at the hospital and raced down the hallway to the elevators to get her to the operating room. The doctors prevented Derek from getting on with her.

"Wait, that's my baby in there!" He yelled at one of the doctors. "What's happening to her?"

"Sir, I need you to stand back. If you want us to save your girlfriend and your baby, let us do our job and please go wait in the waiting room. We'll send someone out to update you as soon as we have an update to give," the doctor said to Derek. He then got on the elevator and Derek watched as the doors closed.

28

Vanessa was back at Temple University's track field. Up ahead, she saw her father walking the length of the track casually. She ran to catch up with him.

"Daddy!" she called out to him. He stopped and turned to her with a warm smile.

"I've been waiting for you, Vanna. But I wasn't expecting you so soon," he said to her.

Vanessa looked at him confused. "What do you mean? We came to the field together." She froze for a second, as if she remembered something she never should have forgotten. And though her father seemed very real to her, she knew that it could not be possible because he had been killed almost eight years prior. Her heart ached as she came to that realization.

Her father smiled before putting his arm around her. "Vanna, I can't tell you what it did to me not being there for you like I planned to be. To protect you, to teach you, to guide you and help mold you into a beautiful, strong and intelligent Black woman."

Yani

"But you did," Vanessa said to him. "Everything I am, it's because of you, Daddy. Everything good I have inside of me, it's because of everything you taught me. I lost myself along the way, and that's not your fault. I could never blame you for what happened to me," Vanessa said to her father as she looked up at him.

"I know baby-girl," her father sighed as they walked on a little longer. "Remember what I taught you before. Be you, be fearless. Don't let a bad experience cause you to shut down and reject love. Be smarter in who you give your heart to. But most importantly, don't punish the next man for what the last man did or because I wasn't around to protect you from what was done to you. Don't lose yourself. Be you, unapologetically," her father said to her firmly.

Vanessa rested her head on her father's shoulder. "No man could ever love me as you do, Daddy. Why can't I just stay with you?"

"We'll be together again. But there is so much more for you to do. Just never forget what I taught you. Promise me that," Vanessa's father said to her.

Vanessa's eyes became teary as she nodded her head. "I promise," she said becoming choked up. Her father wiped her tears away with his thumb and kissed her on the fore-head. "I love you, Vanna..."

Vanessa opened her eyes and he was gone. "I love you too, Daddy…"

• • •

Vanessa felt a gentle kiss on her forehead and opened her eyes. The bright light in the hospital room caused her to squint. When they adjusted to room's lighting, she looked at Derek and smiled.

"It's good to see you with your eyes open," he said to her with a smile. "Someone wants to meet you." He pulled a baby basinet over to her side of the bed and Vanessa's heart almost melted when she laid eyes on the precious baby.

"You have a beautiful son," Derek said softly as he picked the baby up. The tiny baby boy fidgeted in his arms as Derek sat in a chair next to Vanessa. She felt overwhelmed with love and joy as she laid eyes on her brand new son. The brief dream that she had of her father came to her and she was unable to hold back the tears. Derek kissed the side of her mouth before placing him in her arms. "We've been calling him "Baby-Boy L" for the past three days," he told her.

"Three days?" Vanessa looked at him with a raised eye-brow.

"Yeah, you lost a lot of blood. They had to give you two blood transfusions." Vanessa couldn't take her eyes off of her new son. "What are you going to name him?" Derek asked her.

"Darryl Malik Lofton," Vanessa said with a smile.

Derek smiled. "I had a feeling you would." He ran his fingertips over the side of baby Darryl's chubby cheeks and then kissed Vanessa softly.

"Eric…?" she asked hesitantly.

"He's dead," Derek told her. He hesitated a moment. "So is Ms. Vera." Vanessa looked at him with her eyes wide. "I wasn't sure if you wanted to go back to Philly since Eric is gone and he was the only reason you left. But if you decide to stay…" Derek trailed off. "It's no pressure."

Vanessa stared at baby Darryl for a moment and then remembered what her father said to her in her dream. She looked at Derrick and smiled. "I want to stay with you."

Derrick let out a sigh of relief and then laughed nervously. "No lie, if you told me you were going back to Philly, I would've came with you." Vanessa chuckled with him. He kissed her again, this time longer and then leaned his forehead against hers. "I told you I got you, Vanessa."

Vanessa nodded her head. "Thank you." She closed her eyes and took a deep breath. So many people had been hurt and killed through this ordeal, but it was finally over. Eric was dead, and all of the horrible things that had been done to her by him, she let them die with him. She knew she would still need counseling to heal the wounds that were still there mentally and emotionally. But at that moment, she was positive that she would be alright, and that her son would be alright as well.

Yani

Epilogue

George walked into the 22nd precinct carrying a small package. He stopped at the help desk and waited patiently for the officer behind it to finish with her meaningless conversation and actually help him.

"How can I help you, sir?" she asked him in a tone that made her appear uninterested in doing her job.

"I'm trying to get in touch with Detective Jamal Williams and his partner Dante Smith," George replied nervously.

"What's this about?" the officer asked.

"I have a package for him from Officer Felix Montague."

"The officer who was killed in Atlanta about a month ago?" the female officer asked with a raised eye brow.

"Yes, ma'am."

"You can give that to me. I'll make sure it gets into Williams' hands as soon as he gets in."

"No, I was given specific instructions that no one was to touch this package except for either him or Dante Smith. I can wait if that's okay," George replied.

The female officer looked at him clearly annoyed. She waved for him to have a seat in the waiting room. "I'll see if I can locate him at his desk."

George sat in the waiting room with the package in his lap. Almost forty-five minutes had gone by before he felt someone tap him on his shoulder.

"I'm detective Jamal Williams. Are you George?"

George felt like he was standing in front of a celebrity. "I read up on your father, Andre. It's an honor to meet you," he said as he gave Jamal a firm handshake.

"Thank you. What can I do for you today?"

"I was told not to say too much. Everything you need to know is in the package. Felix told me that if anything ever happened to him, to get this over to you and only you," George explained.

Jamal took the thick manila envelope from George. "I'm a little confused. I didn't know Officer Montague personally. I heard what happened to him and I attended his service. I don't understand why he specifically wanted you to give this to me and also, he was killed a month ago. Why are you just getting this to me?" Jamal asked.

George fidgeted for a moment. "Just go through what's in there. And then call the number in the file. I can't say any more than that. And watch yourself..." George got up and walked out of the precinct. Five minutes after he was standing at the corner, a dark Lincoln town car pulled up. He got in the back and the car pulled off.

"Did you give him everything?" Felix asked.

"Yeah. A female officer offered to give it to him for me but I told her I would wait. She seemed a little pissed about it."

"Yeah, you can guess why, too."

"So now what?" George asked.

"Now we wait..."

• • •

Jamal didn't have time to look through the envelope because he was swamped with paper work and he wanted to get it finished so he could get home in time to have dinner with his wife, Tiffany. Their one year old son was having a sleep over with Deisha and Maurice's two children so they could finally have some alone time together. He promised Dante he would drop him off at home first.

"Yo homie, you ready to roll?" Dante asked as he approached Jamal's desk.

"Yeah man, I was just finishing up," Jamal replied as he stood up. He threw his jacket on and was about to walk away from his desk when he remembered the envelope that was given to him by George earlier that day. He snatched it up and he and Dante headed out of the precinct together.

"You never checked out what was in the envelope that dude gave to you earlier?" Dante asked as they walked over to the parking lot.

"Nah, I said I would look at it tomorrow since I'm off. Dude was real secretive about it like it was some Mission: Impossible type shit. It was weird." He and Dante chuckled. Jamal took out his keys and hit the keyless starter. As soon as the car started, an explosion erupted lifting the car from the ground. The explosion caused multiple car alarms to go off and the blast knocked Jamal and Dante back into a wall. Jamal's ears were ringing and his head and back hurt. Dante slowly moved to his knees and looked at Jamal in disbelief. Jamal looked at him wide-eyed.

"What the fuck was that?!" Dante yelled. Other cops ran from the precinct to see what happened.

Jamal shook his head with a look of shock written over his face. "Your guess is as good as mine."

"Nah fuck this. You're looking at that file tonight! Whatever is in it, they don't want you to see it." Dante grimaced. "Here we go again with this bullshit."

Sirens from firetrucks and ambulances could be heard approaching the scene. A Sergeant from IAB stood in the window of the fifth floor looking down at what was going on. His cell phone rang.

"This is Rutkowski," he answered as he continued to stare down below.

"What's the result?" a male asked on the other end.

"Target was missed. We'll get them though," Sergeant Rutkowski replied.

"That's not the answer we were expecting," the man on the phone said.

"I know, sir. My apologies."

"Save your apologies. Next time, be more efficient." The man disconnected the call and Rutkowski put his phone back in his pocket. He continued to stare down at the scenery as the fire fighters put out the flames to Jamal's 2015 Acura RDX as he plotted on his next move against Jamal Williams and Dante Smith…

<u>About the Author</u>

The Author Yani wrote her first novel when she was fifteen years old while attending University City High-School. What started out as just a short story to help her cope with the accidental and devastating murder of a friend, turned into a full length, 893 handwritten paged novel after being encouraged to continue writing more by her peers. Years later, A Thug's Redemption along with its two sequels, became Amazon Best Sellers and featured in Yo! Raps Magazine. Yani had previously been known for her writing through her edgy poetry, which granted her an invitation to the Tri-State's number 1 Hip-Hop and R&B radio station, Power 99FM, to recite her popular poem "Why Tyrone Can't Read" in 2001. Since then, Yani has attended open mic nights, reciting her poetry throughout Philadelphia. Yani has been featured on numerous blogs and has made guest appearances on various blog-talk radio shows. She was also a featured author at the 2013 National Black Book Festival in Houston, Texas. Yani still resides in Philadelphia with her three children and is working on her sixth novel.

Yani

Check out more novels by the author Yani brought to you by Anitbeet Productions.

<u>A Thug's Redemption Trilogy</u>

<u>Obsessive Intimacies</u>